Catlin had witnessed major sandstorms twice—one time outside of Texas, while running down a bail jumper; the other one in Arizona Territory, when coming up on Tucson with a highwayman draped over what had been the outlaw's skewbald gelding—but he'd never been enveloped by one, blinded, deafened, struggling to breathe.

First time for everything, he thought, and didn't like the ring of that inside his head.

Dying, for instance, was a person's first and only time—except perhaps for Lazarus of ancient myth.

Catlin eyed the northern skyline, frown hidden behind his mask as he saw the thunderclouds shot through by lightning were advancing on the Bar X herd. Most times, a sight like that would come complete with blurriness below, a screen of pouring rain. This time, however, he could see a clear horizon line below the clouds, which told him that the clouds were wreaking havoc only with the static electricity and roiling desert winds they'd generated.

Even as he watched, twisters of sand and gravel rose, writhed, and collapsed, as if some huge primeval beast with tentacles in place of legs was clutching at the sky above it, tempting the storm with its living, flailing lightning rods. One finally succeeded, struck down by a blue-white shaft of energy, exploding silently, grit raining down.

A monster that you couldn't fight with guns or hope to run away from on horseback.

He couldn't calculate how fast the storm front might be traveling, but it was miles wide, growing as he watched.

And there was no escape.

RALPH COMPTON

DRIVE FOR INDEPENDENCE

A RALPH COMPTON WESTERN BY
LYLE BRANDT

BERKLEY
New York

BERKLEY
An imprint of Penguin Random House LLC
penguinrandomhouse.com

Copyright © 2020 by The Estate of Ralph Compton
Penguin Random House supports copyright. Copyright fuels creativity, encourages
diverse voices, promotes free speech, and creates a vibrant culture. Thank you for buying
an authorized edition of this book and for complying with copyright laws by not
reproducing, scanning, or distributing any part of it in any form without permission.
You are supporting writers and allowing Penguin Random House to continue to
publish books for every reader.

BERKLEY and the BERKLEY & B colophon are registered trademarks of
Penguin Random House LLC.

ISBN: 9780593100790

First Edition: November 2020

Printed in the United States of America
1   3   5   7   9   10   8   6   4   2

Cover art by Steve Atkinson
Book design by George Towne

THE IMMORTAL COWBOY

This is respectfully dedicated to the "American Cowboy." His was the saga sparked by the turmoil that followed the Civil War, and the passing of more than a century has by no means diminished the flame.

———◆———

True, the old days and the old ways are but treasured memories, and the old trails have grown dim with the ravages of time, but the spirit of the cowboy lives on.

———◆———

In my travels—to Texas, Oklahoma, Kansas, Nebraska, Colorado, Wyoming, New Mexico, and Arizona—I always find something that reminds me of the Old West. While I am walking these plains and mountains for the first time, there is this feeling that a part of me is eternal, that I have known these old trails before. I believe it is the undying spirit of the frontier calling me, through the mind's eye, to step back into time. What is the appeal of the Old West of the American frontier?

———◆———

It has been epitomized by some as the dark and bloody period in American history. Its heroes—Crockett, Bowie, Hickok, Earp—have been reviled and criticized. Yet the Old West lives on, larger than life.

———◆———

It has become a symbol of freedom, when there was always another mountain to climb and another river to cross; when a dispute between two men was settled not with expensive lawyers, but with fists, knives, or guns. Barbaric? Maybe. But some things never change. When the cowboy rode into the pages of American history, he left behind a legacy that lives within the hearts of us all.

—Ralph Compton

PROLOGUE

Las Vegas, New Mexico Territory

THE LAST CHANCE Saloon lived up to its name. It needed paint inside and out, along with rigorous sweeping, new furnishings, the whole shebang. Glasses were spotty, the bartender weary-looking. Its piano likely had been out of tune before some rowdy drunk had fired two bullets through its upper panel. He might have had a human target, judging from some old stains on the barroom's floor.

The Last Chance was a place where people died by violence from time to time.

As more might do today, perhaps.

Arthur Catlin sipped his second whiskey, wondering why anyone had named the town Las Vegas.

He spoke fair Spanish, knew *las vegas* meant "the meadows," but he hadn't glimpsed a bit of grazing land since he'd arrived in town two days ago. Not that he minded. Folks could call their towns whatever they desired. It made no difference to him, but things like that stuck in his mind sometimes, distracting him from work at hand.

But not today.

This afternoon Catlin was focused on the men he'd ridden sixty-some-odd miles to find, along a trail of sorrow they'd left in their wake. Two murders he was sure of, one bank robbed, a coach as well, and one young woman outraged but surprisingly allowed to live.

They hadn't done her any favors there.

The Grimes brothers, in order of descending age, were Lincoln, Leland, and Lucas. Catlin guessed their parents had a fondness for the letter *L*, although their father's name was Rupert and their mother's Abigail.

Again, he couldn't work that out and didn't give a damn.

Standing rewards for capture of the brothers totaled fifteen hundred dollars. Lincoln was worth seven, Leland five, and Lucas just a measly three, but altogether they'd been worth the trip and the two days learning where they went to have a bender and disport with ladies of the evening.

The former was an occupation, while the latter seemed to be a last resort. From what he'd learned while tracking them, Catlin believed their preference was picking up some innocent young woman to terrorize.

Between that and the murders, they were slated for an air dance on the gallows if he brought them in alive. The good news: Catlin could collect his money either way, their "Wanted" flyers having specified "Dead or Alive."

That made it easier.

Just now, the brothers had a table and a whiskey bottle to themselves, the only Last Chance customers besides Catlin, on a sultry afternoon. They all wore pistols, two in Lincoln's case, with knives sheathed on their belts.

Good reasons for deciding "Dead" might be the way to go.

As brothers will, the three Grimes boys were arguing; Leland and Lucas starting off, then Lincoln joining in to keep the fire stoked, maybe for his personal amusement. Catlin had grown up with brothers and he knew how that could be, but when the chips were down, he reckoned they'd be all for one and one for all.

Three men who'd proved themselves killers, and Catlin had six .44-caliber rounds in his Colt Army Model 1860 revolver. He didn't like to use all six, preferring one or two kept in reserve for unforeseen eventualities, but he would play the hand that he was dealt.

Quaffing his whiskey off, he set the glass down quietly and focused on his targets. Leland Grimes had spared a glance at him when the brothers arrived, frowned to himself, then seemed to shrug it off. Whatever the Grimes boys were squabbling about, they had been working on it when they pushed in through the barroom's batwing doors and couldn't seem to let it go.

Not shouting, though; they were keeping their voices down, so Catlin couldn't make out much of what they said.

Again, he didn't give a damn.

As they'd arranged themselves around their table, Leland sat facing toward Catlin, Lucas on his right and Lincoln to his left. When Catlin started giving Leland hard eyes from halfway across the room, it took a minute for the middle brother to pick up on it, but then he lost track of whatever Lucas had to say, giving Catlin a cold stare of his own.

Another minute passed that way before Leland inquired, "You want something, mister?"

"I do," Catlin replied, right hand already on his Colt below his table.

All three Grimes brothers faced him now, regarding him with different measures of hostility. Leland said, "Yeah? And what might that be?"

"Money," Catlin said.

Leland tried smiling but fell short. "You want some change, then? Is that it?"

"I took him for a bum right off," Lucas chimed in.

"I'm thinking bigger money," Catlin said. By then, he had his holster's hammer thong released, his fingers curled around the Colt's curved butt, thumb on its hammer.

"Getting greedy, and we ain't even been introduced," said Lincoln Grimes, making his brothers snort and chuckle.

"Not your money," Catlin said, correcting him. "And if it was, so what? You won't be needing any where you're going."

"What is that supposed to mean?" asked Leland, past seeing the humor in their repartee.

"The three of you have decent money on your heads," Catlin replied. "Thought I might help myself to that."

Slow minds required another heartbeat to connect on that and start reacting. When they did, all three Grimes brothers bolted to their feet as one, tipping their table over, whiskey bottle shattering on impact with the floor. Hands dipped toward guns, liquor hampering their speed.

Catlin kicked over his own table, using it for cover as he drew and cocked his Colt. The pistol weighed a tad under three pounds, was fourteen inches long, and eight of that was barrel. He shot Lincoln first, two guns being the greatest threat, and saw blood spout out of a chest wound just an inch or so off target for the heart.

The elder Grimes went over backward, howling, pistols spilling from his hands and clattering across the barroom's floor. His brothers didn't seem to notice, focused as they were on clearing leather with their own smoke poles while time remained.

But not much.

His second shot plugged Leland through the left shoulder and spun him off to that side, traveling 640 feet per second, striking with 207 foot-pounds of explosive energy. It didn't make the middle brother drop his weapon, though. As Lincoln was reeling, he squeezed off a shot that punched through one of the saloon's front windows.

On the street, a woman screamed.

Catlin had no time to consider that if he intended to survive.

Lucas was lining up his shot, Leland still on his feet but unsteady, with his back turned toward the enemy as Catlin fired again.

At first, he thought he'd missed and only knocked the final Grimes boy's hat off, but then Catlin saw a chunk of skull was airborne with it. Lucas folded like an empty suit of clothes as he collapsed.

Lincoln down and jiggling through his death throes left only Leland fit for battle, if you stretched a point. Turning to face Catlin again, the middle brother saw both of his siblings lying dead or close to it, and a howl of rage ripped from his throat, eclipsing the prior sounds of pain.

His pistol wavered toward its target as the sole surviving Grimes shouted, "Son of a—"

Catlin fired his fourth shot, got it right that time, and stillness fell over the Last Chance battlefield. It took another moment, his ears still ringing from gunfire, before he picked up sounds of female weeping from somewhere outside.

Long strides propelled him toward the shattered

window, where he saw a woman kneeling on the sidewalk, gingham fabric pooled around her, sobbing as she clutched the limp form of a child to her bosom.

A little boy, he saw, blood smeared across his forehead but no longer pulsing from the bullet wound that set it free.

Across the street, a portly man was rushing toward the scene, propelled by legs too slender for the rest of his physique. A tin star on his vest explained the six-gun in his hand.

Catlin holstered his own and muttered to himself, "Well, shit!"

T HE MARSHAL'S NAME was Bradford, with no given name offered. He read the scene inside the Last Chance and could see right off what had transpired. He had no problem deciding that the window shot had come from Leland Grimes's weapon, but he still eyed Catlin like he was a pile of road apples he'd stepped in, giving off a noisome smell he couldn't shake.

"A bounty hunter," he pronounced, as if the words tasted like lemon juice. "See what you've done today?"

"Marshal—"

"Shut up! I know you were within your rights, far as that goes." Standing behind the small desk in his office, Bradford peered down at the "Wanted" posters Catlin had provided, creased from spending three weeks folded in his pocket. "I'll pay up and bill the capitol for reimbursement, like the papers say."

"All right, then."

"But my question to you is, will fifteen hundred dollars soothe Amanda Regner's mourning for her son, Bill Junior?"

"Marshal—"

"You don't know her, but she lost her husband—that

would be Bill Senior—in a mining accident last year. Their son was all she had left in the world."

"I didn't shoot him, Marshal, as you know full well."

"You didn't pull the trigger on him, true enough. But if you hadn't done your hunting at the Last Chance, I suspect that he'd still be alive."

"You want to talk about what might have been?" Catlin replied, tone challenging. "The Grimes brothers— all wanted men on counts of murder, robbery, and rape— have hung around your town at least three weeks before I got here. Once I settled at your fleabag Grand Hotel, it took me one day to find out where they spent time drinking and whoring. Where were you the other twenty days, Marshal?"

"You got me there. My cross to bear, and not the first. You think that lets you off the hook, Catlin?"

"Which hook is that?"

"Depends."

"On what?"

"Whether you've still got any conscience left or if you've burned it all away."

"You ever plan on turning to the pulpit, Marshal, I'd think twice about it."

"I'm no sin-buster, much less a saint. Just wondering who'll help the Widow Regner put Bill Junior in the ground."

"I get it now. How much?"

"For what?"

"The burial. What else?"

"I reckon twenty dollars ought to get it done."

"So, rake it off the bounty. Keep some for yourself, why don't you?"

"That sounds like a bribe, son."

"First, I'm not your son. Second, how can I bribe a lawman to do nothing?"

"No damage to your sense of humor, eh?"

"If you're all done, Marshal . . ."

"Not quite. You plan on staying here in town awhile?" Before Catlin could speak, Bradford informed him, "I expect your answer to be no."

"I'll need my money first. Minus the twenty."

"Right."

Bradford turned to a safe that occupied one corner of his office, crouching down in front of it and wheezing from the effort, blocking Catlin's sight line on the dial. The sound of shuffling money was familiar. When he'd counted twice, Bradford reclosed and locked the safe, then rose and turned around.

He dropped a wad of well-worn currency. Said, "Fifteen hundred minus twenty. Count it."

"I don't need to."

"Count it anyway."

Catlin obliged him while the marshal roughed out a receipt in pencil and set it beside the cash, the stubby pencil lying next to it.

"Sign that," said Bradford, "and the money's yours."

Catlin read it over, then signed, picked up the cash, and folded it, stuffing the wad into a pocket of his blue jeans. He was turning from the desk when Bradford spoke again.

"You've already checked out of the hotel," the marshal said. "I had the manager pack up your things. He's holding them behind the counter for you."

"Much obliged." It was about what Catlin had expected when he'd first glanced through that broken window back at the Last Chance.

"You'll understand that folks are tired of having you in town."

Won't be the first time, Catlin thought. And said, "That's mighty thoughtful of you, Marshal."

"Doing what I can with what I've got."

"Next gang blows into town, you might try stepping up a little sooner. Or you could take off that tin."

"Get on that big old bay of yours and ride," Bradford replied. "You're burning daylight."

Leaving Las Vegas wouldn't be the worst trial Catlin had endured, by any means. He had another six or seven "Wanted" flyers in his saddlebag, men sought for felonies across New Mexico and Arizona Territories, but he didn't feel like starting up another hunt first thing.

No need for that, with fourteen hundred eighty dollars in his pocket and no deadline for another catch. In fact, Catlin was thinking he might take a short vacation. Give his gun a rest.

That wouldn't purge Bill Regner Jr. or mother Amanda from his mind entirely, but forgetting certain things was something of an art form that he'd cultivated over time.

It helped him sleep at night and get through long days on the road.

But would a short break do it this time? Should he maybe start to think about another line of work?

And what would that be? Where would he begin to look?

The answer came to Catlin as he mounted his bay stallion, turning toward the Grand Hotel to pick up his meager belongings.

Santa Fe, the territory's capital, lay sixty-odd miles to the west and slightly northward. Last he'd heard, some forty-seven hundred people occupied the city, with hotels, saloons, and restaurants, bathhouses, barbershops, something for any need that came to mind. Albuquerque, twice as far to the southwest, was just a minor crossroads by comparison, still trying to recover from the Civil War when it was claimed by the Confederacy, then recovered by the Yanks in 1862, eleven years ago.

Why not?

Catlin could find something to do in Santa Fe, maybe someone to hunt.

Or would he maybe find himself a whole new life?

CHAPTER ONE

Saturday, April 5, 1873

Waking to early-morning daylight and a rooster crowing, Arthur Catlin had to take a moment and remember where he was.

A bunkhouse on the Bar X spread, with ten men on adjoining cots, all stirring into wakefulness. Another ten would just be rousing in a second bunkhouse on the property, some forty feet from where Catlin was reaching for his clothes and boots.

Their boss, Bliss Mossman, occupied the big house with his wife, Gayle, and their late-life son just coming up on seven years old. The Bar X foreman, Sterling Tippit, had a three-room house off to himself, and Jared Olney—Mossman's horse wrangler—lived in a smaller one behind the barn, adjacent to the paddock, so he'd hear if anything was troubling the stock at any hour.

The last thing Catlin had in mind when he rode into Santa Fe was joining a cattle drive. He had some limited experience with livestock from his youth, working around his parents' farm in southern Illinois, but nothing on the scale of driving some twenty-five hundred steers from Santa Fe northwestward across Kansas, to be sold at Independence, in Missouri.

Thinking of it now, as fellow drovers started filing out to breakfast, Catlin wondered whether he had gone and lost his mind.

The route they meant to follow didn't put his mind at ease.

Travelers called it the Cimarron Trail, *cimarron* being "wild" in Spanish. In theory, it spanned seven hundred and seventy miles between Santa Fe and Independence, with traffic passing both ways: herds trudging to market from New Mexico Territory, wagon trains of would-be settlers reversing that process westward. Part of the way was a "dry" route, sixty-some miles without potable water between the Wagon Bed Spring, which fed the Cimarron River, to the Arkansas River outside Wichita. Conestoga wagons carried barrels filled with water while it lasted, but a herd on foot would have to tough it out for up to five days without drinking anything, getting moisture—what there was of it—from grass and shrubs along the way.

And if Wagon Bed Spring was dry when travelers arrived, that made things even worse.

Catlin had never traveled over the Cimarron trail, but he'd heard stories of abandoned wagons, sun-bleached bones that might be cattle, horses, even humans. And not all of those who died along the way had passed from thirst.

Hostile Indians were found along the way, as were mixed bands of Comancheros who sold guns and liquor to the native tribes illegally. When they were short on inventory or desired a bit of sport, those low-life raiders sometimes preyed on wagon trains, although they tended to prefer a solitary stagecoach or a smaller group of immigrants—one wagon, say, or maybe two—proceeding without company and poorly armed.

If drought lay heavy on the land, or Indians were on the warpath, travelers each way might take a longer route, adding another hundred miles to their journey, thereby requiring more food, water, ammunition, and the like to make a go of it.

A wild trail any way you looked at it.

A trail herd and a wagon train moved at the same pace, roughly, covering on good days twelve to thirteen miles. "Good" days were those without a skirmish to be fought or rampant Mother Nature to be dealt with, wielding storms of sand, rain, lightning, snow, or sleet, depending on the time of year.

While a herd spent no fewer than sixty-two days traveling, they could expect warm weather all the way, from mideighties through April to the high nineties or hundreds during May and June. That dropped at sundown, possibly as low as freezing, though in record years the mercury had plummeted to ten or twelve degrees. As far as normal rainfall, that might range between three-quarters of an inch per month to double that, but squalls could blow up out of nowhere, bringing thunder, lightning, or cyclonic winds that spooked the steers into stampeding.

Always something new and different, the foreman had advised Catlin when he'd signed on. Not so much an adventure, he suspected, as a trial for men and animals alike.

How many, man and beast, would manage to survive, it was still anybody's guess.

THE BAR X hands had lined a trestle table in the farmyard well before full light encroached upon

the spread. Catlin did not consult his pocket watch to
check the time precisely, satisfied to know that it was
earlier than he normally rolled out of bed to face another day.

Two cooks—one from the house, named Sherman
Toole, and Piney Rollins, who would man the chuck
wagon once they departed, backed by teenager Tim
Berryman, called "Little Mary" in his present role—
served up breakfast to the hands. The menu they'd
prepared included ham and bacon, biscuits and gravy,
fried eggs, and tin mugs of steaming black coffee. No
one complained about the fare or how much they'd received upon their metal plates.

While he ate, Catlin surveyed the other hands who
would be going on the drive with him, their boss, foreman, and Jared Olney. He'd been introduced to all of
them over the past two days while they were getting
ready for the trek to Independence, and he'd always
been a quick study with strangers' names.

Beside him on his left sat Danny Underwood,
roughly Art Catlin's size but balding, though it was
often covered by his hat. He had a port-wine birth-
mark on his jawline but pretended that he didn't know
it; he likely caught hell for years from other kids while
growing up. He wore no pistol at the table but possessed a Springfield Model 1855 rifle that he carried in
a saddle boot when mounted on his palomino stallion.

Next to Underwood and to his left sat Zebulon
Steinmeier, five foot six or seven, red hair graying at
the temples and a paunch hanging over his belt. From
seeing him around the spread, Catlin knew that he had
a matching set of rifle and six-gun produced by the
Volcanic Repeating Arms Company. He rode a rose-
gray gelding when at work on horseback.

Next in line to Catlin's left was thin Job Hooper,
who pronounced his given name the way a preacher

would on Sunday, reading from the Bible book of that same title, not confused with any ordinary job that Mr. Mossman or his foreman might assign. A First Model Schofield revolver rode his left hip, holstered backward, and when riding on his liver chestnut mare, he kept a Springfield Model 1871 rifle sheathed securely in a saddle scabbard.

The next in line, still to the left, was Merritt Dietz, armed with a Colt Walker revolver and an Arkansas toothpick to balance out his pistol belt. He owned a seal-brown bay stallion and handled it with skill, despite his relatively hulking size at six foot five, pushing two hundred fifty pounds.

The last two drovers on his left were Mike Limbaugh and Julius Pryor. Limbaugh was the youngest hand at table and the shortest, maybe five foot seven, with a Beaumont-Adams revolver on his hip. Rebels had favored that pistol, produced in England, during their revolt against the Union, though it hadn't saved them fighting at close quarters. Limbaugh's backup weapon for the trail was a Bridesburg Model 1861 rifled musket, used by both sides in the same conflict. His horse, a piebald mare, made Mike look even more diminutive than usual when he was saddled up.

Pryor was tall and thin, with whipcord muscles and a weathered hide resembling tanned buckskin. His sidearm, a Remington Model 1858 revolver, resembled a Colt at first glance, but its cylinder included "safety slots" milled between chambers, preventing the six-gun's hammer from resting atop a live cartridge that might be discharged accidentally. He owned a chestnut mare but got along all right with other horses from the Bar X herd.

Working back along the table's facing side, seated immediately to Bliss Mossman's left, Catlin's gaze fell on Nehemiah Wolford, owner of a grulla mare and

Springfield Model 1863 rifle. His nose was bent from being broken once too often, and he often snuffled like a man fighting a cold.

To Wolford's left, wolfing his food and keeping quiet while some of the others chattered, Luis Chávez was one of three Hispanic drovers chosen for the journey, stocky in a way that Catlin hadn't often seen among his people, mouth nearly concealed by a walrus mustache. His hands seemed small compared to his physique in general, but Catlin knew that he could throw a lasso with the best of them, without hanging up on his Colt 1851 Navy revolver, whether on his feet or riding his cremello stallion.

The drive's other two Hispanic hands came next in line. Jaime Reyes carried a Colt Army Model 1860 revolver and kept a double-edged stiletto sheathed in one boot for emergencies, readily accessible while riding his smoky perlino mare. Thinner than his friend Chávez, he stood taller than Chávez by three, perhaps four inches.

Next in line, Francisco Gallardo had no pistol showing but normally didn't stray far from his six-shot Colt New Model revolving rifle. Like most long guns in common usage, that weapon had seen its share of service in the Civil War, despite an unfortunate tendency to spray a shooter's forward hand with lead splinters on firing. Most days, Francisco rode a handsome amber champagne gelding.

Next to him, Jerome Guenther was slow to speak, encumbered by a stammer, and quick to take offense if someone mocked him or he only thought they were. Big-knuckled hands were scarred from fighting, though he'd faced no trouble on the Bar X spread so far. His rifle was a Springfield Model 1868, and Guenther backed it with a Colt Model 1862 Pocket Police revolver. His horse, a black gelding, was smaller than some of the drive's other mounts but still bore Guenther's corpulent form easily.

Across from Catlin, catty-corner, sat Bryce Zimmerman, owner of a blue roan gelding and a sixteen-shot Winchester Model 1866 rifle. He was moon-faced and bearded, with arms that seemed longer than normal at first glance. He'd lost most of the little finger on his right hand but it didn't stop him eating crispy bacon two strips at a time.

Last up, seated across from Catlin, was Linton McCormick, who wore a Gasser M1870 revolver—another foreign pistol, standard issue for the Austro-Hungarian cavalry, chambered for 11mm Montenegrin cartridges. Catlin could only guess where he acquired those in his travels stateside, but he'd wasted none of them so far on practice or the shooting contests other drovers staged for fun. His horse, a dun gelding, was getting on in years but still had life left in him yet.

To Catlin's right sat foreman Tippit, who faced their employer at the far end of the table, across twenty feet of swiftly disappearing food. He was a larger man than Mr. Mossman, heavier, but never forgot to treat the Bar X boss with absolute respect, an attitude he'd passed down to the other hands.

It was a mixed bag, but they'd worked together well so far during the short time since Catlin had joined the team. As to what kind of strain they'd have to bear over the next two months and change, Catlin supposed New Mexico would put them to the test.

A NY WAY YOU looked at it, the territory was a work in progress. Sprawling over 29,640 square miles at present, it served up deserts, mountains, rivers, lakes, and forests to delight explorers and encumber travelers. Of course, since politics determined the size and shape of U.S. territories, any measurements were fluid until statehood was achieved, whenever that might be.

As everywhere in North America, the Indians came first, though their date and point of origin was as yet unknown to modern scholars. In the 1540s, Spaniards arrived to steal the land from its original inhabitants, enslaving some and killing many more, searching in vain for the Seven Golden Cities of Cibola glimpsed (or imagined in delirium) by a conquistador, Álvar Cabeza de Vaca, whose supposed sighting of boundless wealth got him promoted to rule a massive chunk of South America the Spaniards called New Andalusia. In his absence, other Spanish nobles tried to settle the region Cabeza de Vaca had barely survived, importing farmers and battling natives including the Apache, Navajo, and Comanche.

Meanwhile, New Spain rebelled against its absentee rulers in 1521, its upstart royals renaming their appropriated home away from home the Mexican Empire. Another 280-odd years elapsed before Thomas Jefferson secured the Louisiana Purchase from France, doubling the United States in size. He sent a party under Lieutenant Zebulon Pike to explore the acquisition's southernmost reaches, but they were arrested and deported by Mexican troops before they'd completed their mission. That insult festered until 1846, when, irritated by events in Texas, America created the provisional government of New Mexico on land stolen from the original thieves.

Congress officially created the Territory of New Mexico in September 1850 but statehood remained elusive, boundaries drawn and redrawn over time, ceding part of New Mexico's land to Texas, lopping off close to half of the region's landmass to create the Arizona Territory in February 1863.

By then, the Civil War had been in progress for the

best part of two years, with two more yet to run. Pro-slavery forces declared the creation of a Confederate Arizona Territory, which was eradicated with General Lee's surrender at Appomattox in April 1865. Since then, four governors had presided over New Mexico Territory, Michigan native Marsh Giddings the latest in line for that thankless job. He hadn't been in office long before heated campaigning for New Mexico's seat in Congress sparked rioting at Mesilla, killing five persons and wounding fifty before U.S. Cavalry troops quelled the mayhem. Now war was brewing in Lincoln County between competing merchants and ranchers, with Giddings seemingly unable to keep order.

All that was simmering one hundred sixty miles due south of Santa Fe, while Bliss Mossman and his Bar X spread were unaffected by the bloodshed yet to come. Though unaffected by the Lincoln County conflict, Mossman's spread required close watching in a territory rife with bandits, rustlers, and hostile red men. Catlin knew there'd never be a "good" time for his present boss to travel more than seven hundred miles from home, taking along half of his hands, leaving his wife to raise their son and ride herd on the men he left behind.

But if he didn't go—or if he failed to reach the Independence stockyards with the steers he raised this past year—the Bar X would soon go broke, dry up, and blow away.

What it came down to in the end was no real choice at all.

WITH BREAKFAST DONE and cleared away, the drovers scrambled to their horses that were standing by. Bedrolls had already been stowed aboard the chuck wagon, less weight for mounts to carry on the trail.

The Bar X specialized in longhorn cattle, bred for hefty weight, intelligence, and even disposition, although handling them still required determination and a fair degree of courage. Though not the fattest bovines, and known for their lean beef, longhorn bulls still tipped the scales between fifteen hundred and twenty-two hundred pounds, with the cows weighing anywhere from eight hundred fifty to thirteen hundred. Thick hooves could crush flesh and bone during a stampede, but the horns that gave the breed its name were the real danger, measuring eight to ten feet tip to tip.

A longhorn might not plan to gore you or another steer at any given moment, but the risk was ever present. A four-foot horn could easily impale all but the stoutest men, and on a long trail drive, with no physician in attendance, any major wound to man or horse could be life-threatening.

On the plus side, longhorns—even bulls—were relatively placid, rarely taking umbrage to the point where they would charge a man deliberately. They also consumed a wider range of grasses, weeds, and other plants than many breeds, a bonus on a long drive with its end point at a slaughterhouse where every pound was money on the hoof.

Mr. Mossman's hands would earn forty dollars a month and "found"—the grub served up by Piney Rollins and Tim Berryman—with no cash in their hands until the herd was sold in Independence. Catlin had an edge on other drovers, still holding about a thousand dollars of the payoff he'd collected for the Grimes brothers, but with nowhere to spend it on the trail.

There were no creature comforts on a drive. Bedrolls meant sleeping on the ground and open to the sky above. Tents weighed too much and took up too much space to bother with. Inclement weather was a cross they'd bear if it caught up with them, whether they wound up drenched with rain, pelted with sleet, or quaking in unseasonable snow.

In that respect, the men had no advantage over the livestock they'd pledged to guard.

As necessary, hands would swap out horses from the drive's remuda. Bar X horses were adept at herding and pursuing cattle, but the private mounts brought to the drive by part-time hands would have to learn that skill while on the job.

While steers and horses lived mostly on grass, the trail boss and his men would pass their meals with salt pork, bacon, beans, and bread, washed down with coffee. There would be no beef unless a longhorn died or had to be put down along the trail.

At an ideal pace, the herd would cover ten to twelve miles daily, cattle grazing as they went, meant to keep up the weight they'd started at as much as possible. They'd drink when water was available—from creeks, streams, possibly a lake somewhere along the way—without retarding progress overmuch. Drovers would keep them pointed toward the northeast, marking Independence as their goal, and watching out for any hazards that arose.

Those could be natural, like cliffs and gullies, rivers that the longhorns couldn't cross without assistance in the face of rushing currents, rockslides, and the like. Four-legged predators included cougars, bears, gray wolves, coyotes—maybe even foxes if the smaller canids felt like nipping at a steer's legs, though they'd likely get trampled into jelly for their pains. As the herd progressed, a changing cast of venomous reptiles would threaten men and animals alike: coral snakes and several breeds of rattlers in New Mexico, more rattlers all the way through Kansas, and copperheads and cottonmouths depending on proximity to water.

Even the smaller animals—like rodents, living off of seeds and insects as they mostly did—could cost the herd in steers and dollars at their point of sale. Gophers and prairie dogs dug burrows that could lame a steer or horse, snapping a pastern, cannon bone, or knee, requiring that the animal be spared from further suffering by point-blank gunfire to its brain. In that case, with a steer, there would be beef at mealtimes while it lasted. With a horse, only the landscape's native scavengers would benefit, while Mr. Mossman bore the loss.

It wasn't hungry predators or deadly snakes that worried Catlin most, however. For his money, the worst threat they might face along the trail would come from other humans bent on stealing Mr. Mossman's herd, attacking any drovers who saw fit to intervene.

At least that was a problem Catlin felt equipped to deal with from his prior experience at hunting men.

An hour past full daylight they were on the move: twenty-five hundred steers, seventy horses, counting spares in the remuda and four yoked to pull the chuck wagon, plus nineteen men. It made an awesome spectacle, the herd alone enough to make a person stare if any strangers had been passing by. Their shuffling hooves raised dust in clouds that might be visible from twenty, maybe thirty miles away against the azure sky, as if announcing, *Here we come. Line up for plunder if you're in a mood to rustle, rob, or just raise hell in general.*

What bad men, whether veterans or rookies, could resist that kind of bait?

Thinking about Las Vegas, Catlin wondered if he'd made a change at all in how he made a living out of death. Suppose they made it through the whole trip without firing off a single shot in anger on the way. So, what? The steers still had no clue where they were going, or to what end—brained with a hammer, butchered, parceled out to end their days on dining plates.

Looked at another way, they'd feed a major portion of America, from robber barons to the laborers in their employ.

But if it came to gunplay down the line, at least Catlin was certain he could count on one thing.

There would be no children in the line of fire.

CHAPTER TWO

Friday, April 11

CAN'T SAY I like those thunderheads," Bert Moss-man said, eyes focused to the north, miles off.

"Could be a problem if they overtake us," Sterling Tippit granted, "but they're ten, twelve miles away, at least. I doubt we'll even hear the thunder as it stands right now."

"It's not the thunder that concerns me," said the Bar X owner.

Even as he spoke, a far-off bolt of lightning arced from the blue-black heavens to the earth below, and Tippit was correct. Mossman heard nothing of the thunder that always accompanied that kind of fire-works in the sky.

"More what it sends us, then," the foreman said.

"You read my mind," Mossman replied.

"You're thinking a dry thunderstorm?"

"I wouldn't be surprised," said Mossman.

And dry thunderstorms were trouble all the way around.

Those were the deadly storms that spawned thunder and lightning aplenty, while most of their rain evaporated in the atmosphere, never reaching the ground below. Since they occurred primarily in regions prone to drought, the lightning strikes often set fire to trees or grasslands, while their gusty surface winds fanned the flames and sent them racing miles away. And with no rain to speak of falling from the clouds, dousing those flames became a grueling task for humans—if they could be stopped at all.

"Not much to burn out here," said Tippit, once again anticipating what might have his boss on edge.

Mossman responded with a question of his own. "But what about the wind?"

"Well, shit."

"That's what I thought."

Mossman wasn't afraid of fire sweeping the desert, though "dry" lightning could do damage to a herd of stock all by itself. He'd seen longhorns cut down by lightning bolts as they grazed peacefully on open land, though it was rare, and Mossman personally had his doubts concerning claims of strikes that cut swaths of destruction through a herd as if some baleful giant in the sky were scything wheat. That seemed improbable to him, like stories of the giant fish that got away, though it was not impossible per se.

"A dust storm, then," said Tippit, sounding glum.

"Just have to wait and see," Mossman replied.

But maybe not for long.

He didn't know the scientific lingo to describe it, but the rancher understood how nature worked against mankind. Or maybe there was no purpose behind it, just bad luck for anybody standing in the way.

Aside from tossing arcs of lightning that could turn

a forest into smoking ash, dry thunderstorms cooled off the air beneath its clouds, changing its weight and density compared to ground-level conditions. That cool air descended rapidly and fanned out when it reached the earth's surface, spreading outward from the storm's eye, picking up whatever dust or sand lay coating arid soil. Sometimes that grit was spun off into whirling dust devils, which could be frightening to man and beast alike but seldom matched the size or strength of a tornado.

But a sandstorm could be bad enough, all on its own.

Mossman had seen the desert's rolling dust clouds form a front that towered anywhere from fifty to a thousand feet or more above flat land, attaining speeds of twenty-five to forty miles per hour within minutes. Flying grit could scour bark from trees and paint from buildings, bullet-sized pebbles smashing through windows and admitting clouds of dust to rural homes. Worse yet, for men and animals caught in the gale-force winds, sand clotted eyes, nostrils, and even lungs. That could result in blindness, fatal choking, or an aftermath of "dry pneumonia" that scarred lung tissue beyond hope of healing properly.

If they were overtaken by a sandstorm, Mossman reckoned, that would be the real danger to his stock and to his drovers. It could spell disaster, and there wasn't much that he could do about it.

Nothing much but getting ready for the worst.

"Best spread the word," he told Tippit.

"I'm on it, sir," his foreman said, and galloped off to warn the Bar X hands that hell on earth might soon be overtaking them.

THE WICKED DUST is coming," the muscular Apache told his fellow braves.

His name, self-chosen, was translated as "Eagle." He had been born Yuma, "Chief's Son," but since his father's death in battle with the white eyes' cavalry when Yuma was himself a child, he had outgrown that name, discarding it as certain Anglos laid aside the postnominal suffix "junior" when their fathers passed away.

Today he was Paco, war chief of a fourteen-man Apache band whose members were oath-bound to spend their lives opposing any further white encroachment on the sacred land that once was theirs.

Patamon, Paco's younger brother, said, "Perhaps the storm delivers opportunity."

Paco nodded, agreeing with his sibling, but he felt compelled to add, "If we are cautious."

They had been following the white man's trail drive for the past two days, attracted first by its dust cloud, keeping a safe distance and watching the herd's progress from concealment atop mesas and peering from dry riverbeds. Paco's plan of attack was still not fully formulated, but there was something to what Patamon proposed.

A desert sandstorm might imperil warriors and their mustangs, but concealment mitigated that inherent danger. If the storm itself was not too strong, not too dangerous, Paco supposed his braves might seize the chance to raid the trail drive, claiming cattle to sustain themselves and even picking off a few whites in the process.

All while hoping none of his own men were slain.

ART CATLIN WAS retrieving two stray longhorns, easing them back toward the main herd, when Sterling Tippit galloped up to him, the Bar X foreman riding on his blood bay mare. Catlin read unaccustomed agitation on the foreman's face, at odds with his normal relaxed expression, but he kept his mouth shut, waiting for whatever bad news lay in store.

"You've seen those thunderheads off to the north," said Tippit—not a question, just assuming Catlin was aware.

In fact, he had seen them and nodded a silent affirmative.

"Boss reckons it's dry thunder and it might be working up a sandstorm, sending it our way."

Catlin was weather-wise enough to grant that proposition, asking Tippit, "What's he got in mind?"

"For now, just cover up the best you can before it hits us. If we need to pull the herd up short, I'll be around again."

"Right," Catlin said, and watched the foreman ride on to the next drover tracking the herd's long northern flank.

First thing he did was doff his hat and shift the chin strap forward, snugging it to keep the hat on if the wind picked up. The neckerchief he wore, knotted in back, was plain black cloth folded into a triangle and tucked inside Catlin's open shirt collar like a mourning ascot, something he might don in preparation for a funeral. For now, he tugged it free and pulled it up until it masked the lower portion of his face from cheekbones to below his dimpled chin.

"I must look like a bandit, pal," he told his stallion. "It's a good thing we aren't passing by a bank."

The stallion, a strawberry roan, paid no heed to his rider, satisfied to whicker at the two errant longhorns and keep them ambling back in line with other members of the herd.

The mask wouldn't protect his eyes if they were assailed by a sandstorm, but he hadn't thought to lay his hands on any goggles when he'd signed on for the drive. Worse came to worst, he could try pulling up the neckerchief and tilt his flat-brimmed hat forward, then squint his eyelids like an old man reading by dim light and hope that did the trick.

Which it might not, he realized.

Catlin had witnessed major sandstorms twice—one time outside of Texas, while running down a bail-jumper; the other one in Arizona Territory, when coming up on Tucson with a highwayman draped over what had been the outlaw's skewbald gelding—but he'd never been enveloped by one, blinded, deafened, struggling to breathe.

First time for everything, he thought, and didn't like the ring of that inside his head.

Dying, for instance, was a person's first and only time—except perhaps for Lazarus of ancient myth.

Catlin eyed the northern skyline, frown hidden behind his mask as he saw the thunderclouds shot through by lightning were advancing on the Bar X herd. Most times, a sight like that would come complete with blurriness below, a screen of pouring rain. This time, however, he could see a clear horizon line below the clouds, which told him that the clouds were wreaking havoc only with their static electricity and the roiling desert winds they'd generated.

Even as he watched, twisters of sand and gravel rose, writhed, and collapsed, as if some huge primeval beast with tentacles in place of legs was clutching at the sky above it, tempting the storm with its living, flailing lightning rods. One finally succeeded, struck down by a blue-white shaft of energy, exploding silently, grit raining down.

A monster that you couldn't fight with guns or hope to run away from on horseback.

He couldn't calculate how fast the storm front might be traveling, but it was miles wide, growing as he watched.

And there was no escape.

Sterling Tippit felt the first raw gusts of northerly wind on his face as he finished his rounds of the herd. He'd spoken to each hand in turn, all riding alone or paired off, sharing idle conversation as they watched the steers. All had agreed to preparation for a storm, and as he eyed them from a distance now most had begun adjusting hats and neckerchiefs to meet the coming storm.

And it *was* coming. Tippit had no doubt of that.

His boss had called it, got the jump on Tippit that time, but the foreman felt no lingering embarrassment. Somebody always had to spot potential danger first, and if that job fell to Mr. Mossman . . . well, what of it?

Tippit had seen the storm clouds but his boss had beat him to the interpretation of their danger to the herd, and that was fine. The only ones who needed warning now were Piney Rollins and Tim Berryman aboard the chuck wagon.

Before he had a chance to speak, Piney called out to him, "Looks like a storm coming."

"I'd say so," Tippit granted as he pulled up even with their bulky rig.

"Saw you talking up the hands," their cook said. "And I've been through these a couple times before."

"All battened down, then?"

"I've got Little Mary on it," Rollins said, and nodded back over his shoulder, toward where Berryman was making noise in back, under the wagon's canvas cover.

Looking at it from the outside, Tippit counted half a dozen places where the canvas had been patched with newer, lighter-colored bits of tarpaulin, secured by heavy stitches.

"Reckon that will hold?" he asked Piney.

"Whether it does or not, we can't do anything about it now, out here," the cook replied.

"Just do the best you can," Tippit replied.

"Same as we always do."

Another gust of wind hit Tippit, threatening to blow his hat off if he hadn't cinched its cord under his chin. This time, small grains of sand rattled against the Stetson's crown.

Frowning, he nudged his blood bay mare toward Mr. Mossman, riding at the herd's vanguard. Nothing remained for Tippit now but to report that he'd done all he could.

M ASKA—"STRONG," AS translated to the white man's tongue—cursed the approaching storm front that he feared would stall their raid upon the cattle drive. Delays were vexing to him, even though he knew that watchful patience was required.

"We lose another day, at least," he groused to Bodaway, rising beside him, to his left.

"We can't be sure of that," Bodaway said. "Paco may have a plan."

Maska swallowed the complaint that came to mind, against their war chief for his way of holding back his plans until the final moment, listening to other options but rejecting any that conflicted with his own.

"Maybe," Maska said, letting it go at that.

"You doubt it?" Bodaway inquired.

A white man would have called him "Fire Maker," the literal translation of his given name to English. Twenty summers old, bearing a knife scar on the left side of his jawline, Bodaway was better known among his fellow warriors for the fires he set in white men's homes than for campfires over which their party roasted meat at night.

And meat, Maska knew only too well, was presently in short supply.

If they could not make off with one or more longhorns

tomorrow or the next day at the latest, hunger would begin to sap their fighting strength.

"The storm may be a gift from the Great Spirit in disguise," he said.

"How so?" Bodaway asked.

"White men are clumsy, easily confused. Remember the last farm we raided?"

Bodaway smiled. Said, "The old man got so excited that he shot himself."

"Only his foot," Maska said.

But that had been enough to leave the farmer helpless, with his wife and children screaming from the house. The woman had been younger than her husband by ten years of so, their son too small to fight effectively, their daughter still an infant in a cradle.

Paco's band had left none living as they rode away.

"If there is wind and dust enough," said Bodaway, "we should be well-fed for a week, at least."

"I'd rather wipe the white men out and take the whole herd," Maska replied.

"There are too many of them," Bodaway reminded him. "At least *nah-kee-go-nay-nan-too-ooh*."

Counting the Apache way, in which two thousand was described as twenty hundreds.

"So?"

"We are too few and know too little about herding stock in such numbers."

"I don't say we should keep them all," Maska said.

"What, then?"

"Why not trade them to Comancheros for more guns and ammunition? Firewater or anything we want."

Bodaway made a sour face. "I hate the Comancheros worse than settlers. We cannot trust anything they do or say."

"As long as their guns work, who cares?" asked Maska. "Someday we'll deal with them as well."

"You wish to fight the world?"

"Only the white man's part of it."

"Be satisfied with what the Great Spirit has given us," said Bodaway.

"I try," Maska said. "But it never feels like enough."

THE STORM CAUGHT up with them half an hour after Tippit circulated with his warning to prepare for it. Art Catlin saw a massive wall of dust advancing on the herd, an airborne avalanche of sorts but dirty brown and gray instead of blizzard white.

Danny Underwood, riding beside him, muttered, "Here she comes, goddamn it!"

And before Catlin could answer back or even think of anything to say, the tidal wave of grit and dust broke over them, enveloping the herd, its mounted guides, spare horses, and the chuck wagon trailing behind and offset to the south.

Piney Rollins tried to avoid the worst trail dust whenever possible, but now he'd have to eat sand with the rest of them.

At first, Catlin's roan stallion sought to shy away from the onslaught, but there was no escaping it. Art knew the horse's eyes, nostrils, and throat would suffer just as much as his—or worse, since there was no way he could mask the animal or shield its eyes from stinging sand. He did his best to calm the animal, keeping a right grip on its reins, but it could plainly sense his own distress and disturbance spreading through the herd.

Catlin couldn't expect livestock, whether horses or steers, to understand the storm as such. The greatest danger, barring any injury the animals might suffer to their eyes or lungs from blowing grit, was panic spreading through the herd and turning into a stampede.

And if that happened . . .

He'd never sweated out a major sandstorm, so Catlin hadn't experienced the charging aimlessly about, the being spooked by a sound or sudden movement, ranging from a gunshot to a rattler's buzzing in the grass. But he had listened to some firsthand stories from survivors of such incidents, and was aware that once the longhorns started running, no lone man or horse could stand before them without being trampled into bloody pulp.

He wasn't even sure that seventeen of them could keep the herd in line, under a semblance of control, but they would have to try their best, knowing the stakes came down to life or death for all concerned.

He glanced across toward where he'd last seen Underwood but couldn't find the other drover now. Dismissing that, he focused on the herd, calling out to the longhorns through his mask, but in the howling wind Catlin could barely even hear himself.

The steers were making frightened noises now. One brushed against his roan but didn't use its horns, bewildered by the sudden loss of visibility and decent air to breathe. In fact, it wasn't just the airborne grit that threatened suffocation; it was the howling wind that carried it, a primal force that made the simple act of drawing breath at all a daunting task.

And how much time was left before that changed from being difficult to becoming an impossibility?

BLISS MOSSMAN HUNCHED over his saddle horn, wind buffeting him and his flea-bitten gray gelding, trying to unseat him from his saddle. If he fell, he imagined it would be the end of him.

That said, remaining mounted wasn't solving any of his problems. He could barely see beyond his horse's ears, the wind rush in his ears nigh on to deafening. It felt like riding through thick tule fog, except in that case he'd be chilled and damp, not sweating through his clothes and the kerchief hiding the lower portion of his face.

Instead of chilling Mossman, though, the gale was stifling hot, as if a giant from on high had thrown the door back on a blast furnace—or possibly a hatchway leading into hell itself.

That grim conceit fell through when Mossman realized that he was still alive, not roasting on a spit Downstairs for sins that he'd forgotten to atone for while alive. Whatever elsc this was, it damned sure wasn't supernatural.

Still, he could understand how ancient men, living in caves or scattered on the open planes, had looked to deities and demons for an explanation of the waking world around them, with its dangers crowding in upon all sides.

Mossman's predicament was relatively simple, once you pared away the risk of smothering, collapsing from his horse. and being trampled by more than a couple thousand longhorns, or remaining on his perch and going blind for life, his eyeballs scoured by flying sand.

To ward that off, he'd narrowed his eyelids to slits, keeping his head down, trusting in his hat's brim to protect his naked upper face. This wasn't something he could fight and conquer, like a rustling gang or pack of hungry wolves. The storm was utterly devoid of conscious thought or feeling as it swept across the desert landscape, wreaking havoc.

Totally insensate, right.

So why did Mossman feel as if it hated him with a malignant passion normally reserved for feudists in a duel whose only end was death?

If that were true, the rancher knew that he must be the one to die. No man could conquer nature, any more than he could reach into the midnight sky and capture distant stars to light his camp.

The steers were making angry, frightened sounds now, building up a head of steam whose only outlet would be rushing toward disaster through the swirling clouds of dust. Mossman had trouble seeing them, but he could *feel* their agitation radiating outward, pushing back against the storm.

For just a second it reminded him of when he'd lived in Texas, years back, near the Gulf of Mexico at Corpus Christi. He remembered wading out a few yards from the beach there, and the way the ocean water surged against him coming in, then sucked sand out from underneath his feet as it retreated. In that moment, Mossman knew that he was helpless against something vastly greater than himself. It could rise up and push him back to shore, or undercut him and, with its riptide, draw him out and drown him in the time it took to manage screaming once, or maybe twice.

Except he'd heard somewhere that drowning was supposed to be a relatively peaceful death. No one could say that for a sandstorm flaying him alive.

AT FIRST CATLIN thought he'd imagined it, a hoarse voice shouting at the storm.

The second time it reached his windburned ears, he realized it was a human voice in fact, but put it down to panic, someone who'd been pushed beyond endurance by the raging storm.

The third time, though, he got its message, recognized it as a shouted order from Bliss Mossman, rallying his men.

"Head off the herd!" Mossman was shouting, interspersed with fits of coughing. "Stop them running, for God's sake! Corral them if you can!"

The bad news: they had no corral, no fence or barrier of any kind to stop the herd from breaking into a headlong stampede. And one they started running in this storm there would be grievous injuries from falls and slashing horns. Beyond all that, some steers might run until their hearts exploded and they dropped, stone dead. Given the roiling clouds of dirt surrounding all of them, many might simply disappear.

Disaster, if he had to boil it down into a single word.

Catlin began to urge his roan forward, snapping the stallion's reins and thumping with his bootheels, even though he wore no spurs. The horse responded, broke into a trot, but wouldn't risk a gallop when it couldn't see the ground six feet ahead.

Whoever said that animals were dumb, thought Catlin, must be next door to an idiot himself.

A pistol shot rang out from somewhere up ahead, around the herd's front ranks, immediately followed by a medley of voices telling the shooter to put up his iron and stop acting a damned fool with longhorns already stoked up for a breakout. Catlin couldn't recognize the windblown voices and he didn't care to try.

Men sometimes panicked in a storm, the same as livestock, sometimes worse. Loud noises frightened animals, but with their limited imaginations they, at least, weren't prone to conjure devils in the dark.

A good thing, too. Just now, the truth was bad enough.

When Catlin reached the forefront of the herd, the longhorns were already slowing down, ranks telescoping from the southwest to northeast and crowding one another. Mounted drovers alternately shouted at the steers or spoke in what they hoped were soothing voices, sometimes barely audible above the storm. A few were brandishing their lariats like rolled-up bullwhips, stopping short of striking any steers but seeking to distract them from the gritty wind.

And as he joined them, Catlin reckoned it was working. Slowly, by degrees, the longhorns pressed together, seemed to gather strength from numbers, and instead of running with it, hunkered down into a mass the sandstorm couldn't blow away.

Not yet, at least.

But Catlin knew that situation wasn't permanent, by any means.

If the winds kept on blowing for the next few hours, maybe stretching into days as he'd heard tell of while he drifted through the Arizona Territory, even stolid animals would reach a breaking point.

And if that happened, Catlin knew there would be hell to pay.

CHAPTER THREE

Sunday, April 13

T HE STORM DIED around midnight, rolling over into Sunday morning, leaving everybody on the trail drive short of sleep.

Art Catlin guessed the steers and horses were as weary as the men in charge of them, but there was no escaping the fact that a new day was upon them and they had a full morning of work ahead before thcy even got around to breaking camp.

Piney Rollins managed to pull off a minor miracle by having breakfast ready as dawn's first light broke over the wind-scoured flats. Catlin tucked into it, expecting a side order of sand with his bacon and beans, but he was pleasantly surprised to find the simple fare unsullied by their recent ordeal.

Mr. Mossman had the drovers eat in shifts, so half of them were riding herd and counting steers while their companions ate as fast as they could manage, gulping down hot coffee strong enough to clear the dust out of their heads.

At least for now.

Catlin had no doubt that the long night would catch up with him by noon, latest, but there was nothing he could do about it, no exemption he could claim for pulling his own weight along with every other Bar X hand.

Bliss Mossman and his foreman clearly hadn't caught a wink of sleep all night, but they set an example for the drovers, wolfing bread and bacon down while mounted, circulating to assess how the longhorns were holding up. Against all odds, none of the cattle present and accounted for at dawn were seriously injured, though a goodly number of then wheezed and coughed, still clearing dust out of their sinuses and lungs. Catlin imagined many of them would be bleary-eyed all day, as would their handlers,

Once he had checked his guns for fouling dust and satisfied himself that his strawberry roan was fit to face another day, Catlin swung up into his saddle and joined Nehemiah Wolford on a search for any longhorns straying westward from the herd. More two-teams were headed south and east on that same errand, leaving ten men with the main herd, Jared Olney checking over mounts in their remuda as he got them ready for the trail.

"How many would you guess we lost?" asked Wolford as they left the camp behind.

"Guessing won't get us anywhere," said Catlin, "but I wouldn't be surprised to learn it was a dozen, maybe more."

"Not bad, as many as we started with," Wolford replied.

"But money out of pocket for the Bar X, even so, meaning there's less to go around."

"I guess we'd better try 'n' find some, then."

"Sounds like a plan," Catlin agreed, already checking out the landscape for a longhorn's silhouette.

"You figure last night's blow will be the worst we have to deal with?"

"If we're lucky," Catlin answered. "But I wouldn't count on it."

"Each day a new adventure, then."

"One way to look at it."

"And what's another?" Wolford asked him.

"Take a job and see it through, then move along to something else."

His problem being that he never knew what "something else" might be.

Before he'd turned to bounty hunting, Catlin had spent six months working as a deputy in Abilene, before he ran into a rich man who believed he was above the law and owned the marshal Art was serving under. He had cleared that obstacle but found himself obliged to leave or face a term in prison on a framed manslaughter charge. From there, he'd found it easier to hunt men down without a badge or rule book to confine him, shrugging off the obvious disdain most people felt toward his profession, keeping to himself.

Cowpunching was an honorable job, comparatively speaking, and the men it tended to attract weren't known for prying into the affairs of strangers, which he liked. As far as making it a long-term occupation, though, Catlin couldn't imagine it.

The good news: he'd gone nearly three weeks now without a gunshot fired in anger, no one bent on killing him.

Which meant nobody's children in the line of fire.

"There's two of 'em," Wolford announced. "Off to the left, there."

Sleepy-looking longhorns. Seeing them brought

Catlin back to the here and now—the only time and place that mattered for the next two months or so.

B LISS MOSSMAN WASN'T happy, but he knew their situation could have been much worse.

This morning's head count told him seventeen longhorns were missing since the storm forced them to a halt, but Mossman had his fingers crossed, hoping that some of those, at least, would be recovered by midmorning, fit to travel on.

Beyond that, thank whatever deity you chose, he and his hired men had come through the sandstorm without any lasting injuries. Jaime Reyes had fallen from the back of his smoky perlino mare but hung on to the reins, stopped it from bolting, and was back aboard as soon as he regained his bearings. Otherwise, the Bar X hands, horses, and chuck wagon all seemed to be in decent shape. Some men and beasts were still coughing and likely would be through this day, into the next, but that discomfort only proved that they were still alive.

Mossman hadn't gone out on the search for strays himself, believing that his presence with the main herd was required after their setback from the weather yesterday. He pulled his weight most days, except for standing watch over the sleeping steers at night, but that exemption was an owner's privilege after the long years he'd devoted to carving a spread out of the wilderness, stocking longhorns, and nursing them through seasons when he didn't have enough to market profitably, waiting for their numbers to increase.

This made his fourth year driving herds to Independence, while the hands he'd left behind watched over bulls and cows handpicked to be the sires and dames of next year's herd. Choosing the men who stayed behind had proved as critical as hiring others who would help him on the trail. And that, in turn, brought Mossman's thoughts circling around to settle on his wife and son at home.

Gayle Mossman had worked close beside her husband as they built their desert home with visions of an empire in the making. If anything, he would have said she'd worked harder than he had, since her basic tasks including cleaning up around the house they'd built together, cooking all the meals, and never once complaining that she couldn't get it done.

That kind of life inevitably took its toll, and they had given up on having kids until a happy accident presented them with Danny seven years ago. He was the light of Mossman's life, intended heir of all his parents had achieved since settling in New Mexico—but if he chose another path when he was old enough to know his mind, Mossman had vowed to be supportive, not a stubborn obstacle.

On trail drives, Mossman missed his wife and child through every waking hour and he sometimes dreamed of them at night. It troubled him, being so far away from them when there were mortal dangers to be faced at home, ranging from lawless men and hostile Indians on down the scale to wildfires, storms, and rattler bites. Mossman couldn't protect them personally while he pushed their herd hundreds of miles away from home, which left only the element of trust.

Bliss trusted Gayle to love and cherish him beyond question. He trusted Hardy to obey instructions, do his chores, and shun trouble as well as any boy could manage growing up. As for the men he left behind, Bliss trusted them to guard his wife, their son, their property, and sacrifice themselves if need be in that cause.

If any of them ever let him down in that regard, they knew there would be hell to pay and no escaping it while they were drawing breath.

He spotted Sterling Tippit riding toward him on his

blood bay mare, calling from twenty yards away, "Four head recovered, Mr. M!"

Good news after a rough patch.

Now they only needed thirteen more to make the heard complete.

A SINGLE LONGHORN WASN'T much, but on the other hand, Paco knew it could feed him and his braves for days on end.

That spared them hunting deer and pronghorn antelopes or smaller game while granting more time to examine and pursue the larger herd that trespassed over land Paco's ancestors had considered home, a sacred place where they could live in peace aside from periodic feuding with Comanches. There had been no peace since the *tsayaditl-ti* arrived—his people's name for white men—and considering the losses that Paco's nation had suffered since that time, he had no expectation of another day without some conflict preying on his mind.

That was a warrior's lot in troubled times, and he made no complaint, felt no resentment for the obligation handed down by elders of his tribe, all murdered now or caged on reservations that destroyed their spirits even if their bodies clung to life.

Paco could feel his warriors growing more and more restive with each new sunrise. They craved battle, greater opportunities to strike back in retaliation for the pain and misery inflicted on their people by invaders from a land across the seas. He shared that eagerness and understandable impatience, but at the same time, as war chief, Paco was required to counsel patience, careful planning, and development of strategy.

The steer they'd captured overnight was tethered to a hemlock tree inside a small canyon where Paco's band was presently concealed from prying eyes. The braided rope around its neck allowed the beast to graze at will within a six-foot radius, its forage spared from blowing dust during the storm by yellow sandstone walls that boxed the canyon on three sides.

The canyon was their desert sanctuary for the moment, but it could become a death trap if white cowboys should discover them. Paco believed that raging winds must have erased their tracks before the storm ended last night, but just in case, he'd posted Patamon and Kuruk—"Bear" in English—to stand watch atop the looming cliffs.

"When may we eat, Paco?" a voice behind him asked.

Turning to face Abooksigun—"Wildcat" as he'd been named at birth—Paco said, "After sundown, when the white men pitch another camp. This place will hide the fire we build, and afterward there will be smoked meat for the trail."

"And are we settling for just the one?"

"My plan remains unchanged," Paco replied. "We strike again when circumstances favor our success."

"To take more cattle," Abooksigun declared.

"To teach a lesson that the whites will long remember," Paco said, correcting him. "To make them bleed and learn to live with fear."

T HAT LOOK LIKE three to you?" asked Nehemiah Wolford.

Catlin had to spend a moment longer staring down into the weed-choked gully that had been a creek's bed sometime in the past. At least two steers had tumbled down its bank during the storm last night and never made it out again, covered in dust and grit that smothered them and now served as a shroud of sorts.

"It's two, for sure," he told Wolford.

"I'm counting legs and I get nine."

"I grant you eight," Catlin replied.

Pointing from where he sat aboard his grulla mare, Wolford said, "No, I'm pretty sure that's nine."

A closer look told Catlin he was right. A ninth hoof, with its dew claw and a portion of its hock, protruded from the drift of sand, as if the longhorn in extremis had attempted to escape the crushing weight of other blinded strays who'd stumbled down on top of it.

"You're right," he said. "Nine hooves, it has to be three steers."

"All dead," said Wolford, squeezing in the obvious.

"No doubt about it."

They had collected three live steers so far that morning, but discovering three dead ones now brought Catlin's spirits down.

"Should we just leave 'em here?"

"What's the alternative?" Catlin inquired.

"Try fetching one of 'em, at least, before they start to rot. Means beef for supper and a few more meals besides."

Catlin glanced back at the three longhorns idling twenty feet away from them and frowned. "We try to drag one up and butcher it while they stand watching us, they could take off again. Besides, where would we put the meat?"

"So, how about one of us rides back to the camp and takes these three along. Fetch Piney and his kid back here and bring that sled they haul around for fetching firewood and the like? The other waits here, so they spot him coming back, and that way keep the buzzards off 'em, too."

It made good sense to Catlin. "Fine by me," he said.

"You wanna flip a coin for who does what?"

"No need," Catlin replied. "I'll stay and stand watch over them. Just get back here quick as you can."

"Well, if you're sure . . ."

"Go on ahead."

"Okay, then."

Wolford didn't delay for further conversation, and rode over to the three stray longhorns, urging them back toward the camp and herd located half a dozen miles northwest of where the desert gully had become a make-shift tomb. Catlin watched man and animals recede into the distance, then checked out the clear sky over-head for any vultures circling a potential breakfast.

So far, he and his strawberry roan were alone with the dead.

That situation wouldn't last long in the desert, nor would fresh meat on the carcasses from last night's storm. Insects would find the longhorns first, predom-inantly ants and flies, but as the morning passed there might be foxes and coyotes; maybe something larger would home in on the smell of blood and death.

Nature let nothing go to waste, and if the plan for salvaging at least one steer proved viable, it meant Piney Rollins, maybe with his adolescent aide, would have to shake a leg and claim whatever they could carry before serious decomposition set in. Beyond that point, contaminated beef could be life-threatening to any cowboys who partook of it.

Catlin surveyed the land around him, saw no scav-engers as yet, and figured he should let Rollins decide if they could use the beef or not. If Catlin doubted its digestibility, he could beg off at suppertime, sticking with beans and bread.

They doubtless would face other hardships on the trail to Independence, and he didn't plan on going down from any self-inflicted injuries.

STERLING TIPPIT RODE from camp with Piney Rollins, traveling southwestward with two horses from the drive's remuda trailing them. In place of saddles, Jared

Olney had draped blankets on the spare equines, to
cover each between its withers and its croup, better to
drape each animal with slabs of beef while sparing
them from injury.

Rollins had brought along a fair selection of his cutlery wrapped up in chamois cloth. Tippit had watched
him pack a butcher's knife, a meat cleaver, a boning
knife, a skinning knife, and a sharpening steel to employ if a blade lost its edge while he worked.

Three dead steers was a blow to the herd and to Tippit's employer, but if they could salvage a supply of beef
for eating on the trail over the next few days, at least
the sacrifice would not have been a total waste.

They spotted Catlin waiting for them at a distance
of two hundred yards, not able to make out his features
yet, but Tippit recognized the drover's horse and reckoned no one else would be that close to where Wolford
had placed him on a map scratched in the dust. To play
it safe, though, just in case, Tippit released his holster's
hammer thong and let his right hand rest atop the
curved butt of his Colt Dragoon.

When they were close enough to speak without straining their vocal cords, Tippit backed off preparation for
a fast draw, telling Catlin, "Wolford says you've got three
down."

"We came to that by counting hooves that we could
see," Catlin replied. "I doubt there's any more than
three. The gully isn't deep enough."

Peering down into it from horseback, Tippit saw
that he was right. If any more longhorns had fallen in,
their bodies should be lying in plain sight.

Turning to Rollins, Tippit said, "Okay, Piney. What
happens now?"

Dismounting from a sorrel mare, Rollins removed
his wrapped-up tools and peered up into Tippit's face.
He said, "I gotta get in with 'em, see what shape they're

in. Whichever ones we salvage, you two pass me down your lariats with running nooses tied in both of 'em. I'll fasten them to one steer at a time, around the horns if I can manage it, then you-all drag 'em up on top. From there, I'll dust 'em off and see what's what before I start in cutting."

Catlin had his noose tied seconds before Tippit did, and both men tossed the ropes to Piney, watching as he caught them. After setting down his cutlery, still bundled up, Rollins slid down the gully's nearer bank and grappled with the steer on top, working both nooses over its long, curving horns.

When he was set, their cook backed off and signaled with a liver-spotted hand. In unison, Tippit and Catlin backed their horses from the gully, lariats gone taut and straining as hemp took the steer's deadweight. It took a good five minutes before they had landed it on level ground, then they repeated the procedure to exhume a second lifeless animal. Instead of going back for number three when that was done, Piney released their lariats and watched the mounted drovers reel them in.

"Two's more 'n we can handle as it is, roped to the extra horses. Nothing more for you to do until I'm finished skinning 'em and figuring which cuts to take."

Tippit finished coiling up his lariat and tied it to his saddle with a rope strap dangling from the horn. Catlin was finished tying up his own a moment later, and they turned to watch Rollins at work.

It wasn't pretty, but for anyone who'd ever set foot in a butcher's shop, there was no mystery or shock involved. First, Piney skinned one of the steers, then gutted it before he started etching out a side of beef for taking back to camp. When that was done, it proved a three-man job to put each slab in place atop one of the riderless remuda horses, taking care that neither one was laden down so heavily that it might suffer muscle strain or other injury.

When that was done, Tippit asked Piney, "Do we have to make a round trip from the camp and go through all of this again?"

"No point, sir," Rollins said. "Too much and I can't cook it fast enough to keep it fresh. Don't want it going ripe and stinking out the wagon."

"No," Tippit agreed. "We don't."

"We'd best be starting back, then, or the boss might think we're lost and give Tim Berryman my job."

THE FINAL WORD on longhorns scattered by the sandstorm came to three dead, thirteen brought back to the herd, and one still missing when they broke camp, pushing on.

Bliss Mossman reckoned that the one who'd disappeared without a trace was also dead, its carcass lying someplace that his search parties had missed. If it was still alive, odds were that it would either turn up at some local homestead craving water or would die from causes unrelated to the storm—raw thirst, a rattler's bite, or drinking from a waterhole contaminated with some creature's rotting corpse or arsenic that leached out of the desert soil.

One down after a full week on the trail was something Mossman understood as natural attrition, often unavoidable. If they were spared from any further freakish weather, the landscape should be more forgiving once they'd crossed the border into Kansas. That might lead to other problems, though, of the distinctly human sort, including thieves and interference from survivors of the Civil War who'd hung on to their lives but lost all claim to common decency.

And that would mean the kind of fighting Mossman had been hoping to avoid.

At least, the Bar X owner thought, they would be having beef tonight for supper, with more coming for the next couple of days. He hated losing any steers in transit—and the money that it took out of his pocket at trail's end—but if he couldn't save the steers, at least he'd make good use of them.

They'd lost time on their trek today, as Mossman had expected, waiting for stray longhorns to be found and brought back to the herd, waiting while Piney Rollins butchered two that hadn't made it through the night and rode back with sides of beef draped over horses pulled from the remuda. By the time the herd moved out, they barely had a half day's light remaining, and he'd sent Tippit ahead—no rest for foremen on a cattle drive—to find a likely campsite for tonight.

The spot selected offered water from a running stream, with forage adequate to keep the longhorns happy overnight. They would eat damned near anything, from scrub grass up to Juneberries and big sagebrush, but it needed to be devoid of native hazards such as locoweed and toadstools. Overall, the spot struck Mossman as a decent place to overnight and let the herd recoup some of its energy that the storm had blown away.

They should be fine if nothing else cropped up to spoil his plans.

And that, as Mossman knew from grim experience, was one big if.

PACO'S APACHES ATE their stolen beef, cooked on a spit, but even with their mouths full they continued planning for a raid against the white man's cattle drive.

Each brave had his opinion, naturally, and Paco allowed each one of them to speak in turn, while never letting them forget that his plan was the final word. Debate helped vent frustration, but as war chief, he was careful not to let it shift from a sharing of ideas into a deadly argument.

And sometimes, unexpectedly, he heard a fresh idea that seemed to him more useful than his own.

Maska and Kuruk favored an attack by night, catching most of the cowboys in their bedrolls, killing them before they had a chance to wake and arm themselves. Paco had counted nineteen members of the trail crew altogether, thus outnumbering his band by five, but a surprise assault could shift those odds dramatically. From his surveillance of the herd before the sandstorm, Paco knew that three riders stood watch in shifts, two hours each, thereby allowing every man to sleep before they broke camp in the morning and moved on.

Also, a night strike could be doubly effective since most whites seemed to believe Apaches feared to join in battle after sundown. Some fool had convinced them that a morbid dread of dying after dark, and thus losing direction to the Happy Hunting Ground, prevented braves from mounting night campaigns.

Unfortunately for the white men who relied upon that superstition, nothing could be further from the truth.

Against the plan advanced by Kuruk, Maska, Bodaway, and Yuma suggested an assault upon the herd at dawn. Their notion did not spring from dread of darkness, rather noting that white men were generally at their worst and weakest as they roused from sleep, trying to clear their eyes of grit, their minds of last night's dreams. If Paco's braves could close in on the camp unnoticed, choosing easy targets as the first light of a new day broke, they might annihilate enough cowboys with one quick fusillade to swing the battle in their favor.

But if they were spotted moving in . . .

Hototo ("Spirit Who Sings") and Biminak ("Slick Roper") suggested following the herd without an actual assault against its drovers, picking off a few more longhorns each night, possibly dispatching sentries individually. Such a gradual, prolonged engagement should spread fear among the white men who survived, seeing their numbers dwindle night by night, unable to retaliate against elusive enemies.

Paco listened to each idea in turn, including a suggestion raised by Dichali—"Speaks a Lot"—that they leave the herd alone and go in search of other targets, isolated trading posts or homesteads that they could surround and plunder without facing nineteen hostile guns. While no one else among his braves endorsed that cautious plan, Paco was pleased that all refrained from branding Dichali as a coward, thereby touching off a lethal brawl.

When everyone had spoken and consumed his fill of beef, Paco explained why they must follow his original decision.

First, raiding the herd would send a message to white men at large, kindling fear inside their hearts and minds. Second, although the odds favored their adversaries slightly, they were only *tsayaditl-ti* and thus inferior to native children of the soil.

And finally, his plan prevailed because it was *his* plan. Paco was their war chief and would remain so until he was killed in battle, either by white men or by a challenger from his own band.

He left that part of it unspoken, scanning faces by their campfire's light until he satisfied himself that none were yet prepared to face him down for leadership.

And so the plan was settled. They would strike again when he decided it was time, with Paco in the lead, riding to triumph or to death, whichever was their destiny.

CHAPTER FOUR

Saturday, April 25

THE BAR X herd was crossing its first borderline since setting off nearly three weeks ago. There was no marker on the trail, no striking change in the landscape, but Bliss Mossman had shown his men a map last night and pointed to the spot where they would cross a short time prior to noon.

Officially, they were no longer in the Territory of New Mexico. Their route to Kansas and beyond cut through the far western corner of Indian Country, crossing the tip of what scattered white settlers liked to call the panhandle.

And the change, at least to Arthur Catlin's mind, meant they should be on watch for danger from all sides.

For starters, as its name implied, Indian Country had been set aside—at least in theory—for defeated native tribes uprooted from ancestral homelands far and wide. Catlin hadn't made a study of it, but he knew that some of the resettled tribes included Cherokee and Chickasaw, Choctaw and Creek, Cheyenne and Kiowa, even some Seminole driven from southern Florida. Officially, all were confined to reservations mapped out by the U.S. government, but no one with a lick of common sense believed that every native dropped there with a military escort was abiding by the Great White Father's rules.

Congress had passed various laws to keep potential enemies in check—no liquor sales, restrictions on the ownership of firearms, hunting regulations—but those august men in Washington still hadn't bothered to make the region a territory, overseen by an appointed governor and ruled by courts of law. The nearest court was located in Fort Smith, Arkansas, dispatching U.S. marshals to patrol some seventy thousand square miles, either singly or in pairs. Against that widely scattered force, the district teemed with outlaws of all races and extractions, confident that the odds weighed heavily against their capture.

And then, as if that wasn't bad enough, the so-called panhandle was marked on Mossman's map as a "Neutral Strip," assigned to no tribe, where intrepid settlers drawn from Texas and New Mexico, Kansas and Colorado, had arrived and put down roots on land that Uncle Sam had seemingly forgotten on his westward rush.

And "neutral," in this context, often meant no law at all. It was the Wild West in a nutshell, and a man with property of any value—like a cattle herd—had best be ready to defend it on his own.

If that meant cowboys fighting for their lives and for their boss's stock, there were no referees, no heroes in blue uniforms arriving in the nick of time to save their hides.

With that in mind, Catlin was glad he wouldn't be

on guard duty tonight. Rotating shifts were parceled out among the drovers, Mr. Mossman spared from any, while his foreman took an occasional turn, but on a given night two drovers were excused from lookout duty and allowed two extra hours of sleep.

Catlin was looking forward to that respite from routine, but he would not forget about his duties to the Bar X and its stock. He couldn't literally sleep with one eye open all night long, but he would keep his weapons handy, tucked under his blanket, just in case.

And if someone should ask, "In case of what?" he wouldn't have an answer for them. All he knew was that a man caught sleeping *and* unarmed was ripe for killing. On three occasions from his bounty-hunting days, Catlin had managed to surprise fugitives sought on warrants charging murder, robbery, and horse theft. One had given up without a fight; the other two had tried to kill him but wound up taking their last ride draped across their horses, trailing Catlin's stallion.

From them, he'd learned to take whatever edge might be available and run with it, showing no mercy when his life was on the line. That was a lesson he kept foremost in his mind, whenever tempted to let down his guard.

It hadn't failed him yet.

PACO KNEW THAT his warriors were on edge. They had consumed the last meal of their liberated beef two nights before and were again reduced to hunting quail and rabbits to sustain themselves.

Paco felt natural, predictable impatience building up among his braves with every passing day. Even his own brother, Patamon, had begun to chafe against his elder sibling's counsel of restraint until the perfect time arrived.

But would there ever be a perfect time to face a larger group of *tsayaditl-ti* and try to steal their herd? The sheer mechanics of it—first killing the drovers, then escaping with two thousand steers or more—made Paco wonder if he had bitten off more than a man, even a chieftain, could digest.

If he was just content to steal a few more longhorns, even one or two per week, it would be simpler, easier to carry off, and he suspected none among his band would criticize him harshly when they'd filled their stomachs. But as the days wore on without a sign of progress, nothing to suggest a victory impending . . .

Paco was conscious of the fact that any member of his band could challenge him for leadership, with victory decided by the death of one combatant or the loser's plea for mercy, marked down as a coward and exiled to roam the land alone. Alternatively, if the whole group turned against Paco, he might be overwhelmed, assassinated, and left to feed the turkey vultures and coyotes of the plains.

Better, he thought, if that must be his fate, to lead them in a cataclysmic battle with the *tsayaditl-ti*, slaying as many as they could before the pale-skins cut them down. At least, that way, they were assured of a reunion with their ancestors and songs among their fellow tribesmen of the war that they had waged.

Paco knew he would not be ranked as equal with the Chiricahua chief Geronimo or Barranquito of the Mescalero, but in these days when the great war chiefs were either dead or hiding from the bluecoats, he was all the remnant his starved and slaughtered people had to call their own.

And Paco meant to make them proud, no matter what it cost him.

As shadows lengthened into dusk and Paco's men

began to set up camp, he called them to him, interrupting their collection of firewood and preparation of four rabbits they had caught the day before, dressed out for cooking in advance. The others gathered round him, watchful, waiting, and the war chief took his time before continuing.

"I have decided," he informed them. Watched them hanging on his every word, expectantly. "We are no longer in the territory called New Mexico. Our enemies call this Indian Country, and where better to begin the reclamation of our land?"

A murmur made its way around the ring of braves surrounding him. This would have been an apt time for his adversaries to attack, but they were hanging on his words now, watching him.

"We wait no longer," he advised them. "Tonight we strike."

"And do you have a plan?" asked Helaku—"Full of Sun" in the white man's tongue.

"Silence and speed," Paco replied. "Once it begins, there may be time to liberate more steers, or there may not be. Either way, we fight."

Now heads were nodding in agreement with his order. None saw fit to ask for any details at that moment, thinking only of the fight to come. Paco trusted each one of them implicitly, never considering that one of them would fail him when the time came.

Battle tested, all were killers primed for conflict against enemies who had demeaned, murdered, and degraded their people for generations, and tonight they could achieve a reckoning.

Whether they came out on the other side alive or not, Paco believed, was now beside the point.

One man's hopeless gesture was another's victory, and he would leave the final judgment to his ancestors.

* * *

So, KANSAS COMING up," said Sterling Tippit as he sipped his strong black coffee.

Bliss Mossman nodded, finished mopping his plate with half of a biscuit before he replied, "Tomorrow with luck. Day after at the latest, if we don't run into any snags before we hit the border."

Crossing into the Jayhawker State was a milestone of sorts, though most of the journey would still lie before them. They'd still have some four hundred seventy miles yet to travel, but after the sandstorm and the tension that always came over him when passing through Indian Country, crossing an invisible line on a map would still feel like a victory of sorts.

Of course, they weren't clear yet.

It was a rancher's lot on trail drives to see problems where they might arise, even if none were evident. A wise man who'd accumulated property was constantly on guard against threats that could snatch it from him without warning.

Every stranger they encountered on the trail was a potential thief or scout for rustlers who might swoop down on the herd. A drifting puff of smoke—maybe a farmer burning leaves, a housewife cooking breakfast, or a wildfire sparked by lightning—might turn out to be a signal between bands of red men lying in ambush.

"A penny for 'em," Tippit said.

"For what?" Mossman replied.

"Your thoughts, boss."

Mossman clucked his tongue, then said, "The same as always on a drive. I wonder what in hell tomorrow may throw at us when our backs are turned."

"We've done okay so far, considering," his foreman said. "Even that storm could have been worse."

"You're right," Mossman agreed. "And that's the problem."

"Meaning what?"

"I can't relax until we're at the stockyards. Till then, even when we hit a rough patch and get through it, I keep waiting for the other shoe to drop."

"At least Kansas is settled," Tippit told him.

"So they say."

Mossman knew better. Sure, they would be skirting towns along the way, but every settlement they passed was a potential nest of livestock rustlers. Dodge City had barely gotten off the ground when last year's drive went through, but it was growing like a weed and had a wicked reputation for its gunfights and rowdy saloons. Great Bend was slightly older, founded back in 1851, but still on the wild side.

The other towns they'd pass, Salina and Topeka— "T-Town" to its residents—had law in place, but that was no insurance against trouble. Every human settlement from coast to coast, from New York City to the pueblo of Los Angeles in California, harbored its share of bad men, shady women, and peace officers who used a badge to lord it over folks they didn't give a damn about.

That was the problem with humanity as Mossman saw it: everyone you had to deal with turned out to be human, all beset with faults that overcame them in the end.

Including me, he thought, and finished off the dregs of coffee that were going cold in his tin cup.

"We've only had a problem crossing Kansas that one time," Tippit recalled, trying to put his boss's mind at ease.

"And that was bad enough," Mossman reminded him.

They'd been a day southwest of where Dodge City stood, a year before its first saloon and church were

built, a pair of whitewashed monuments to sin and vir-
tue. Three men had approached the herd, asking for
work, but Mossman hadn't liked the look of them,
He'd turned them down, saying he had all of the hands
he needed, wishing them good luck.

At that point, smiling to his face, the three strangers
had tried to draw their pistols but fell short. Mossman
and Tippit got there first, along with Rowdy Lathrop,
one of that year's drovers. When the smoke cleared, all
three highwaymen were dead or dying, Lathrop had a
bullet in his brain, and that had soured the drive for
Mossman. Even when he got a record price for beef at
Independence, it felt like blood money in his hand.

And sure, he'd gotten over that—mostly—but he'd
learned one thing that afternoon that never left his mind.

Trust no one but your family and keep an eye on
everyone in case they sell you out.

"You've got the night watch set?" he asked Tippit.

"All done, boss."

"Right. Guess I'll be turning in."

"Tomorrow morning, then."

His foreman nodded. Said, "I'll see you then."

H OW MUCH LONGER must we wait," Wanikiya whispered to Kuruk.

"Until Paco signals," Bear replied.

Wanikiya refrained from answering, trying to swal-
low his impatience as the night wore on.

In English, his name meant "Savior," though the
young brave could not think of anything he had saved
since he'd fled the reservation to become one of Paco's
raiders. Since then, he'd killed one white man and had
witnessed half a dozen others being killed. Their
deaths had not disturbed him as he first expected,

thereby proving to his satisfaction that he'd been correct in choosing war over the settled, "civilized" existence that his parents had adopted.

Wanikiya's problem: to his mind, waiting was not war. Only the thrill and heat of battle qualified in that regard.

Still, since he was not the band's war chief and likely never would be, what else could he do but wait?

Paco had planned the strike in detail, starting with a signal he would issue in the form of a screech owl's cry—a series of short whistles, rapidly accelerating, closing with a long trill falling slightly at end. The call was unmistakable, but not too hard to mimic. It should fool most *tsayaditl-ti*, but only one had to see past it for the plan to fall apart.

"If we are not successful—"

Wanikiya meant to say more, but Kuruk was quick to interrupt him, asking, "When has Paco ever failed us?"

That was fair enough, but Wanikiya could not quell his own misgivings. "He is only human, like the rest of us."

"You'd take his place?" Kuruk inquired.

Wanikiya did not have to pretend surprise. The thought had not emerged from his subconscious previously, but Kuruk now forced him to consider it.

"I do not say so," Wanikiya answered back.

"But you are thinking it. I know you," his best friend replied.

"What does it matter? No one would support my challenge."

Kuruk had his chance, then, to speak up and back Wanikiya's half-formed idea. His silence, on the other hand, spoke volumes. If Wanikiya challenged Paco, he should not count on Kuruk to support him.

Kuruk was trying to compose an answer, something

neutral but assertive in a subtle way, when both braves heard the screech owl's call wafting above the long-horn herd and dozing camp.

"You wanted action," said Kuruk. "Now it begins."

Wanikiya tightened his grip upon the Sharps carbine he carried, rising from his crouch behind a thin line of mesquite trees. Kuruk stood beside him, met his eyes by moonlight, before both braves swung aboard their mustangs, riding bareback, braided buckskin ropes serving as reins.

Mounted, both young braves began advancing toward the herd. Wanikiya could not see any other members of their war party but knew they must be closing in as ordered once the signal came.

They would obey Paco's instructions and his plan might prove successful. If it did, Wanikiya would be among the first to praise their war chief for his wisdom as a strategist.

But if it failed . . .

A loss would fuel dissent within their party, and if no one else stepped forward to contend for leadership, why not Wanikiya himself?

Why not, indeed?

Whichever way the plan worked out, he stood to profit from it, either by saluting Paco or by challenging his right to lead their band.

But first, Wanikiya knew he must make it through this night alive.

A RT CATLIN HAD the night off from guard duty and intended to relax.

With sixteen drovers on the duty roster, two men were relieved of night watch every third day on the trail. Tonight was Catlin's turn and Danny Underwood's, the latter seeming bent on sitting up to shoot the breeze until sleep overtook him. Catlin, for his part, had bedded down after a second helping of salt pork and beans, taking it easy on the coffee so caffeine wouldn't keep him awake.

Time off from herd patrol was one thing, though; forgetting all about the risks they faced was something else entirely.

Underneath his blanket, Catlin had his Colt Navy six-shooter unholstered, within an easy six inches of his shooting hand. Off to his right, and also covered, as a hedge against whatever morning dew might manifest itself, his Henry rifle lay in readiness for any challenge that might face him overnight.

That habit, always being armed and ready for a spot of trouble, carried over from the days when he was tracking men with bounties on their heads. During those years, whenever someone challenged Catlin's choice of lifestyle, his response had always been the same: he hunted men who preyed on others and were wanted by the law, even if lawmen never seemed to have the time or wits to run them down. Catlin regarded it as something of a public service, and the fact that he took money for it—payment volunteered by state authorities, no less—had never bothered him.

At least, it hadn't till he faced the Grimes brothers last month, in Las Vegas, and one of them, not even meaning to, had killed a little boy.

From time to time, Bill Regner Jr. still turned up in Catlin's dreams. He'd never seen the boy alive but saw him while he slept the same way as the child had looked when Catlin noticed him, his blood staining a weathered sidewalk's boards.

If anyone had pressed him on it, Catlin would have said the accident—not even his mistake, in fact—had wrought no changes in his view of life and death. No boy could come of age out west without having grasped that life was fragile, likely to be snatched away whenever someone least expected it. Nor had he come to think that outlaws should be free to roam around the countryside at large while lawmen sat behind their desks and claimed that legal jurisdiction bound their hands.

The Bar X drive was simply a vacation from the life he'd led till now, no more, no less. He wasn't counting on cowpunching as a new career, far from it. He was taking some time off, trying a little something new, and he could always go back to the other if and when he felt like it. But in the meantime, it was something new and different.

A screech owl's raucous cry caught Catlin on the threshold of a dream and snapped him back to wakefulness before he could discover whether young Bill Regner might be waiting for him on the other side, silent and staring in the moment when a thunderclap snuffed out his sad, short life.

Catlin lay waiting for the owl to call again, but it had fallen still. Instead, he heard men talking near the campfire, Jaime Reyes singing softly to the longhorns, lulling them to sleep. Catlin wasn't sure about the song, being in Spanish, but thought it sounded like a ballad, something on the mournful side. He couldn't picture anybody dancing to it, maybe sitting at a bar somewhere and staring down into a whiskey glass.

Catlin had lived through days like that himself, but always managed to come out the other side intact.

So far.

Lulled by the tune, despite Jaime's off-key delivery, Art closed his eyes again and drifted off to sleep.

PACO WAITED IN darkness, watching as his braves closed in around the white man's herd. Each warrior was within a few yards of the place assigned to him, not bad for moving over unfamiliar ground at night while trying not to make a sound.

So far they'd been successful. Only two cowboys watched over the longhorns as usual, one of them softly crooning to the animals in Spanish while the white man on the far side of the herd rode silently among them, seemingly alert to any threat of danger.

But he clearly had not recognized it yet.

And any moment now, it would be too late for him to recover. He had almost reached the point of no return.

Paco had drilled the plan into his warriors' minds: a shriek to signal the attack, and they would fall upon the drovers like a mountain rockslide, using every weapon they possessed to slash the odds against them. If their luck held out, perhaps they could annihilate the party and escape with enough livestock to sustain them in their flight, with some to sell for cash.

And if they failed? In that case, Paco would be reunited with his ancestors, proud to declare that he had not surrendered to the white men and their pony soldiers. Even dying, he could be a symbol of resistance to his people who lived on.

Paco carried a dead man's rifle, lifted from a settler he had killed and scalped between Las Cruces and El Paso. It was a Winchester, the Model 1866 some whites referred to as the "Yellow Boy" because its receiver was cast from a bronze and brass alloy. Its magazine held fifteen rounds of .44-caliber rimfire ammunition, with a sixteenth in the firing chamber. All he had to do was cock the rifle's hammer with his thumb—or, incidentally, strike hard objects with it, which could trigger the first shot by accident.

Before this moment, with his braves advancing on all sides, Paco briefly fantasized about slaying fifteen of the herd's cowboys by himself, dropping each one in turn with single well-placed shots that struck them down before they realized that death had come to call. He knew that was ridiculous, if not impossible, but every man—regardless of his race—harbors at least one treasured dream unlikely to come true.

In fact, he would be satisfied if his war party could dispose of half the drovers in tonight's ambush. The rest—their numbers whittled down, unable to seek aid from bluecoats or the residents of scattered settlements—would then be easier to finish off with long-range rifle shots, swift arrows in the night, or sharp knives drawn across their throats.

That might not rival victories achieved by Mangas Coloradas or Cochise, but it would be a start. Cochise was now retired and living on a squalid reservation, while soldiers had tortured and murdered Mangas at Fort McLane, claiming he'd tried to "escape" custody, then boiled his head and sent the skull to a New York phrenologist.

Paco might die tonight, but he would never yield or plead for mercy from his enemies. If by some chance he drove a stolen herd of cattle to the Mescalero reservation south of Ruidoso, he might manage to achieve a double victory. His people would have beef to eat for the first time in months, and when the cavalry arrived from Fort Bayard to take back the survivors, some of Paco's tribe might find the nerve to stand and fight.

That, he decided, might be victory enough, even if he was not alive to see what happened next.

What true Apache would not choose a death in battle with the *tsayaditl-ti* over some foul disease from Europe while his loved ones starved before his very eyes?

In fact, Paco thought, he would bless his fellow Mescaleros with another chance to live as men and die, if need be, with a vestige of their honor still intact.

CHAPTER FIVE

T HE FIRST GUNSHOT roused Bliss Mossman as he was drifting off to sleep beside the campfire. Weary from another long day on the trail, he'd been about to seek his bedroll near the chuck wagon when suddenly the crack of rifle fire snapped him out of a fuzzy waking dream.

What visions had his mind been conjuring before all holy hell broke loose?

Later, in retrospect, he couldn't say and didn't give a damn.

Mossman still wore his gun belt with a Schofield revolver holstered on his left hip for a cross-hand draw, and he was reaching for it as he dropped his empty coffee cup and stood, scanning the darkness for some sign of where the shot had come from. Others in the camp were casting off their blankets, donning boots and grabbing weapons, shouting back and forth for answers to the same insistent question.

Mossman had his saddle thrown over one shoulder

and was jogging toward the camp's remuda and his flea-bitten gray gelding, when more shots rang out, causing the herd to shift uneasily, some of the longhorns voicing their displeasure in loud voices. This time, he saw muzzle flashes in the night, illuminating reports from rifles and revolvers as they crackled overhead.

Some of the shots were being fired from outer darkness, toward the Bar X camp, while several of Mossman's drovers were returning fire. He doubted whether they were hitting anything so far, but what else could they do until they had something approximating clear targets?

Five minutes seemed to take forever, Mossman grappling with his saddle, clambering aboard his gray, and ducking as a rifle bullet whispered past his face, its hot tailwind ruffling his hair beneath the wide brim of his hat.

Too close for comfort, that one, but the Bar X boss knew that he couldn't duck and cover when his men were on the move, exposed to hostile fire from unknown enemies. The raid was bad enough all by itself, without the drovers losing faith in him.

He called out to the drovers just arriving. "Rally round and listen up, boys! I don't know who's shooting at us, but we need to stop it, pronto. If the herd starts running, we could lose a week trying to get 'em back, if all of 'em are even still alive."

"How 'n hell are we supposed to do that while we're taking fire?" Linton McCormick asked, forgetting to add "sir" or "boss."

"Take care of that the best you can," Mossman replied. "Don't bother trying to take any prisoners. If you can't drop the shooters, run 'em off at least, but keep a sharp eye on the stock while you're about it."

Murmurs told him that the men had understood his message—namely, shoot to kill, but make it quick and clean if possible. The longhorns had to be their top priority after survival.

That said, Mossman galloped off to meet his enemies and do his best to stop them stone-cold dead.

Hᴏᴛᴏᴛᴏ'ꜱ ᴘᴀʀᴇɴᴛꜱ ʜᴀᴅ been murdered by Comanches when he was a child of only seven summers, during one of countless skirmishes between their warring tribes. He had not asked them why they'd named him "Poet," and that chance was lost forever to him now.

Not that he cared today, at age nineteen, when he had never spoken any rhyming words and could not even tell a simple story very well, without losing its drift and circling back around to where he'd started from. Despite whatever hopes his parents might have had for him—perhaps a shaman with the gift of prophecy—those dreams had died with them, unrealized.

He was a man of action now, and happy to be facing white men on a battlefield.

But in that case, why did he also feel afraid?

Somehow, he had imagined that the cowboys would be shocked and dazed by an attack at night, but that did not appear to be the case. Most of them had recovered quickly and were firing back, although it did not seem that they had spotted any solid targets yet.

How long could that go on?

How long before a bullet found him without even being aimed in his direction?

Hototo had a Burnside carbine, .54 caliber, widely used by both sides in the white man's Civil War. The single-shot breechloader measured thirty-nine inches from muzzle to butt plate and weighed seven pounds with a round in its chamber. Its iron sights allowed a skilled shooter to hit man-sized targets from two hundred yards away.

So far, in this engagement, Hototo had not fired the carbine, but he had a target lined up now. The drover was dark-skinned, perhaps a Mexicano, although Hototo could not say with certainty. It made no difference to him, in any case.

No one of any race who served the white man was a friend, and enemies deserved to die.

He framed the horseman in his carbine's open sights and cocked the Burnside, snugged its butt against his shoulder, his index finger curled inside the weapon's dual trigger guards that also served the carbine as a lever for unloading empty cartridge casings.

Hototo took a breath and held it, waiting for his pony to stand still beneath him, then squeezed off a shot from sixty yards away. At the last moment, no more than a fraction of a second, something made the drover's horse rear up, his bullet ripping through the animal's muscular neck and bringing it squealing down. His human target rolled away, seeking cover from the herd while blood pumped from his horse's mortal wound, leaving the animal to die.

Hototo cursed fate and sloppy marksmanship, reloading while his pony shied a bit and then fell back in line.

If Hototo's target showed himself again, he still might have a chance to make it right.

ART CATLIN GUIDED his strawberry roan away from camp and into darkness, moving toward the fight before it came to him. Eyes grown accustomed to the darkness scanned the herd in front of him, tracking the horsemen whom he recognized, looking for strangers in their midst.

He still had no idea who had attacked the camp or

why, but such details could be resolved some other time, when Mr. Mossman's crew had beaten back the raiders. And a new moon on this Saturday cast no light on the battleground to help him spot his unknown enemies.

Whoever they might be, there had to be more than a dozen of them, judging by the sounds and muzzle flashes of their firearms. He had rarely faced a situation like it heretofore, and never when he had no clear idea of who was bent on killing him.

It stood to reason that whoever mounted the attack had plans for Mr. Mossman's herd. The Bar X drovers were an obstacle in that regard, and killing some—or all—of them would make it easier for renegades to make off with the steers. Should gunfire set off a stampede, it might play just as well into the raiders' hands.

Of one thing Catlin had no doubt: the Bar X drovers couldn't mind the herd while fighting for their lives.

And stopping gunmen in their tracks was one thing he knew how to do.

The way to go about that, in his case, was spotting one opponent at a time, then acting swiftly to eliminate the threat. How much he could accomplish in pitch-darkness with lead flying all around him was a question unresolved so far.

To start, he chose a random target, fixed upon a rifle firing toward the camp and chuck wagon from eighty yards or so away. Urging his roan in that direction, Catlin drew his Henry rifle from its saddle boot and held it ready, braced across his lap, the hammer down for safety's sake until he had a clearer mark in sight.

There was a chance, he knew, that someone else would pick him off before he moved in close enough to aim and fire, but Catlin had to take that chance. He had to play the hand that he'd been dealt, even if that meant drawing to an inside straight.

* * *

PACO AIMED HIS Remington Rolling Block rifle toward
the white men's campfire, paused to let a drover pass
before the flames in silhouette, then fired the weapon's
single .50-70 Government round and instantly began
reloading with another cartridge.

From a distance, in the dark, he could not say whether
his shot had struck a living target, but at least it made
some of the other cowboys duck and scramble as they
struggled into trousers, boots, and gun belts.

For the moment, that was good enough.

The Remington had come to Paco from a homestead
raided nine months earlier, near Portales in New Mexico.
It measured fifty inches overall, tipping the scales at nine
and one half pounds. A breechloader used widely by
white buffalo hunters, the piece could kill a man or other
big game at two hundred yards, presuming that a shooter's eyes could frame a target at that range using the
rifle's open sights.

As he reloaded, Paco scanned the night with narrowed eyes, seeking his raiders scattered through the
darkness, trading shots with their white enemies, seeking to kill as many as they could or, at the very least,
provoke a stampede that would spread the longhorns
out for several square miles.

Whether or not they left some of the drovers living,
Paco's braves had vowed to claim as many cattle as
they could before they fled the scene.

For his next shot, Paco decided on an easy stationary
target, sights fixed on the wagon standing off a few yards
from the campfire. That, at least, should be impossible
to miss, and while he did not know if anyone remained
beneath its darkened canvas covering, he hoped to
damage some of the trail drive's supplies, perhaps leave
its survivors hungry if they managed to survive the raid.

The rifle bucked against Paco's shoulder, and this time he could mark the slug's progress from rippling canvas as it struck. Someone crouching behind the wagon fired back in his general direction—with a pistol, by its sound—but it was wasted, coming nowhere close to Paco or his unshod pony.

As he slipped another round into the rifle's smoking breech, he called out to his warriors with another screech owl's simulated cry, urging them to hurry up their efforts and prepare to disengage before the white men rallied to go on a counterattack.

Some of his braves heard and responded with wild hoots and chirping of their own, while others failed to answer. Were they wounded? Dead? Simply preoccupied with fighting for their lives?

Paco could not have said, but logic told him they were running out of time.

The raid was not proceeding as he'd hoped it might, which would reflect upon his judgment as a leader with the other braves—assuming, that is, that they managed to survive, escape, and sit in judgment on him at some future date.

If they were all gunned down tonight, it would not matter. Only Paco and his disappointed ancestors would care, and likely none of them for any longer than it took a fleeting thought to vanish from all memory.

As war chief—while he still retained that title—Paco had a choice to make without further delay. His raiders could fight on, perhaps inflict a few more casualties before they were finally annihilated, or he could command them to break off and flee into the night, perhaps to live and fight another time.

The choice was gut-wrenching, a frank admission of defeat, but Paco only took another second to decide. Cupping both hands around his mouth, he shrilled the fierce scream of a red-tailed hawk, hoping his warriors heard it over crackling gunfire and the anxious lowing of two thousand steers.

If they did not—if none of them responded to his cry and disengaged from combat—he would have no choice but to remain and die beside them in the dark.

Foreman STERLING TIPPIT fired his Sharps carbine into the night and knew almost before the hammer fell that it would be another wasted shot. He didn't have a target, only winking muzzle flashes from the hostile guns around him, and with each new blast he worried that the herd would bolt into a mad stampede to nowhere, trampling all before it.

Still, he couldn't just stand by without responding to the gunfire Mr. Mossman's crew was taking in their camp. After he had the Sharps reloaded, Tippit spurred his blood bay mare into the darkness, seeking closer contact with the enemies he hadn't seen yet, to at least find out who was intent on panicking the herd and killing off its drovers.

Were they white men, hostile Indians, or raiders up from Mexico? He didn't know and didn't care while lead was flying all around him. All that mattered was their criminal intent and crushing them before they could do any further damage.

Tippit knew one Bar X drover had been hit so far and guessed they would be lucky if he proved to be the only one. A slug had grazed Francisco Gallardo's left thigh, an inch or so above the knee, but one of his amigos, Jaime Reyes, had been quick to tie it off with a bandanna before too much blood was spilled. The last Tippit had seen of him, Gallardo had been lying prone beneath the chuck wagon, returning fire toward their attackers with his Colt New Model revolving rifle—

and most likely having no more luck than any of the other Bar X hands.

That had to change, and Tippit reckoned it was up to him, since he'd lost track of Mr. Mossman in the fracas. Keeping that in mind, he started shouting to the other mounted drovers, calling any who could hear him to form up around his bay and join him in a charge against their faceless enemies.

It could be foolish, and it might well get him killed, but at that moment Tippit saw no other way to turn the tide.

DENZHONE HAD NEVER understood what made his parents choose his name, translated as "Beautiful" in the white man's tongue. Throughout his childhood it had been a burden, constantly inviting other boys to tease him, asking whether Denzhone's father wished that he had been a girl instead.

After tonight, at least, he thought that mockery would cease.

A rifle bullet from the darkness had ripped into Denzhone's face, slicing across his left cheek from an inch or so beneath his eye down to the jawline, spilling blood over his buckskin shirt and nearly toppling him from his pony on impact.

Somehow, he'd stay atop the animal and hung on to his Snider-Enfield rifle, though he'd been unable to reload the .577-caliber weapon after his last shot before he was wounded. Dazed and groggy, with his head throbbing as if someone had used it for a tom-tom signal drum. His ears rang, and Denzhone's left eye was nearly swollen shut. In short, he was a bloody mess and feared he might lose consciousness at any moment.

Even so, he heard Paco's call for retreat. No red-tailed

hawk would be soaring abroad by night, so what else could it mean?

And in that instant, Denzhone was ashamed to feel a swift rush of relief.

He was no coward. Denzhone had proved that repeatedly since joining Paco's war party last year, but now, disfigured and still losing copious amounts of blood, he was relieved to be recalled from combat that was ill-conceived at best, futile at worst.

If he could only manage to escape now, Denzhone thought he might survive to sit in judgment of the chief who had squandered their party's strength to no result.

He hoped to live that long, at least, and possibly to fight again some other day.

ART CATLIN PUMPED the lever action on his Henry rifle, quickly aimed, and fired a .44 round from behind one of their mounted enemies, watching the shadow figure tumble from his mount onto the ground.

He felt no more compunction about back-shooting this raider in the darkness than he would have gunning down a fugitive from justice in pursuit of a reward. The faceless stranger clearly meant to murder Catlin and his fellow drovers, likely to obtain the Bar X herd, so he was asking for whatever mayhem came his way.

After he'd jacked another round into the Henry's chamber, Catlin rode up on the man he'd shot, confirming from his silent, prostrate form that he was either dead or on his way. It took another moment, short of moonlight, to discover that the raider wore buckskin and had hair longer than some women's splayed across his shoulders and around his face where it was pressed into the turf.

There was no need to roll him over and confirm the

raider was an Indian—which told Catlin the others were as well.

He could have shouted out that information to the other Bar X hands within earshot but saw no point to it. Race and specific tribe were things to talk about after the fight had been concluded to his satisfaction, but just now it made no difference.

Armed men had set upon the camp and herd. They must be stopped at any cost, regardless of their skin color, the language that they spoke, or any other aspect that distinguished them from Mr. Mossman's crew.

The first and foremost rule of any gunfight was to kill or be killed. All else was a potentially lethal distraction.

And one thing Catlin didn't plan on tonight was getting killed because he couldn't focus on what mattered—namely, taking down his enemies.

The next nearest among them was some fifty yards away, firing a shotgun, likely a ten- or twelve-gauge. That ruled out the shooter being one of Mr. Mossman's hands, and gave Catlin his next target of opportunity.

Now all he had to do was manage the approach without tipping his adversary off and taking deadly fire before he had a shot lined up.

Whether he could accomplish that was anybody's guess, but Catlin was obliged to try.

And if he failed . . . well, Art supposed he'd never know the difference.

MASKA—"STRONG"—WONDERED how much longer he could stand his ground before a white man's bullet brought him down.

It was not in his nature to be frightened, quite the opposite in fact, but neither was he fool enough to leave himself exposed to sudden death if there was any viable alternative. And now, hearing their war chief's high-pitched call for a retreat, Maska knew he must obey.

But was it shameful that he also felt relieved?

He fired the second barrel of his ten-gauge coach gun toward the white man's camp, not bothering to aim from sixty yards but trusting the buckshot to spread and find whatever targets were available. A kill at that range was unlikely, but before he turned and fled, Maska hoped he could at least wound one of the *tsayaditl-ti* cowboys before his pony bore him off into the night.

And would their enemies pursue them?

Likely, he supposed, although they probably would wait for sunrise, pausing first to calm their livestock, then perhaps draw lots to see who would give chase. They would not dare to leave the herd and camp unguarded altogether, and that fact might draw the white men to their deaths.

If their commander split his force in half, they should then be outnumbered by Apaches—or at least they would if all Maska's fellow braves were still alive and fit for battle.

And if not?

Then he supposed that neither he nor any of his comrades would survive.

Maska, galloping away with shots still ringing out behind him, had no morbid fear of death per se. He had lost friends and loved ones—some to violence, others to old age or disease—and knew what lay in store for all at their life journey's end. He was content in the belief that fighting for his people, even in a losing cause, assured him of a place with his ancestors on the Other Side.

But truth be told, he had no wish to die *tonight*.

At least, not without taking white men with him as he fell.

When he had covered half a mile or more beyond the white men's camp, Maska paused and slipped fresh cartridges into the breech of his coach gun. He still remembered prying it out of a dead man's fingers after their war party ambushed a stagecoach along the Gila River, outside Tucson in the Arizona Territory.

That had been a proud day—eight whites slain and four horses acquired for later sale—boosting the spirits of Maska and his fellow braves.

Small victories, but when resistance fighters made war on a giant like the U.S. government, with all its horse soldiers and settlers swarming westward, any triumph was a cause for celebration.

Would they celebrate tomorrow, or be wiped out by their enemies?

Only the rising sun could tell, and Maska was none too thrilled by what it might reveal.

W HAT TRIBE'S HE from?" asked Piney Rollins, bending closer to the prostrate body, lamp in hand.

Bliss Mossman rolled the corpse onto its back, revealing streaks of war paint on the cheeks and forehead of its flaccid face. "Apache," he told the assembled drovers. "Mescalero, by the look of him."

"Not rustlers, then," said Merritt Dietz, still mounted on his seal-brown bay stallion.

"I wouldn't go that far," Mossman replied. "They likely meant to make off with as many steers as possible, after they put us down."

"Is this the only one who didn't make it out?" Sterling Tippit inquired.

"The only one we've found so far," Job Hooper said. He'd led a brief pursuit of the escaping raiders on his liver chestnut mare, but with his two companions—

Zimmerman and Guenther—gave it up and doubled back to camp after three quarters of a mile or so.

"There must have been a dozen of 'em, likely more, from counting muzzle flashes," Mike Limbaugh chimed in.

"So, what now, boss?" Linton McCormick asked.

Bliss Mossman answered with a question of his own. "We've got the stock under control for now?"

"Yes, sir," the foreman said.

"All right. I would say we move on and clear out of here come daybreak," Mossman said, "but that means leaving hostiles on the warpath hereabouts." He hesitated, then pressed on. "Some of you might say that it's not our fight, beyond what happens to the herd, and I can see that side of it. But can we just ride off without repaying them for what they did tonight, letting 'em run wild through the territory as they please?"

When no one answered, Mossman filled the silence. "I believe we ought to hunt 'em down, but I'm not making it an order. Anybody who agrees—up to, say, eight of you—could follow them at daybreak, try to overtake 'em, and be done with it. Or, failing that, stop at the first homestead you come to, tell 'em all about it, and leave them to spread the word. What do you say?"

It took a moment, standing in the wan lamplight, but all of them eventually nodded, though Art Catlin thought the gesture was a grudging one from several. Mossman nodded in turn and said, "Okay, then. Any volunteers right off?"

No one had answered when the boss turned to face Catlin, asking, "You dropped this one, Arthur?"

"Yes, sir."

"Are you willing to go after them that's left?"

It seemed a long two seconds before Catlin heard himself reply, "I might as well."

"All right, then," Mossman said. "Sterling, I'll put

you in the lead. Now all we need is six more hands to ride along."

Already, Catlin was asking himself, *Why in blue blazes didn't I use common sense and just say no?*

CHAPTER SIX

Sunday, April 27

A SUNDAY MORNING, but for Catlin it would be no day of rest. After a hasty breakfast, he was on the move with Sterling Tippit and the other drovers who'd been picked to run down the Apache raiders: Luis Chávez, Nehemiah Wolford, Merritt Dietz, Linton McCormick, Julius Pryor, and Zebulon Steinmeier. Those they left behind, their trail boss in command, would drive the herd as far as possible and camp as usual, near dusk, in hope the hunting party would catch up with them before another dawn. Keeping their fingers crossed that everyone they'd said good-bye to after breakfast would return alive and in one piece.

Art Catlin wondered whether that was likely.

Despite the herd milling about last night and mounted riders racing every which way, they had little difficulty picking out the trail that their assailants left behind while fleeing south and westward. From the direction they'd gone, it was clear the renegades weren't running toward a reservation in the territory's so-called Neutral Strip, but if they'd covered enough ground last night, they could be halfway back to Texas or New Mexico by now.

Catlin was hoping they'd have stopped to camp out overnight, licking their wounds—if any—or at least mourning the brave they'd lost. The other side of that coin: if they'd ridden through the night, or till their horses threatened to collapse, pursuing them might be a futile enterprise.

At that point, Catlin had another thought that troubled him, although he kept it to himself. There was a slim chance, maybe one out of a hundred, that the war party had faked its getaway, planning to double back and strike the herd a second time while Tippit's hunters wasted time and covered miles pursuing a false trail.

Art hoped that wasn't true, but he stopped short of praying for it, since he'd never seen that work for anyone. Catlin had learned that anything he couldn't manage to accomplish with his hands or tools available most likely wasn't getting done at all.

During a momentary stop to rest their horses, some two hours on the trail, McCormick raised a question, asking none of them specifically. "How many of 'em do you think we're after, anyhow?"

When no one tried to answer right away, Tippit took it upon himself to try. "Can't say for sure, the way this grass is trampled down," he granted. "Guessing, I suppose there has to be a dozen of them, anyway."

"Got us outnumbered, then," said Pryor. "Creeping up on two to one."

"Your point is . . . ?" Tippit asked him.

"Nothing, boss. I'm just saying."

"Saying *what*, exactly, Julius?"

"Forget it."

"That's a thought," the foreman said, "considering you knew the odds might be against us when we saddled up."

"I'm here, ain't I?" A whining tone had entered Pryor's voice.

"In body," Tippit granted. "But I need your heart and mind for when we catch up to 'em."

If we do, thought Catlin, but he kept it to himself.

"I'm with you," Pryor said again.

"All right, then. Anybody else who's thinking that we ought to turn around and just forget about last night, I'll tell you here and now. Cross Mr. M on this, you might as well light out from here and keep on going. There won't be a place for you with the Bar X, not on this drive or back at Santa Fe."

A silent moment passed before Luis Chávez spoke up to ask, "So, are we doing this, or what? The more we sit around palavering, the farther we'll be chasing them, eh?"

At DAWN, PACO led his surviving warriors in a mourning song for Yuma, who was no longer among them. During the attack last night, a white man's bullet had erased Chief's Son from this plane of existence and dispatched him to his ancestors.

Denzhone did not join in the song but stood by watching while he held a piece of blood-caked fabric to the ravaged left side of his face. It was a fluke, Paco saw now, that Denzhone had been spared from death. Another inch or less, and rather than being disfigured, he would likely have been killed outright.

Was that a blessing or a curse?

Paco had glimpsed the young man's face, or what was left of it. Assuming that he healed without contracting an infection that poisoned his blood and brain, he would have difficulty speaking and his given name—already cause for passing merriment among his fellow braves—would turn to outright mockery.

Whether he lived or died, Denzhone would nevermore be found attractive among sighted men, women, or children.

The Apache word for "face" was *shinii'*, but offhand, Paco could not recall a term for "hideous." In Spanish, "Scarface" was Caracortada, but could Denzhone bear to change his name so drastically?

That was a personal decision, for Denzhone to make in due time, if and when his wound healed. Paco supposed it was a blessing that none of his other braves had suffered injury during the raid last night, although he half expected someone to dispute his leadership after the grim result his planning had achieved.

No white men killed, as far as he could tell, and they had brought no longhorns with them when they fled the camp. His scheme had failed, costing them one man and perhaps another, if Denzhone's wound festered.

And were trackers from the trail drive chasing after them right now?

As if reading his thoughts, Nashota—"Twin," whose sibling died at birth—inquired, "How many will pursue us, Paco?"

The war chief had pondered that all night, while sleep eluded him. Now he replied, "Enough to fight us while the herd moves on. They drive the steers to market, hoping to make money from their flesh. Each day without progress defeats their purpose."

"Might they all stay with the herd, then?" Kuruk sounded almost hopeful, but his face did not reflect that optimism.

"I do not believe so," said Paco. "We should expect another fight. The only question now is whether to keep running or face them on ground of our own choosing."

"You are war chief," Bodaway reminded him. "The choice is yours."

Paco considered that and nodded, frowning.

"I am tired of running from our enemies," he said at last. "We stand."

STERLING TIPPIT REINED in his blood bay mare and asked the riders closing in around him, "Everyone see that?"

In fact, it was impossible to miss: a thread of smoke rising into the washed-out sky before them, something like a mile ahead.

"You think it's them, boss?" Nehemiah Wolford asked.

"That, or it's something that they set afire," Tippit replied. "A homestead, maybe, but I doubt there's smoke enough for that."

In fact, it looked more like a campfire's output, although too far off to say how many individuals—if any— might be clustered around it. Would the raiders he'd been sent to find make camp out in the open and invite attack this way?

"So, what we gonna do now?" Zeb Steinmeier asked.

"Much closer and they're bound to see us coming," Arthur Catlin said.

Tippit considered that, removed a telescopic spyglass from an inside pocket of his coat, and held it up for all to see. Finally said, "Move in a little more and have a look at 'em through this. If it's not Injuns, we ride on a bit and try to keep after their trail."

"And if it *is* them?" Lint McCormick prodded him.

"Close into rifle range and take 'em out," Tippit replied.

A long-range duel wasn't ideal, he realized, and the Apaches likely had some rifles, too, along with one shotgun they'd used during the raid last night that couldn't close the distance. Ditto any bows or sidearms they were carrying, which should be visible once he'd applied the telescope. With any luck, his drovers could pick off their riflemen first thing, and pot the rest from there.

"Just shoot 'em from far off without a call or anything?" asked Merritt Dietz.

Nearly fuming, Tippit answered back, "You hear 'em give us any warning when they hit the herd last night? When they plugged Frisco in the leg? Who figures that we own 'em any kindness now? Come on, speak up!"

None of his riders spoke. Facing back toward the smoke spiral rising from the plain ahead, the foreman nodded. Said, "That's what I thought."

He drew the spyglass out to full extension, raised it to his right eye, following the smoke down to its point of origin. From that range, he saw men and horses, no one mounted up as far as he could tell for sure, but all other details were lacking.

"Still too far away," he told his posse. "I need to gain another two, three hundred yards on 'em before I get to counting heads and weapons, much less saying if they're red or white men."

Cautiously, he led the way forward, counting his blood bay's strides as they progressed and marking off the distance covered in his mind. When they'd reduced the distance to three quarters of a mile, he tried the telescope again and this time found himself nearly transported to the outskirts of the distant camp.

"It's them, all right," Tippit declared. "I count thirteen of 'em. One's got a messed-up face. He's stanching blood."

"Still too far off, I'd say," Wolford opined.

"We'll take it up another hundred yards," Tippit replied. "Dismount and walk the horses up from here. As soon as we're in range, we go to work."

* * *

Denzhone, no longer suited to his given name, gently removed the crusty patch of buckskin from his mutilated cheek and saw only a few fresh smears of blood.

Not bad, considering the damage done.

If there had been a stream nearby, he might have washed his face, but he was not about to waste the drinking water from his half-empty canteen—another trophy taken from a white homestead that Paco's war party had set ablaze after its occupants were massacred. They had killed seven whites that day, including four young ones. Denzhone himself had slain a boy of nine or ten years and experienced no guilt from doing so, accounting it an act of self-defense on his people's behalf.

Around him, other members of the war party had settled down to wait for whatever was coming, be it riders from the trail drive seeking vengeance or some idle travelers who happened by and found their luck exhausted.

Either way, Paco clearly intended that the day should not elapse without more white blood being spilled.

Denzhone sat on dry grass, cross-legged, with his Snider-Enfield rifle braced across his lap. He had confirmed that it was loaded, primed to fire at need, and he almost wished that their pursuers would appear sooner rather than later, to relieve suspense that only added to his suffering.

Firemaker was approaching him, offering pemmican and asking whether Denzhone wanted some. He did not, but accepted it nonetheless, in the knowledge that he needed food to keep his strength up and to generate replacement of the blood he'd lost.

Chewing on the uninjured right side of his jaw, Denzhone stifled a groan as that most basic action sent fresh bolts of pain rippling across his wounded face and down his neck, cramping the muscles in his left shoulder. Instead of gnawing on the pemmican, he then resolved to let it soften from saliva in his mouth, until it was more manageable.

Glancing up, Denzhone saw Bodaway retreating toward the campfire, striding easily until he seemed to stumble, stagger, lurching to his right. At the same instant, Denzhone beheld his fellow warrior's head bursting as if it were a melon shattered by a tomahawk. A crimson mist of blood and brains hung in the air for just an instant, then Bodaway's lifeless body toppled to the sod.

At the same time, the echo of a gunshot caught up with the bullet that had slain him, fired from what Denzhone supposed must be one hundred yards or more away.

While those around him scrambled, seeking cover, Denzhone flattened on the grass, swallowed another groan of agony from that sudden exertion, and stared off to the northeast, seeking his mortal enemies.

A RT CATLIN AND the other drovers waited while their foreman took the first shot, lying prone and sighting down the barrel of his Sharps carbine. The weapon roared and bucked against his shoulder, by which time its .52-caliber slug weighing twenty-four grams flew downrange at some eighteen hundred feet per second.

Catlin didn't have the telescope and didn't need it, as one of the Apaches standing upright crumpled and collapsed, leaving a pink cloud where his skull had been two heartbeats earlier. The booming gunshot rolled along behind its fat projectile, catching up just as the other hostiles went to ground, clutching whatever weapons they possessed.

Catlin had time to pick a target from the dozen-plus Apaches still alive in camp. None bolted toward their horses, tethered off to one side at a cluster of mesquite trees. He chose a warrior who was kneeling with a long gun at his shoulder, aiming at the assailants who had overtaken his war party.

Catlin almost felt that he had locked eyes with his enemy across the intervening distance, though he realized that had to be illusory. He could make out the warrior, roughly judge his weight and stature, but his features were a smudge devoid of any detail. That was fine, since when he fired at human targets from a distance, Catlin always tried to choose a spot mid-torso, which increased his chances of a hit with maximum effect.

He took a deep breath, released half of it, and held the rest, hearing his pulse throb in his ears, his index finger taking up the Henry rifle's trigger slack. The weapon kicked, but just a little, most of its recoil absorbed by stock and butt plate before nudging against Catlin's clavicle and deltoid muscle.

By the time that happened, Catlin's .44 slug was airborne. It weighed eleven grams less than Tippit's .52-caliber and traveled seven hundred feet per second, give or take, but it was still more than enough to drop a man if he scored any kind of solid hit at all.

And so it did.

Catlin would never know the hostile's name, nor was he interested. Whatever he was called, the renegade had tried to murder Catlin and his friends last night, and this was the result of it.

Don't start a fight unless you were prepared to see it through.

* * *

Paco lay belly down, aiming his Remington Rolling Block rifle toward the attackers a hundred yards out from his war party's camp. He could see them at that distance, but could not distinguish one man from another at that range, in terms of faces or the clothing that they wore.

On top of that, the riflemen shifted positions constantly, making it difficult for their Apache enemies to draw a bead on any one of them. Paco had fired three shots since the firefight began, and knew his rounds were wasted, flying past his targets, off across the prairie into nothingness.

Now, with a fourth fresh cartridge in the Remington's chamber, he had a paltry nine rounds remaining. When he had exhausted those, what could he do to help his warriors or himself?

It was ridiculous to think of charging toward his foes across the intervening distance with his hunting knife in hand; he'd be cut down before he'd cleared a dozen running steps forward. On the other hand, Paco could not abide the thought of simply staying where he was, waiting to die.

The Apache war chief cleared his mind of doubts and speculation, concentrating on his aim before he sent his next .50-caliber slug downrange, powered by seventy grains of black powder. His aim *felt* better to him this time, but he missed again, cursing as his target dropped to a crouch just as Paco's finger depressed his rifle's trigger.

"Chi wat!" Furious, if only at himself, he cleared the weapon's breech and thumbed another cartridge— two and one quarter inches long—into the firing chamber. Paco knew that he could still slay every foe who stood before him with the rounds remaining to him,

but he had to make them count without wasting another single one.

And firing from the safer prone position had not worked for him so far.

All right, then.

With his rifle primed and cocked, Paco rose to his full height, turned in profile toward his enemies, thereby making a smaller target of himself while simultaneously compensating for the Remington's recoil. He could absorb the weapon's kick, his upper torso rotating off-center, then come back into alignment with his targets by the time his bullet found its mark.

Aiming his rifle, with its rear ramp and leaf sight and a blade sight at the muzzle, seemed to take forever, but Paco knew that in truth he'd barely spent two seconds on the process, maybe less. He chose a cowboy as the first man he would kill today, held steady on the distant form, and slipped his index finger through the weapon's trigger guard—when something struck him in the chest and knocked him over backward to the ground.

Paco had heard the white man's words of wisdom more than once: *You never hear the shot that kills you.*

Now he understood that was another of their countless lies.

Sprawled on his back, his perfect shot wasted on fluffy clouds passing above him, Paco clearly heard the echo of the gunshot that had felled him. At the same time, when he tried to draw a breath, the sucking chest wound he'd received taught Paco how it might have felt to drown in warm, deep water.

No. Not water.

By the time he realized that he was drowning in his own life's blood, Paco was beyond earthly help. His eyes locked open, no longer responsive to his brain's commands, he watched the vast blue field above him dwindle to a fading speck of black and then wink out.

* * *

I GOT ONE OF the bastards!" Merritt Dietz cried out, exultant. "Any of you boys see that? Damn, what a shot!"

Art Catlin thought Dietz had begun to dance a happy little jig of celebration for his marksmanship, but then he heard a soggy slapping sound and Merritt went down in a boneless heap. He landed on his right-hand side, giving Catlin a glimpse of bright blood pulsing from a blowhole in his throat.

Maybe the gunshot's sound reached Catlin's ears a second later. He supposed it must have, but with all the firing back and forth, he couldn't have sworn to it.

"Dietz?" Tippit rushed over to the fallen Bar X hand and knelt beside him, feeling for a pulse along the jawline. When his fingers came back red and dripping, Tippit scowled and wiped them on the prairie grass.

"Stay down!" he shouted to the six drovers still living, but he could have skipped that warning. All of them, Catlin included, were renewing their acquaintance with the sod beneath them, minimizing the silhouettes they offered to Apache rifleman trying to pick them off.

Catlin was already more than halfway through his Henry rifle's load, if he'd been counting properly since he and his companions brought the hostiles under fire. He'd started with a live round in the chamber, and he'd fired his ninth shot just as Dietz went down, meaning he had eight rounds remaining in the Henry's magazine.

Unlike the later Winchester repeaters, Henrys had no wooden forearm to protect a shooter's hand when steady firing heated up the rifle's twenty-four-inch barrel. Catlin compensated with a leather glove he'd slipped on when they spied the raiders' campfire smoke, and therefore had no fear of blistering his left-hand fingertips.

Not that it mattered now.

With one man down, the half dozen members of the hunting party still alive were focused on elimination of their enemies at any cost, without further delay.

It finally came down to blind luck, rage, and butchery.

Despite their being one day short of three weeks on the trail together, Catlin couldn't say he'd known Dietz well or felt particularly close to him. They'd worked night watch together once, luck of the draw, and now he'd never hear the drover tell another of his odd off-color jokes again, supplying laughter on his own part when his fellow cowboys didn't see where he was going with it. Now his rowdy voice was stilled for good.

The rage derived less from a sense of loss than fear, Catlin supposed. He'd felt its like in other killing situations, desperate to be the last man standing when the gun smoke cleared, translating fear to anger that could serve him, rather than leaving him helpless in the face of mortal danger.

In that moment, as at other times, Art understood how U.S. soldiers must have felt at Sand Creek, four years later on the Washita River, and during all the other massacres of red men, women, and their children over time. Sometimes, he realized, that feeling sprang from pure race hatred. Other times—at least for him, as now—it was a natural response to being frightened that the next minute or two could leave him dead and bleeding out, beyond all human aid.

He fired and fired again, saw human targets dropping in the hostile camp downrange, and kept on pumping lead into those twitching human forms until the Henry's hammer snapped down on an empty chamber and he either had to pause, survey the killing field, or else reload and start firing again.

Their foreman's voice spared Catlin from that choice.

"Hold fire!" Tippit commanded, pushing to his feet and peering through his spyglass at the now-silent

Apache camp. Then said, "They're down. Come on with me, and let's make sure."

THE HOSTILE CAMP was still as Tippit led his men across green grass toward turf now sprayed and spattered crimson from the thrashing dead. Seeing his adversaries laid out of the ground in twisted shapes repulsed him, but it also sparked another feeling in the foreman's chest.

He felt relief.

Why not?

He was alive, with all but one of his subordinates. He'd followed Mr. Mossman's orders, done his job, repaid a raid against the Bar X herd, and made damned sure the men responsible would threaten no one else.

Tippit remained alert as they drew near the camp, in case one of the warriors had decided to play possum and try one last shot at members of the Bar X crew before they finally finished him off. None stirred as he and his companions passed among them, though, and Tippit finally relaxed his guard, easing the hammer down on the Sharps carbine in his hands.

Men slain by violence collapse in different ways. Tippit preferred the facedown posture to those lying on their backs or sides, some with dead eyes fixed open, staring through and past him to the dark void of eternity. He knew they couldn't see him, much less raise a hand against him, but the gaping stares were so damned creepy that they made his skin crawl.

Someone's walking on my grave, he thought, an ancient superstition from his childhood, but the image still required him to suppress a shiver as he moved beneath the warm sun overhead.

You ain't dead yet, he told himself. *And no one knows where you'll be planted, come that day.*

All true, but still not reassuring as he walked the killing ground.

"What should we do with 'em?" Linton McCormick asked.

"Nothing," Tippit replied. "We'll take their guns and any ammunition back with us so no one else can use them. Turn the mustangs lose and let's get moving."

"No graves, then?" Nehemiah Wolford asked.

Tippit stared back at him as if Wolford had lost his mind and answered with a question of his own.

"You think they would have buried you?" With no response forthcoming, Tippit said, "I didn't think so. We need to finish here and pick up Dietz, then get back to the herd."

CHAPTER SEVEN

Friday, May 2

Ford County, Kansas

NINETEEN DAYS NORTHEAST of Santa Fe and the herd was making fair time. Ford County was a sparsely settled area for 427 residents for its 1,099 square miles of area at the last census, three years earlier, most of those inhabiting Dodge City and the immediate environs.

What that meant for Arthur Catlin and the Bar X cattle drive was ample grazing land watered by springs and streams that kept the county green through spring and summer, rife with game, including elk, whitetails, mule deer, and pronghorn antelopes. The predators they had to watch out for ranged all the way in size from foxes to coyotes, wolves and pumas, black bears, and a few grizzlies that farmers hadn't managed to exterminate so far.

Again, as elsewhere on their chosen route of march,

the greater danger would be posed by humans. Mr. Mossman planned to pare that threat by staying well outside Dodge City, barely one year old this spring, already with a reputation for attracting gamblers, pimps, and harlots, spawning drunkenness and fights that often ended up with one or more men lying dead.

Catlin had never been to Dodge and didn't see that as a detriment. He'd seen enough towns like it in his bounty-hunting days to figure that he wasn't missing out on much of anything. The trail drive's hands might not agree, but they were under orders from their boss. Whoever strayed to wet his whistle or whatever in Dodge City might as well keep riding when he'd finished and forget about his job with the Bar X, including any pay he'd earned to date.

Hard rules for a tough journey through an unforgiving land.

Job Hooper sidled up on Catlin's left, aboard his liver chestnut mare. He asked, "You seen that, Art?"

Instead of asking what he meant, Catlin followed the drover's gaze farther along their path and knew immediately what Job had in mind.

"That dust, you mean?"

"What do you reckon that to be? Another herd?" asked Hooper.

"Heading in the wrong direction if it is," Catlin replied. "It's coming our way, not to any market hereabouts."

"So, what then?"

Only one other answer came to Catlin's mind. "Likely a wagon train," he said. "They follow this route westbound, headed to New Mexico and west from there, far as the California coast."

"Sodbusters," Hooper said dismissively.

"Most anything, I guess," said Catlin. "Miners, shopkeepers, take your pick."

"Or painted ladies?"

"Well . . ."

"Be funny, wouldn't it? The boss won't let us make a side trip into Dodge, but what if someone brings the doxies out to us?"

"Don't get your hopes up," Catlin cautioned him,

"Did anybody ever tell you you're a spoilsport?"

"It's been said of me," Catlin allowed.

"There's nothing wrong with hoping, is there?"

"Not a thing," Art said.

Thinking, *At least until it lets you down and leaves you flat.*

A S FOREMAN OF the Bar X and its present trail drive, Sterling Tippit had his orders from the boss. Specifically, he was supposed to ride ahead and meet whoever was approaching them this afternoon, either confirming Mr. Mossman's hunch that it must be a wagon train or, failing that, bringing back other news.

Now, as the train came into view, he realized that Mr. M was right again, as usual. All that remained now was for Tippit to forewarn the wagon master, making sure his train and Mossman's herd didn't collide and make a mess of things.

As wagon trains went, in his personal experience, this one didn't impress Tippit much. He counted thirteen Conestoga wagons rolling one behind the other, with a smaller chuck wagon behind them, bringing up the rear. He took for granted that the leading vehicle would be the wagon master's home on wheels, maybe shared with his scout, and guessed that meant a dozen families en route to settle somewhere in the open West. Some trains he'd seen or read about had anywhere from fifty to a hundred wagons trailing, strung across a mile or more of countryside. This outfit, by comparison, was small indeed.

Approaching slowly while a scout rode up to meet him, Tippit wondered if the train had fallen on hard times since leaving Independence on its long trek into the unknown. Not Donner Party trouble, or the gruesome Mountain Meadows kind, but still . . .

Reining his mare in while he waited for the scout to reach him, Tippit went back over what he knew of long-range wagon travel in his mind.

Each Conestoga, also known as a "prairie schooner," was constructed as a mobile world unto itself. To start, each was like a ship of sorts, its floor curved upward at each end to stop the wagon's contents shifting, tipping over, each end slanting to prevent a family's belongings spilling out while climbing or descending hills. The average wagon, including its tongue for the team that hauled it, measured roughly eighteen feet in length, depending on the craftsman's preference, while being four feet wide. Its height—tough canvas fastened over curving arches patterned after the ribs in a ship's keel, but open at front and rear until a flap was closed at night or during storms—stood some eleven feet in height. Each wagon's body seams were caulked with tar to stop leaks when they forded rivers and progressed through rain or snow.

Conestoga wagons were built to transport loads that might top out around twelve hundred pounds, including occupants, their furniture, and various supplies—multiple water barrels, food for weeks on end, a toolbox and a feed box for the team—all of which determined how a wagon master charged his customers for time and distance traveled. That could vary, Tippit knew, depending on the obstacles expected while in transit, but the average was something like one dollar per mile traveled, *after* acquisition of a wagon and supplies that might exceed one thousand dollars prior to starting out. On top of that, a fully loaded Conestoga would require six draft horses or two oxen to haul it overland, which sold for twenty dollars and upward per head.

Most families, as Tippit understood it, sold their homes, along with any other items they could spare, to make the trip out west, pursuing an uncertain future. If they had to purchase land upon arrival, they added that to the total when they started making plans.

On balance, he supposed a drover's life was easier and cheaper all the way around.

The scout, a freckle-faced, broad-shouldered man, had reached him now, not smiling as he asked, "What can I do for you?"

A GOOD TWO HOURS passed before Bliss Mossman saw his foreman riding back to join the herd. They were already aiming for a place to spend the night, a sort of meadow where the Bar X crew had spent a night with last year's herd, assuming that the stream Mossman remembered hadn't dried up in the meantime. Barring that, he thought they ought to be all right.

"Sorry it took so long, boss," Tippit offered as he slowed his mare beside Mossman's flea-bitten gray. "Afraid I got to jawing with the wagon master."

"So, it *is* a train, just like we thought," Mossman replied.

"Not much of one. Twelve families from Scandinavia, plus one that fell behind to fix a busted wheel."

"Just thirteen wagons, and they rode away from one?" The thought of it made Mossman frown.

"I know. The wagon master—Thomas Redden, never heard of him before—was set against it, but the other men outvoted him."

"A train that size, he lets them vote on who gets left behind?"

"He says these Swedes have been a headache from day one. First time they've been out west, but every one of 'em thinks he's an expert. Half of 'em were threatening to dock his pay for leading them across unless he kept on schedule, no matter what."

"Well, if he lets them call the tune, what else can he expect?"

"I hear you. Anyway, he wants to know what you think about camping out tonight, the train and herd together."

Mossman's frown deepened on hearing that. "What's that about?" he asked. "Man can't control his passengers, and now he wants us riding herd on 'em besides the stock?"

"I didn't get that feeling from 'im, boss. More like he hopes passing some time with other people might help calm the herring chokers down a little."

"Did he sound like they'd be wanting beef for supper? I can tell you right now, that ain't gonna fly."

"No, sir," Tippit replied. "He never mentioned anything like that."

Mossman was thinking past that, to the other problems camping with the wagon train might cause him. If the Scandies stuck to eating their own food, that still left liquor and potential trouble over females he would have to guard against.

"This Redden's counting on an answer, I suppose."

"Hoping for one, more like. By now, it's just a mile or so round trip, if I ride back to fill him in."

"Free country, I suppose," Mossman allowed. "But I want two things clear, up front."

"Yes, sir?"

"The first is booze. I don't want any Bar X hands

with sore heads in the morning, from that aquavit or whatever the Nordskis drink. I don't care if they wanna chug it down all night. They can't be sharing it around our men."

"Got it. What else?"

"The women, girls, whatever. I expect some of our men are leaning to the randy side, knowing we won't be stopping off at Dodge. We need to minimize contact between them and whatever females may be riding with the wagon train. They need to understand that any trouble on that score means getting fired straight off."

"I'll talk to 'em as soon as I get back, boss."

"Okay, then. Take it easy on that mare of yours, with all this riding back and forth."

"No problem, sir."

I hope not, Mossman thought as Tippit rode away, back toward the train.

"A LL SET, THEN, boss?" Chad Sturgis asked. The wagon master, Thomas Redden, nodded thoughtfully and told his scout, "Seems like it. Their man says the trail boss, guy named Mossman, out of someplace in New Mexico, is worried about liquor getting to his men and maybe 'female trouble,' as the foreman put it, since they've been out on the trail awhile."

"I don't see any problem there," Sturgis replied.

Redden knew all about the Scandihoovian affinity for aquavit or *akvavit*—"water of life"—which was clear liquor distilled from spuds or grain and flavored with a range of herbs and spices, frequently tasting primarily of dill or caraway. It packed a punch, all right, running to eighty proof or better, but the Olafs mostly handled it all right—at least until one of them tipped the scale and ran amok.

That hadn't happened yet, on this trip west, and Redden hoped he'd seen the last of it for good and all.

As for the female side of things, he'd trust the Nordski fathers to ride herd on wives and daughters, if the Bar X trail boss could control his itchy drovers. Beyond that, Redden saw no way that he could be deemed responsible for any improprieties.

His bigger problem, as the wagon master saw it, was his shortage of employees on the train. Aside from Sturgis serving as his scout and hunter, he had Marlon Frank running the chuck wagon and Hector Davos, a soft-spoken Greek who doubled as a handyman and a mechanic on the trail.

Those were the only three men under his direct command. The rest, his paying customers until they reached trail's end, consisted of eleven families—five Norwegian, four Swedish, three Danish—with forty-nine all told, including children. One more Swedish family of four, the Bjorlins, was a day behind them, working to repair a broken wheel. The husband had declined Redden's offer to lend him Hector Davos for the job, insisting he could work it out himself.

That rankled, but the other clans had cast their votes supporting Axel Bjorlin in his stubbornness and pressing on, which caused Tom Redden to consider whether they had any sense of a community at all.

"One other thing," he told his scout, just then remembering.

"What's that, boss?"

"This Mossman character sent word they won't be sharing any beef with strangers met along the way."

"Makes sense," said Sturgis, shrugging. "Figures that he'd want to pinch a penny till it screams."

"No doubt. I'm just surprised he thought it needed mentioning."

"I guess it take all kinds."

"Still, before we get to camp, I'll mosey down the line and tip these fools to what they can expect."

And won't that be delightful, Redden thought, turning his black buckskin stallion to double back along their line of march.

THEY GOT A cook that serves the train?" asked Piney Rollins. "Or is it each family serving themselves?"

"I couldn't answer that," Tippit replied. "I saw a chuck wagon but didn't ask about their feeding schedule."

"I just thought we could share a bit, depending on their stores," Rollins explained. "Guess I won't bring it up, though."

The foreman couldn't tell if Piney sounded disappointed or relieved. Bearing their boss's words in mind, he cautioned Rollins, "Keep an eye out for the Bar X hands trying to cadge a drink of anything aside from coffee, though. Boss doesn't want 'em getting three sheets to the wind and playing sick tomorrow."

"Wouldn't mind a touch of that myself," Piney confided. "Just for tasting purposes, o' course."

"Uh-huh. Don't let that 'tasting' make you late for fixing breakfast in the morning, eh? And if you're smart, I wouldn't make it obvious to Mr. M."

"I hear you, boss," Piney replied. "Can't set a bad example for my Little Mary, either, don't you know?"

"Heaven forfend," Tippit replied, and nosed his mare off toward a circuit of the Bar X drovers, planning to impart the same advice he'd shared with Rollins.

It could be a touchy subject, telling grown men how to spend their leisure time, such as it was. He owed that much to Mr. Mossman, though, and would make plain the rancher's order that his hands be on their best behavior while consorting with the travelers whose path had intersected theirs.

That, in its turn, made Tippit think about the family left behind to mend its broken wheel and catch up with the wagon train as soon as possible. In ordinary circumstances, that might be all right, but there were still bad men at large in Kansas, and the Bar X herd might well erase the other wagon tracks before their lagging group tried catching up.

It wouldn't take much in an unfamiliar land to make them stray and lose the trail their fellow countrymen were following to the southwest. And having lost their way . . . well, damned near anything could happen next.

Forget it. Not my problem, he decided.

But he still thought he might have trouble dozing off to sleep this night.

*T*ACK GUD, THAT'S done at last," said Axel Bjorlin, wiping grease from his stained hands onto a tattered rag.

"We did a good job, eh, Papa?" His elder son, Nils, beamed up at his *fader*, seeking praise.

Before Axel could answer, his wife, Rowan, spoke up for him, saying, "Yes, you did, Nils. Very good indeed."

"Det är bra," Axel granted, though he normally refrained from lavish praise for work expected to be done correctly. How else would a boy absorb the burden of daily responsibility?

"I want to help next time," their younger son, Arvid, chimed in.

"There should not be another time," Axel advised. "Not if the work is done correctly."

Standing next to Rowan, middle child Kirsten, eight years old, evinced no interest in maintenance of Conestoga wagons. Nor, her father thought, should she. Women and girls had duties of their own to keep them occupied, whether housekeeping on a farm or serving menfolk from a house on creaky wheels.

"Can we catch up now to the other wagons?" Rowan asked.

Peering into the west, Axel responded, "No, it's too late in the day for that. We must camp here tonight and get an early start tomorrow."

Rowan wore a disappointed look but did not question Axel's judgment. In their Lutheran religion—Sweden's formal church of state since 1580—wives were subservient to husbands as dictated in the gospel and from pulpits nationwide. In some respects they stood on nearly equal footing—naming children and the like—but when it came to major choices, such as emigrating to a new land, then embarking on a trek to parts unknown on the frontier—wise women kept their opinions to themselves.

It was a man's world, after all, as planned by the Almighty from day one.

"Will we be safe out here alone tonight?" asked Kirsten, sounding close to tears.

"Of course," Axel assured her. "I will stand watch with your brothers to assist me; eh, boys?"

"Ja, Papa!" his sons cried out as one, clearly delighted by inclusion in the role of family protectors.

"Nils," he said, "go fetch my Comblain from the wagon, son."

"And take care with it," Rowan added.

"He'll be fine, wife," Axel cautioned her.

Nils returned a moment later, reverently carrying his father's M1870 Belgian Comblain rifle manufactured in Liège and sold as a military weapon to farflung governments including Chile's and Brazil's. It used a falling-block action, chambered for .42-caliber rounds, and measured fifty-one inches, weighing nine and one half pounds. A skilled hand, like Axel, could manage ten single shots per minute, striking man-sized targets beyond three hundred yards in daylight, using the rifle's iron sights.

With the Comblain, Nils also carried a leather ammunition pouch filled with rimfire cartridges, each weighing an ounce and one half. So far, since leaving Independence, Axel Bjorlin had shot deer to feed his family and had no doubt that he could do as well with human targets if the need arose.

Wild Indians for instance, though they'd seen none on the trail so far. If anyone at all threatened his loved once or his property, Bjorlin meant to be prepared.

Turning to Rowan with the rifle in his hands, a broad smile on his face, Axel inquired, "What shall we have for supper, wife?"

A RE THEY STAYING put?" asked Oren Dempsey.
"Fixing up a meal, looks like," Melvin Halstead replied, grinning.

"I hope they made enough for all of us," said Dempsey, giving in to mirth and chuckling.

Halstead ranked as second-in-command of Dempsey's Comanchero band, so called because they'd started out by trading manufactured goods—tools and cloth, tobacco, various foodstuffs—to the Comanches in exchange for livestock, hides, and slaves. From there, they'd branched out to commune with other tribes: Pueblos, Apaches, Kiowa, and Navajo. Their stock-in-trade had also broadened, drifting to supplies that U.S. law forbade to red men, namely liquor, guns, and ammunition.

That made Dempsey and his eleven followers outlaws, for all intents and purposes, although they didn't give a tinker's damn about such legal niceties. In fact, they didn't shy away from rape, murder, or highway robbery, and had been known to cross the southern border on occasion, selling "hostile" scalps to military buyers acting on behalf of Mexican president Sebastián Lerdo de Tejada.

It was just coincidence—and a convenient one—that Mexican scalps were mostly indistinguishable from Indian hair and brought the same welcome price: $100 for men, $50 for women, and $25 for children. And why not? Wasn't it Colorado's Colonel Chivington who'd issued orders to his cavalry at Sand Creek, only nine years previously, telling them to "kill and scalp all Indians" because, as God assured him, "knits make lice"?

Dempsey's mélange of renegades was a mixed bag, cutting across all ethnic lines. As they stood right now, their group included six Anglos, five Mexicans, and one Celestial—a former railroad coolie and opium addict called Wu Yanbin. They'd had a black man with them for a while as well, but he'd been gutshot back in January, when they'd tried to rob a mail coach and Dempsey had left him for the buzzards, howling at them to come back and finish him, at least.

Why bother, though, when cartridges cost money and a flock of vultures worked for free?

"We gonna take 'em now?" asked Zachary Bodine.

"Hold off a bit, I reckon," Dempsey said. "They're fixing supper for us. We can wait until it's done."

"The sodbuster's *mujer* is easy on the eyes," Juanito Calderón observed.

"Remember why we're mostly in this," Dempsey chided all of them. "This is a business first. The fun comes afterward."

ART CATLIN FELT a rising sense of expectation from his fellow drovers as they put the herd to bed and drew assignments for the night watch. Yesterday had been another day off for him, and tonight he drew the late shift, carrying from two a.m. till dawn.

He hadn't been surprised when Sterling Tippit drew the night's lookouts aside and handed them an extra chore, watching the other Bar X hands as best they could, to bar what Tippit and his boss called "fraternizing" with the wagon train's immigrant families.

That was a sensible request, to Catlin's mind. Meetings with strangers on the trail were rare and often fraught with peril to the herd, while happening across a woman—much less more than one—was roughly the statistical equivalent of being struck by lightning from a cloudless sky. Art heard the campfire talk that he'd expected, drovers boasting of their prowess with the fairer sex, however unlikely that seemed depending on the individual.

When lonely men were paired with women they had never met and likely wouldn't see again, particularly overnight and well beyond the bounds of civilized society, it didn't take a mastermind to see that sparks might fly.

And sparks out on the prairie could ignite a wildfire in the time it took blink your eyes.

Catlin hoped there'd be no trouble—and particularly none on his watch—but he'd keep an eye peeled, just in case. The last thing Mr. Mossman and his drovers needed was a fight erupting with road-weary immigrants who likely had no understanding of the West, its ways, or the tremendous pressure it could place on lonely men trying to earn their keep by any means available.

A brawl between the Bar X hands and members of the wagon train would be unfortunate, to say the least. A shooting, much less a fatality, could tie the trail drive up for days on end and leave the team shorthanded if the county sheriff felt like jailing those involved.

By the same token, Catlin didn't want to draw down on a cowboy he'd been working with for more than three weeks now. That didn't mean he wouldn't do it in a pinch, but the bad blood resulting from it would most likely lead to someone being fired.

Better to nip a problem in the bud, and better yet if they had no problems at all.

At least, he thought, *not when the burden falls on me.*

CHAPTER EIGHT

B Y MUTUAL AGREEMENT of the men in charge, the wagon train and Bar X camp were situated fifty yards apart, in theory to minimize the drift of individuals from one group to the other overnight. Aside from watching over the longhorns and their remuda, hands on lookout were supposed to make passes through the intended no-man's-land from time to time and head off any stragglers.

Catlin hoped that it would work but wouldn't bet his paycheck on it.

Or his life.

Supper turned out to be a potluck kind of meal, with Piney Rollins dishing up his usual, the wagon train's cook grilling venison, and the train's several families adding a variety of dishes from their stores. Catlin had no experience to speak of with the foods of Scandinavia, but found that he enjoyed Norwegian pickled herring and potato dumplings known as *kumla*; Swedish meatballs, *raggmunk* (fried potato pancakes), and *gravlax* (dill-cured salmon); Danish *stegt flæsk* (fried pork-belly strips), *kartofler* (boiled potatoes), and *karbonader* (ground pork patties).

Overall, he wound up eating more than usual and didn't mind passing up the offered cup of aquavit that Mr. Mossman had forbidden to his men. At least a few of them would likely wind up sneaking it, and that was their problem if they got caught. Catlin's only concern involved a sneaky drunk sharing his watch that night, putting the herd and Bar X hands at risk.

What would he do if he caught on to someone being tipsy while on guard? Likely not much, beyond suggesting that the boozer trade his shift with someone sober and stay mum about the reason for it. If the souse in question balked at that, Catlin could only keep an eye on him and try to pick up any slack.

The very last thing he would do was carry tales and tip Mr. Mossman or Sterling Tippit to a private lapse. That kind of snitching wouldn't earn him any thanks and might just make his life a misery for the remainder of the drive. Worst-case scenario, the man he squealed on might get fired and wind up calling Catlin out for that, which meant that one of them would likely wind up dead.

Art had no fear of any other Bar X drover shading him, but until you saw another man in action, fighting for his life, who really knew for sure?

To hell with that, he thought, and focused on the loaded plate in front of him, black coffee on the side.

With any luck, the night would pass without any untoward events that led to grief, and Catlin could preserve the memory of their time spent with the members of the wagon train as a pleasant surprise.

So far, his life hadn't served up many of those, and Catlin kept them filed away upstairs, retrievable as time and circumstance allowed. During a long night's watch for instance, when a couple thousand longhorns on the verge of sleep ignored Catlin as if he were invisible.

Someone had got a fiddle out, one of the Swedes who looked like he was in his thirties, with a halfway pretty wife and five children. Catlin couldn't have named the tune that he was playing, even when another immigrant—one of the Danes, Art thought, but wasn't sure—jumped in to back the fiddler with a Jew's harp. Married couples started dancing, children getting in on it a moment later, while the Bar X men stayed out of it or clapped from the sidelines, nobody cutting in.

So far, so good.

Catlin sat watching, listening, until he'd cleaned his plate and finished off his coffee, then got ready to turn in. With luck, he'd have the better part of five hours to sleep before his turn on watch, and then the tag end of the night would pass without a ruckus that could force Art's hand.

Tomorrow was another day and he would take it as it came.

AXEL BJORLIN WAS not musical. He'd never learned to play an instrument of any kind, and when he tried to sing in church, it seemed to come out wrong somehow, causing other parishioners with talent greater than his own to wince as if in pain.

His answer to that problem was abstaining from all musical pursuits. Back home in Halmstad, Sunday services were not required by law, but custom certainly demanded his attendance with the other members of his family. When time arrived for singing, Axel Bjorlin held the hymnal for his wife and moved his lips without making a sound.

Rowan was onto his charade, of course, but never

mentioned it. If other members of the congregation noticed, they refrained from giving any sign that might offend Axel, provoking angry words.

Or possibly, he sometimes thought, they were relieved.

Tonight, with supper done—they'd eaten *köttbullar* (meatballs seasoned with herbs) and a potato casserole with onions and pickled anchovies, known as *Janssons frestelse*, translated as into English as "Jansson's temptation"—Rowan and Kirsten had cleaned the plates and cookware, leaving Axel to his pipe and rifle.

He enjoyed a smoke around sundown. As for the firearm, while he hoped that it would not be needed, he had double-checked to make sure it was loaded, just in case.

In case of *what*?

He thought their campfire should keep any cougars and wolves at bay, although Bjorlin was not certain about bears. They'd seen one at a distance, midway through their third week out of Independence, and he didn't relish facing one but thought he should be equal to the task with gun in hand.

The night was reasonably warm—better than nights around Halmstad in spring, with chill winds blowing inland from the Kattegat—and with a pot of coffee on the fire, Axel believed he could remain alert throughout the hours of darkness to protect his family and all their worldly goods.

If not, how could he even call himself a man?

That train of thought reminded him of Rowan, bundled up in what passed for their bed since they had taken up residing in a Conestoga wagon, pushing off to face the wild frontier. He might have crept into their wagon then, awakened her to soothe him, but Bjorlin knew it would disturb the children and he didn't need them eavesdropping.

Granted, Swedish children knew the facts of life before they started school, but knowing something and observing it firsthand were very different.

A sound he couldn't place distracted Bjorlin from his reverie. He peered into the dark beyond his campfire's fitful light, imagined he saw something moving there—or was it some*one*?

Rising from the captain's chair he'd carried from the wagon, Axel clutched his rifle, staring down the prairie night.

H OW DO YOUR people carry all this food?" asked Piney Rollins, sitting on the tailgate of the travelers' chuck wagon next to new friend Marlon Frank, the wagon train's load cook.

Frank was a slightly younger man than Rollins, maybe thirty-five or -six to Piney's forty-something. He was half a head shorter than Rollins, carrying an extra thirty pounds or so that seemed to make his shoulders slump, pushing his head and face forward so that he generally looked inquisitive, about to ask some question that his tongue resisted voicing. Bald on top, he compensated by letting what hair he had grow longer on the sides and back, where it covered his collar.

"Most of what they eat is smoked or canned and pickled," Frank replied. "Seems like it lasts forever, though I wouldn't always hazard trying it. Taters and such they pack like anybody else, but for that taste of home its brine or dill,"

"You don't cook for 'em, then, at all?" Piney inquired.

"Nope. I've only got three customers besides myself: the wagon master with his scout, and Davos, what you'd call a jack-of-all-trades, fixing things."

"What kind of name is 'Davos'?" Piney asked, before he shoved another spoon laden with beans into his maw.

"Some other kind of European, not a Scandie," Marlon told him. "I wanna say he's Grecian, but I may not have that right. Talks English, though, and eats the same as anybody else you might run into."

Piney switched to something else that had been on his mind. "Your train's smaller than what I'm used to seeing, passing up and down the Cimarron to Independence. Mostly, we've run into forty, fifty wagons, sometimes twice that many."

Frank nodded and bit off half a biscuit, but it didn't stop him answering.

"You got that right," he said. "The boss—that's Mr. Redden—normally leads more across, but this come to him through what he calls a broker."

"Ain't familiar with it," Piney said.

"I wasn't, neither. It's some kind a middleman hooks people up with buyers, based on that they got to sell. This one, from what I gather, drums up newcomers and people sick of living in the eastern cities, sells 'em on a dream of going west, and steers 'em toward a wagon builder. Takes his piece o' that and same thing when he books 'em on a westbound train. These Nordskis stick together, even if they ain't all from the same place starting out, and Mr. Redden charged 'em extra to make up for the light load."

"So they've got money." Piney stated it as given fact, not asking.

"Seems like. Around them Scandie countries, people call it *kroner*, meaning 'crowns' as one of 'em explained it to me. Not identical from one place to another, but they kind a look alike if you ain't watching close. I couldn't tell you what that means in U.S. dollars, though."

"Nothing to me," Piney replied. "But since you mentioned sticking close together, how'd they come to leave one wagon back?"

"It's funny you should ask that," Frank replied. "A broken wheel, you'd normally expect Davos to fix it up, but herring chokers are an independent bunch. The *fader* of that family—that's 'father,' but it sounds like 'fodder'—reckoned he could do the job himself and didn't wanna hold the others back. They bickered for a while, then took a vote and finally agreed with him. I can't say Mr. Redden liked it, but he got half of their cash up front, so . . ."

Instead of finishing the statement, Marlon rolled his shoulders in a shrug.

"You think they'll make it? Catch up with the train again?"

"I couldn't rightly answer that," Frank said. "But either way, it's no skin off my back."

The Comancheros were on foot, their horses left some eighty yards behind them to be watched by José Calderón, one of the outfit's Mexicans and elder brother to Juanito. Moving cautiously and quietly, they'd closed within an easy gunshot of the wagon standing on its own, a man on watch outside, with the remainder of his kinfolk under cover.

Oren Dempsey had been crystal clear about his orders before breaking camp and moving in to box their prey. Eleven strong without José along, they were to form a ring of sorts around the Conestoga, then let Dempsey say his piece before they went to work.

"I want this understood," he'd told them, while Jack Runyon and Ardil McManus doused their fire by peeing on its embers. "I intend to be the only one who talks first thing. Got that? Nobody pitching in to scare 'em, anything like that."

"You're taking all the fun out of it," Lubie Grant had said.

"This ain't a picnic," Dempsey had replied, hard-eyed. "It's business, people. I'm in charge, and anyone who can't remember that should get the hell out here and now."

That stopped them grinning at him, and Dempsey accepted victory as no more than his rightful due. With that established, he'd tossed them a bone. "O' course," he'd finished up, "once we've disarmed Daddy, that don't mean that you can't enjoy yourselves a bit."

Now, closing on their target from the darkened plain, Dempsey could feel the old excitement that aroused him every time they carried off another job. It raised goose bumps along both arms and stirred the short hairs on his nape.

From camp they'd come loaded for bear. Each Comanchero had a new Springfield model 1873 "trapdoor" rifle chambered for .45-70 Government rounds, part of a stolen army shipment, with the rest sold off to Indians with raiding on their minds. Each rifle measured fifty-two inches, sporting a thirty-two-inch barrel, and despite being a single-shot breechloader, they could get off eleven or twelve rounds per minute in skilled shooters' hands.

Besides the Springfields, Dempsey's Comancheros carried various handguns they'd either bought or stolen in their travels through the West. That raised some issues where providing ammunition was concerned, with some of the exotic pistols being foreign made, but they had firepower enough to take one wagonload of travelers stranded along the westbound trail, abandoned and apparently forgotten by fair-weather friends.

When Dempsey judged his men should be in place, he stepped out of shadows crowding close around the single wagon and its team, advancing until the lone man on watch could see him by the fading campfire's light.

He raised his voice, calling, "Hello the camp!"

In front of him, the man apparently stood with a rifle in his hands, at what the soldiers liked to call port arms, slanting across his chest diagonally with its muzzle to the stranger's left.

"Vem är det?" the watchman asked, and then remembered to try English. "Who is that?"

"A weary traveler, much like yourself," Dempsey replied, smiling. "I saw your fire and wondered if you could abide some company."

"I must say no," the gunman answered, sounding shaky. "We have nothing here to share."

"Okay, if you say so." Dempsey smiled a little wider as he asked, "But who's this 'we' you talk about?"

The lookout stiffened. Said, "You must move on now."

"I could do that," Dempsey granted. "Or, how's this? If you don't lay down that piece right now, me and my boys will shoot that wagon full of holes and see whose blood leaks out."

Y OU'RE SURE THEY were Apaches?" Thomas Redden asked.

"No doubt about it," Bliss Mossman replied.

They were seated by a blazing campfire, each boss with his second-in-command. The news of hostiles taking on the Bar X herd clearly had Redden worried for the families he was conveying westward.

"And they killed one of your men?"

"Before we wiped them out," Sterling Tippit chimed in.

"For sure? You got 'em all?" asked Chad Sturgis.

"All of 'em that tackled us," Tippit replied. "And we lost one man in the process."

"Any indication that the savages were part of something more? A bigger war party, let's say?"

Mossman nodded to Tippit, let him field that question.

"Nothing to suggest it," said the Bar X foreman.

"One brave shot when they attacked our camp, and thirteen more when we caught up with 'em next day. I can't swear that they don't have friends lurking around, but no one from the raiding party got away. That's fact."

"And you aren't worried that we may be in for any kind of larger uprising?" asked Redden.

"Not until we see 'em coming," Mossman said.

"All right, then. I suppose we'll have to keep our eyes open and guns handy from here on in," said Redden.

"Good advice for anybody traveling along the Cimarron," Mossman agreed. "Speaking of which . . ."

"You want to ask about the family we left behind," Redden predicted.

"Now you mention it, I do," replied the Bar X boss.

"First off, know that it wasn't *my* idea. First time I've ever rolled away and left a family like that, except the time three years ago. Those were Italians, twelve in all, who came down with the smallpox two weeks out from Independence. That came down to sparing the majority of fifty-seven families. They were supposed to turn around and head back to Missouri, but I asked around later and nobody knew any more about 'em."

"On this other deal . . ." Mossman prodded the wagon master.

"Just a busted wheel," Redden replied. "We could've all pitched in and fixed it for 'em, but that Axel Bjorlin is an odd duck."

"Meaning what?" Tippit inquired. Added, "In case we run across him later on the trail."

"He's proud, for one thing," Redden said, "but you could say that about all the Vikes. With Bjorlin, it was like, he'd handle any problems that his family might have, and if you offer help—what he'd call 'charity'—he'll go off in a huff."

"Pride's one thing," Mossman said. "But can he back it up?"

Redden responded with a shrug. "He's armed, I know that much. A rifle from back home, the old country. Whether he's any good with it in an emergency, I couldn't tell you."

"Any luck," Sturgis chimed in, "he might not need to be."

"With any luck," Mossman allowed. "But if his luck runs out . . ."

"He's screwed," said Tippit. And the other three could only nod.

A XEL BJORLIN LIKED to think he was a man afraid of nothing and no one. He made a show of confidence, even bravado, but deep down he knew that most of that was just for show.

And right now he was very much afraid—not only for himself, but for his wife and their three children, still too young to look after themselves.

Counting the gunmen now surrounding him—eleven of them, all with evil etched into their sallow faces—Axel thought that this might be his last night on the planet. And if he went down, he did not even want to think about his wife and offspring, what they'd suffer afterward and how long it would last.

Still, even now—outnumbered, hopelessly outgunned—he could not toss aside the mask he wore to face the world. By now, he knew that Rowan and the children would be listening with rapt attention, fearful, likely weeping. Bjorlin knew he must be strong for them, at any cost.

"We have nothing to share with you," he said again, eyes flicking from the outlaw leader, back and forth along the firing squad.

"Well, now, you don't know what we're after, do

you?" asked the raiding party's spokesman. "And besides, it's only sharing if we leave you some."

That made some of the other gunmen laugh. Axel could feel his cheeks starting to burn, a sign of rage that he could ill afford just now.

"If you do this," he challenged all of them at once, "the law will hear of it."

Their leader snorted. Said, "Hell, I'd be disappointed if they didn't. We be worth more than their 'Wanted' posters claim, the way it is. I think we ought to rate a couple thousand at the very least."

"Or hanging ropes," Axel retorted.

"Most of us got nooses waiting as it is," the leader said, his smile a mockery. "Still getting sold short on rewards, though."

"I implore you one last time to go and leave my family in peace."

"What's that 'implore' mean?" asked a fat man standing to his leader's left.

"A fancy word for begging," their mouthpiece replied.

"Huh." The fat man scratched his beard, keeping his rifle aimed at Axel's torso in a firm one-handed grip. "So, if he's begging, shouldn't he be on his knees?"

"I hadn't thought of that," the leader said. "Thanks for reminding me, Lubie." And then, to Axel: "Well, boy? Are you gonna do it right, or not?"

Bjorlin knew that he should curb his anger, bite his tongue, but rage was boiling over in him now.

"I kneel to beg for no man," Axel answered through clenched teeth.

"Well, then," the leader said, "I guess that settles it."

He raised his rifle, sighting down its barrel, while his comrades did the same. Staring into eleven dark gun muzzles, Axel knew he only had two choices left. He could surrender, begging for his life, and likely

draw more laughter before he was shot and swept
aside.

Or he could fight, expend his final breath cursing
his enemies.

He swore at his assailants while he swung his rifle
into line with their apparent leader's face.

The bad men got there first, their gunshots nearly
simultaneous, and Axel Bjorlin's world went black.

ART CATLIN HEARD the distant gunfire halfway
through the second hour of his graveyard shift.
He guessed that it had come from ten miles off, at least,
and only reached his ears because several large-bore
weapons had been fired at once.

What did it mean?

He thought about the solitary wagon left behind by
Tom Redden's advancing train and knew the distance
was approximately right. One family alone wouldn't
explain the thunderclap of shots unless someone had
come upon them by surprise and sought to rid themselves of inconvenient witnesses.

And what could Catlin do about it?

Nothing.

Glancing toward their campfire and chuck wagon,
he saw no one stirring. They were either fast asleep or
else had chosen to roll over and ignore it, rightly judging
that the sound of shots, cut off after a single fusillade,
posed no immediate danger to them or Mr. Mossman's
herd.

The longhorns, for their part, had barely stirred
at all.

Turning his stallion toward the circled wagons fifty
yards or so away, he saw a lamp come on inside the
wagon master's prairie schooner. Seconds later, Redden stepped down from the tailgate, wearing trousers,

boots, and roll-brimmed hat but bare-chested in the pale light from a quarter moon.

He held the lamp in his left hand, a pistol in his right, but found no targets readily available.

In lieu of waking Mr. Mossman for no reason, Catlin urged his roan closer to Redden, waiting for the man to notice him, hoping he wasn't so keyed up that he might fire a shot Art's way. Instead of that, when Redden noticed him, the wagon master shoved his six-gun down inside the waistband of his pants and raised the newly emptied hand in greeting.

"You heard that, I guess," said Catlin, when he'd moved in close enough to speak without disturbing any of the dozing immigrants.

"Rifles," Redden replied. "On back the way we came from."

Catlin didn't state the obvious, that Redden likely wouldn't see the missing Swedish family again. At least, Art thought, he was unlikely to be seeing them alive and well.

"You think it was the Bjorlins," Redden said, as if reading Art's mind.

Catlin allowed himself a shrug. "Could have been anybody," he suggested.

"Sure. Maybe the governor was passing through and someone picked him off." Art recognized a man disgusted with himself as Redden added, "We both know exactly who that was."

"On the receiving end, maybe," Catlin agreed. "That doesn't say who tangled with 'em."

"No. It doesn't."

"Meaning they're ahead of us, same way we're going, while you move on south and west."

"Luck of the draw," Redden replied. "I'd like to get my hands on 'em, but not with all these other folks caught in the cross fire."

"I was planning to let Mr. Mossman sleep," said Catlin, as if speaking to himself. "But now I guess I'd better not."

"Bad news dislikes waiting around," the wagon boss opined.

"Good night, then," Catlin said, already turning from the wagon circle when its boss called out to him.

"You find the Bjorlins, if it ain't too much . . ."

"I'll ask," said Catlin, "but I can't promise you anything."

"I figured that but had to ask."

"If Mr. Mossman needs you . . ."

"He knows where I am. It ain't like I'll be getting any sleep from here on in."

CHAPTER NINE

Sunday, May 4

A NOTHER SUNDAY ON the trail, and while there was no pause for a religious service, no one on the Bar X crew complained. One day was like another on a cattle drive, hours of labor and monotony spiced up with threats that had to be contained and dealt with, like dashes of seasoning added to spice up a leftover stew.

The hour was approaching noon when all that changed.

It was their second day since camping with the westbound wagon train, and in that time the herd had traveled sixteen miles or so from that night's bivouac. So far, they'd found no sign of the Bjorlin wagon left behind to mend a broken wheel—that is, until the Bar X foreman came back from a scouting mission to report a grim discovery.

Art Catlin wasn't close enough to eavesdrop on the

conversation between Sterling Tippit and Bliss Mossman, but from the expressions on their faces, he didn't
require a gypsy mind reader to tell him both men were
upset. They'd galloped off together, Mossman coming
back alone after a good half hour, keeping any news
about what he had witnessed to himself.

That time around, the boss was solemn faced, as if
he'd just received an invitation to an old friend's funeral.
Instead of riding up to Mr. M and asking him about it,
Catlin concentrated on his job, trusting passage of
time to clarify the reason for their leader's funk.

Some twenty minutes later, it was plain enough for
all to see.

A burned-out Conestoga wagon stood before them
like a monument to tragedy, with vultures circling overhead, frightened to land and feed while Sterling Tippit
sat astride his blood bay mare, Sharps carbine in his
hand, its butt plate resting on his thigh, muzzle directed
skyward toward the circling scavengers.

Considering the wagon's blackened state, Catlin
surmised the fire had died out sometime Friday night
or early morning Saturday, before the drive marched
on from camping out with Thomas Redden's train. A
stench of ash and roasting flesh hung on the air, fainter
than Art supposed it must have been on Saturday, but
still offensive to the Bar X riders' nostrils.

Catlin had smelled death before, of course—some
of it caused by his own hand—but this struck him as
somehow being worse.

He didn't have to wait long for an answer as to why.

The five Bjorlins, big and little, had been massacred. Art had to guess at how they'd died—whether by
bullets, slashing blades, or something else—since coyotes and buzzards had been at them, feasting and ob-
scuring their mortal wounds. The woman—Mrs. Bjorlin,
he assumed—was naked, while her husband and their

three children were fully clothed except where wildlife had torn through their garments, seeking flesh.

Another glance around the family's last campsite showed Catlin no sign of arrows that would pin the slaughter on a native war party. Sadly, that didn't narrow down the range of suspects very much. He realized a single lunatic could have performed these heinous crimes, but if he'd had to place a bet on it, Catlin would have put his money on a roving gang of butchers.

Men no different from those he'd hunted for the prices on their heads.

Riding up beside him, Nehemiah Wolford asked, "Do you believe this?"

"Seeing's believing," Catlin answered.

"Yeah, I guess. But honestly, what kind of scum would leave a mess like this?"

"The kind we're better off avoiding," Catlin said.

"Maybe. I wouldn't mind having a shot at this bunch, though."

Be careful what you wish for, Catlin thought, but he kept that to himself.

"You think the boss will want to stop and bury 'em? Maybe send someone back to warn the others on that wagon train?"

"Guess we'll just have to wait and see," Catlin replied.

He doubted whether Mr. M would send a message to the wagon train. That meant at least a two-day journey, out and back, for the selected rider, and to what result? No wagon master in his right mind would reverse two full days' travel to return and bury murdered stragglers. And, that being true, why even share the news with Redden in the first place? There was nothing he could do about the massacre, and if he tried, Redden would only put his other immigrants at risk.

In time, maybe returning to his base of operations

in Missouri, Redden would discover what had happened here after he left the Swedish family behind. However he contrived to live with it was out of Catlin's hands, nothing for Art to fret about.

Right now he worried more about what Mr. Mossman might decide to do.

W E BURY 'EM," said Sterling Tippit, "it'll cost us half a day's travel."

Bliss Mossman nodded. Told his foreman, "I'm aware of that. It's still the decent thing to do."

"I hear you, boss. It's your call, either way."

"I want it done. Also, I'd like to find the men responsible and make 'em pay."

"You want me to," Tippit replied, "I'll ride to Dodge and tell the county sheriff what's happened."

Mossman frowned at that. After another moment he said, "What I had in mind was going after 'em, running 'em down ourselves."

His foreman blinked at that. "All due respect, sir," he replied, "that ain't our job."

Mossman considered that for two or three heartbeats, then said, "Correct me if I'm wrong, Sterling. I understand *your* job to be whatever I might say it is."

That brought a tinge of color into Tippit's cheeks, either embarrassment or anger, possibly a bit of both. Clearing his throat, the Bar X foreman answered back, "I ain't a lawman, boss. Neither are you, nor any of the drovers."

"Does it take a badge to do the decent thing, Sterling?"

"I never said that, sir."

"You didn't argue against going after the Apache war party."

"That ain't the same at all," Tippit replied. "First thing, they came at us. And second, that was back in the Indian Country. Kansas was a state before the war. Counties elect lawmen to handle things like this."

"And what if we just leave it to the sheriff. What's his name, again?"

"It's Charlie Bassett, till the next election, anyway."

"Bassett. I recollect him, now."

"He's bound to have a deputy or two."

"And by the time you reach him with the news, whoever did this crime will have another two days' lead."

"Boss—"

"It's settled, Sterling. Pick a couple men to ride along with you. On second thought, you'd better make it three. If it'll ease your conscience, ask for volunteers."

"And if I don't get any?"

"Then I'll reconsider making it an order," Mossman said.

"Okay, boss. Just a couple other questions, though."

"I'm listening."

"First thing, how long do we spend on their trail, leaving the herd shorthanded?"

"If you haven't run across 'em in two days, then double back. I'll let it go at that."

"All right, sir. And what happens when we find 'em? *If* we find 'em?"

"You could always try a citizen's arrest and take 'em into Dodge, but I don't see that happening."

"You figure on them fighting, then."

"It wouldn't shock me."

"Then we kill 'em?"

"You defend yourselves, the same as if they'd come after the herd."

"I see. You have a preference for who should come along, boss?"

"Any of the boys who helped with the Apaches would do fine."

"Except for Dietz, sir."

"I regret his death the same as you do, Sterling. But there's no connection to this other deal."

"Except the others who were in on that may not be keen to roll the dice again."

"Seems I remember you saying Art Catlin used to be a manhunter."

"Yes, sir. Claims that he came along with us hoping to put all that behind him."

"But he did all right with the hostiles."

A shrug from Sterling. "Did his share and then some. Doesn't mean he likes it, though."

"Nobody in his right mind *likes* it, Mr. Tippit. Ask him, all the same."

"Just as you say, sir. I'll get started on that now."

"And pass the shovels out," Mossman reminded him. "Whoever stays behind needs to get busy on those graves.

Devil's Crossing, Kansas

Oren Dempsey didn't have a clue how Devil's Crossing got its name and didn't care. If he'd been called upon to speculate, he might suggest that being built astride the border between Ford and Hodgeman counties was responsible, a quirk allowing wanted men to stroll across Main Street and thereby immunize themselves against arrest for any violation of one county's or the other's local laws.

That wouldn't stop a bounty hunter jumping them, of course, but for the moment, Dempsey—drunk and halfway happy with his lot in life for now—wasn't concerned about that possibility. He had eleven men, all hardcase killers, standing by to back him up in case of any danger.

That is, if the other members of his gang were even fit to stand by now.

Dempsey suspected all of them were either soused or sleeping off a bellyful of booze, unless they still had energy enough to roll around with one of the Red Dog Saloon's resident hookers. Dempsey's personal choice, a chubby blonde who called herself Jasmine, omitting her surname, was snoring loudly in her rumpled bed while Dempsey watched her from the crib's lone chair, nursing a bottle of Old Overholt and watching her asleep, as naked as the day she'd come into the world.

Things could be worse.

After they'd finished playing with the Swedes and started picking through their personal effects, one of the Comanchero gang—Nestor Carrasco, just turned twenty-one—had found five hundred thirty dollars hidden in a cedar hope chest stowed aboard the Conestoga prairie schooner. Dempsey, as their leader, had relieved Carrasco of the cash, then shared half of it out among his men and kept the other half himself.

Rank had its privileges.

Eyeing Jasmine and wondering if he could go again so soon after the last time, Oren spared a brief thought for the immigrants they'd killed.

Death held no mystery for him. It was a part of life, awaiting anything that walked, crawled, or drew breath, and Dempsey knew the reaper would be calling on him someday, maybe someday soon. His way of living put him constantly at risk from law dogs, victims who resisted being robbed, and even from his own backstabbing Comancheros. Hadn't Dempsey risen to his present leadership position by eliminating his ex-boss, the late and unlamented Eustace "Killer" Kane?

Indeed he had, and now Dempsey expected nothing better from the men he bossed around.

Thinking about the silvertips they'd sent to Swedish hell the night before last, Dempsey wondered whether anyone had found them yet. Would strangers bother planting them? Would they have checked the burned-out wagon first, to see if any trinkets still remained inside it? Afterward, would they have scuttled off to tell Ford County's law?

Dempsey had no fear of a posse, since Ford County's sheriff couldn't follow fugitives beyond his legal jurisdiction. Vigilantes posed a greater threat to Dempsey's kind, but he was confident he and his men had left no useful clues behind at their latest crime scene.

For all intents and purposes, Dempsey reckoned they should be free and clear, at least for Friday night's fiesta. Beyond that . . .

Thinking of the time he'd had with Mrs. Swede, Dempsey felt a stirring in his loins and reckoned going down to breakfast in the Red Dog's little dining room could wait awhile longer. Rising, he walked three strides to reach the bed and prodded Jasmine's buttocks with his trigger finger.

When she whimpered, still half dreaming, Dempsey told her, "Wake up, sleepyhead. I've got a surprise for you and mean to get my money's worth."

Ford County

Sterling Tippit was surprised to find that following the killers wasn't all that difficult. He guessed the sparsely populated county gave them no cause to believe they'd be pursued right off, or maybe they were just so all-fired arrogant they didn't give a damn.

In any case, despite the better part of two days passing since the wagon massacre, the tracks left by an estimated dozen mounted men were etched into the prairie, indicating that they'd ridden off at speed to wherever they had planned to go after the bloodletting.

A dozen horses, give or take, and Tippit began to wonder if his unofficial posse was shorthanded for the job they'd been assigned.

He'd asked Art Catlin first about joining the hunt and was a bit surprised when the ex–bounty hunter readily agreed. Catlin didn't appear to be fired up about it, but he hadn't tried to shirk the job, either. He was handy with a shooting iron, had proved it in their fight with the Apache braves, and Tippit reckoned Art would more than pull his weight.

The foreman's other volunteers were Julius Pryor and Zebulon Steinmeier. Zeb carried his matched Volcanic rifle and six-gun, while Pryor only had his Remington revolver. Counting Tippit's and Catlin's weapons, that made three rifles and four sidearms, while they'd likely be outnumbered four to one by enemies who'd proved their willingness to kill.

How would his riders overcome those odds, assuming that they ever caught up with the murderers? The only plan that came to Tippit's mind was a surprise attack, harking back to their raid on the Apache camp nine days ago. Whether or not that turned out to be possible depended on a list of factors Tippit had considered while they rode mostly in silence on the killers' trail.

For instance, it would make a difference where they found the fugitives. If they were camped out on the prairie, an approach to them would be more hazardous than if they'd taken shelter in a town, with innocent bystanders blundering into the line of fire.

That thought, in turn, made Tippit voice the first question he'd asked since riding off to leave the Bar X herd behind. "Do any of you know if there's a town in this neck of the woods?"

"Dodge City," Pryor said.

"Not likely they'd go there," Tippit replied. "Unless

they're idjits, they won't try to hide out in the county seat."

"It's in the wrong direction anyhow," said Steinmeier. "But there's another coming up, the way we're headed. Not much of a town, I grant you, but it still might do."

"What town is that?" asked Tippit.

"Devil's Crossing," Zeb replied. "It's more a wide spot in the road—or would be, if they had a road—but last time I was through there, they had a saloon, a livery, and a dry-goods store."

"You figure they'd accommodate a gang of killers?" Tippit asked him.

"All depends," Steinmeier said. "They might deny knowing the men we're after murdered anyone, much less the rest of what they done. Another way to think about it, they might not have guts enough to go against a gang of thugs."

"How far ahead of us is Devil's Crossing?" Tippit asked.

"I'd say another six or seven miles, smack on the county line. A settlement divided, as you might say."

"Is there any law there?" Tippit asked Steinmeier.

"None I ever heard of," Zeb replied. "They've only got a hundred people, give or take. Last time I passed through Devil's Crossing, no one seemed to think the cost of hiring on a deputy was worth it."

"All right, then," their foreman said. "Unless the trail we're following veers off some other way, it looks like we'll be heading on to Devil's Crossing. What's the name of that saloon you mentioned?"

"Red Dog," Zeb replied. "Funny, considering I never seen a dog in town the whole time I was there, much less a red one."

"Don't give up just yet," said Tippit. "They may have some mad dogs with 'em now."

Devil's Crossing

Lonnie Kilgore, the Red Dog's proprietor, had never planned to run a whorehouse and saloon far from anywhere worth mentioning. It surely wasn't what his parents had in mind for him when he was just a little shaver on their farm in Iowa.

His parents wanted Lonnie to grow up and run the place, to make something out of it that his old man never could. But by the time he came of age to light out on his own, Kilgore was sick to death of plowing, seeding, harvesting, and milking cows. He hadn't spoken to or heard from anyone back home in twenty years and reckoned they were likely dead by now, or else had given up and moved on to some other patch of unforgiving dirt.

Running the Red Dog was another sort of life entirely. It had its ups and downs, but nothing by comparison to waking up each morning at cockcrow, knowing your day would be as long and tedious as every other day that went before it.

Drunks and whores, at least, provided some variety. Kilgore had learned to handle both and turn a profit from it, though he wasn't rich by any means. Most nights he shared in the frivolity downstairs, although he sometimes had to fake enjoying it. Mornings, unless there was a problem to be dealt with, he slept in till ten o'clock or so.

But not when Comancheros came to town.

They were a rowdy bunch but paid their way without complaint and rarely tried to get one over on him. With a gang of them in town, there might be scuffling, sometimes outright brawling, but Kilgore employed a bouncer who could settle most problems by glaring, rarely having to knock anybody out.

And if it started going south, Kilgore was armed
and ready, with a sawed-off shotgun underneath the
bar, another one upstairs, and an Apache revolver he
kept in his pocket. That was an ingenious weapon. It
folded in upon itself to roughly four and one half
inches, .27 caliber, with six rounds in its cylinder, had
a knuckle-duster for a pistol grip when opened, and a
two-inch, double-edged blade tucked beneath its
stubby barrel, ready for extension as a kind of bayonet.
Kilgore had used it three, four times on rowdy customers, never on local folk.

And he would never pull it on a bunch of Comancheros, either.

That would wind up being shotgun work, if things
went bad.

Cletus Robard was preparing breakfast in the Red
Dog's kitchen when Kilgore got there, poured himself
a mug of black coffee, and sat back to watch. The smell
of frying bacon grease put Kilgore off eating and followed him as he retreated to his backroom private office, where he shut the door and settled down behind
his cluttered desk.

If he was lucky, Kilgore thought, the Comancheros
would be out and gone today, or else tomorrow at the
latest. As a rule of thumb, they didn't like to stay
around a settlement for long, maybe afraid some civi-
lizing tendency might rub off on them or—more
likely—that someone might come along behind them,
seeking to avenge some grievous wrong they'd done.

And when it came to enemies, Kilgore would bet
that Oren Dempsey's raiders had a longer list than
most.

In fact, if called upon to name someone who didn't
fear or hate them, Kilgore doubted he could list a single living soul.

The good news: Dempsey's gang only showed up in

Devil's Crossing when they had money to spend, and Lonnie Kilgore got the lion's share of that. Granted, from time to time one of their guns went off, drilling a wall or shattering a windowpane, but they had never injured anyone in town, unless you counted putting hard miles on the girls upstairs.

And every time Kilgore heard bedsprings creaking overhead, it meant more money in his pocket.

A few more hours, then—another day at most—and he'd be rid of them until they made another score. And if the greenbacks they gave Kilgore for his liquor and women had a few rust-colored stains on them, so what?

For all he knew, it could be spilled ink or a smattering of chicken blood.

T HE SUN WAS westering, maybe an hour shy of dusk, when Zebulon Steinmeier said, "That's it."

"You're sure?" asked Sterling Tippit.

"There ain't no mistaking it."

Nor, Catlin thought, could they mistake the tracks that they'd been following, which made a beeline right across the plain toward Devil's Crossing.

"All right, then. Everybody double-check your guns," Tippit ordered. "We should be getting in there right around sundown."

"And what then?" Julius Pryor asked.

"If Zeb's right," Tippit said, "there's only one place we should have to look for 'em. They'd make for the saloon and whorehouse if I've got them figured right."

Pryor pressed him. Said, "I mean how do we go about it?"

Tippit thought about that for a moment while he spun his Colt Dragoon's cylinder, checking loads, then said, "Look first. A dozen men together ought to stand out in a town that size, especially in the saloon. If we

don't spot 'em right away, I'll have a word with whoever's in charge."

Pryor couldn't seem to let it go. "And if they ain't
down in the barroom?"

"Then we'll need to head upstairs. Knock on some
doors," Tippit replied.

"The owner won't like that," Steinmeier said.

Tippit considered that and asked, "What kind of
fella is he?"

"Only saw him for a minute," Zeb replied. "If it's
the same guy I remember, he'd be on the hefty side but
soft-looking. O' course, that don't mean that he wouldn't
fight."

"Armed, was he?" Pryor asked.

Steinmeier thought about it, shook his head, and
answered, "Not that I recall. Remember it's a barroom,
though. I'd be mighty surprised if there weren't guns
around there somewhere."

"The question," Tippit said, "is whether he'd see fit
to back a customer while knowing what they did to
that poor family."

"I couldn't judge his mind," Zeb said. "If it's a matter
of us barging in and telling him we're after murderers
and worse, he'd likely ask by what authority."

"Let's put it this way, then," the foreman said. "We
nose around as best we can without declaring anything.
If challenged, let me do the talking. If the landlord or
whoever wants to side with Comanchero scum, it's his
lookout."

Art Catlin didn't like where this was going but he
knew they'd come too far to turn back empty-handed.
Instead of questioning their foreman's judgment, he
asked no one in particular, "And what about after?"

"After?" Tippit was frowning at him. "After what?"

"Say we come up against them and we don't get shot
to hell, what happens then? We stay around and plant

them, or just head back to the herd and leave a mess behind? The county sheriff may not like it, either way."

"I'll tell you what," Tippit replied. "If he shows up, I'll hand the problem over to him and be glad to see it go. Until then, let's quit wasting time and get it done. That suit you, Art?"

"Sounds fair enough," Catlin agreed.

"Okay, then," said Tippit. "Let's ride."

CHAPTER TEN

The Red Dog Saloon

HALFWAY DOWN THE staircase leading to the Red Dog's second story, Oren Dempsey paused to scan the barroom. First, he saw Lonnie Kilgore seated at a solitary corner table, cutting up a blood-rare steak with fried potatoes on the side. He concentrated on his food like men will when they haven't eaten in a week, putting the beef and spuds away with focused energy.

Out in the middle of the room, four Comancheros had their minds on poker, five-card draw with Lubie Grant dealing. Across from him, Ardil McManus eyeballed four cards in his hand and drummed his fingers on the tabletop, waiting to get his fifth. The outfit's brothers, José and Juanito Calderón, sat facing one another, José on Grant's left, Juanito to his right. Each man had anted up a silver dollar, but they hadn't started betting yet.

The barkeep was a hulk named Spencer Poe, six five or six at least, broad shouldered, barrel-chested—just the sort of bruiser that you needed tending bar if your employer was too cheap to hire a backup bouncer. Eyeing his scarred knuckles and the billy club that dangled from his left hip on a leather thong, Dempsey imagined Poe could look out for himself.

That shouldn't matter if somebody put a bullet in him, though.

Oren had no such plan for Poe just now, but it was something that he thought about, so he'd be ready just in case.

You never knew.

The Red Dog's only other customers so far this evening were a couple of old-timers, townies with a worn-out look about them, like they'd have to study on remembering the last time either of them had occasion for a smile. Their skin and clothes looked dusty, gray hair showing underneath the felt hat each man wore pulled down to shade his face from lamplight.

Dempsey wandered over to the owner's table, and didn't ask before he pulled a chair out and sat down where he could watch the Red Dog's batwing doors and his four gunmen playing cards.

Kilgore made no protest at the intrusion. Looking at him, Dempsey recognized a man who'd learned you go along to get along.

Which didn't mean that if push came to shove, Lonnie wouldn't be dangerous.

"Good steak?" Oren inquired, not really caring one way or the other.

"Fair," Kilgore replied. "Ain't Kansas City prime, but it'll do."

The pleasantries concluded, Dempsey asked Kilgore, "You have our tab writ down?"

"Yes, sir. Will you be leaving us tonight?"

"First thing tomorrow," Dempsey said. "Might have some breakfast for the road."

"Cletus can do that for you. Most days he gets up by six, six-thirty."

"Reckon you'll be sad to see the back of us."

Kilgore rolled his meaty shoulders in a kind of shrug. "You're always welcome here," he answered, with his mouth full.

Meaning that their loot was always welcome, and what more could Dempsey ask? People who knew him— or imagined that they did—stayed focused on whatever profit they could turn from dealing with him. Strangers had a tendency to take one look and shy away, as if some sixth sense let them see the bloodstains on his hands.

"Say nine o'clock, then, give or take?"

"I'll be here," Kilgore said. Then, almost wistfully, he followed up. "I'm always here."

Rising, Dempsey replied, "It could be worse."

"Amen to that," Kilgore said, and went back to sawing at his steak.

A RT CATLIN SCANNED the one and only street that ran through Devil's Crossing. On the west side, to his left, stood the Red Dog Saloon, while to his right, or east, he saw the livery and dry-goods store Zeb Steinmeier had described. Sunset cast the saloon's shadow across the dusty thoroughfare, shading its neighbors as night fell.

"Reckon they'll have their horses in the livery," their foreman offered.

"If they're here at all," Julius Pryor said.

"We'll find out soon enough." Reining his blood bay to a halt when they were still a hundred yards outside of town, Tippit informed his men, "I think it's best that we split up. Zeb, you ride around behind the livery and have a look. Don't rouse the hostler, though, if you can help it. Try to count the horses. See if there's enough of 'em to match the tracks we're following."

"Yes, sir."

Turning to Catlin, Tippit said, "Art, see if you can get around behind the Red Dog. Don't go in unless you hear a ruckus, but be ready if it happens."

Catlin nodded. Said, "No problem."

"Where do you want me?" Julius Pryor asked.

"You go with Zeb, but don't stop at the livery. Ride on around it, so that you can watch the northbound road. Cover the street from there and keep an eye peeled if somebody tries to make a break for it."

"Got it," Steinmeier said. "And what about you, sir?"

"Thought I might mosey into the saloon and have a drink," Tippit replied. "Best way that I can think of to eyeball the clientele."

"And what if they ain't here?" asked Pryor.

"Then," said Tippit, "we should have another think about whether we keep on chasing them or let it go and head back to the herd. Any more questions?"

IT WAS A load off Lonnie Kilgore's mind to hear the Comancheros would be riding out tomorrow morning. If they settled up their tab—which Oren Dempsey had always done before, without complaint—Kilgore could bid the gang farewell and wipe his mind of any thoughts about what they got up to when they were away from Devil's Crossing.

But if Dempsey tried to skip out on the bill this time, or if his riders spent their last night at the Red Dog raising holy hell, Kilgore reckoned that he should be prepared for anything.

After he left his supper plate with Cletus Robard in

the kitchen, Lonnie circled back to have a word with Spencer Poe behind the bar. Poe saw him coming and broke off from wiping down the bar's top with a dirty rag.

"You notice Dempsey jawing with me over there?" Kilgore inquired, nodding in the direction of his corner table.

"Yeah, I saw him."

"Claims him and his boys are lighting out tomorrow morning, maybe after breakfast."

"Suits me," said the barkeep.

"Anyhow, we've never had a problem with them paying up before, but just in case . . ."

"Did he say something, boss?"

"Like what?"

"To make you think he'd try 'n' cheat you."

"No, nothing like that."

"But you're still worried."

"Let's just say I like to be prepared."

"Makes sense, a bunch like them."

"And what I *don't* want is to light a fuse I can't stomp out. You hear me?"

"Sure."

"So, in the morning, what I need's a tab on whatever they've had to drink, how many bottles—keep the empties till they're gone—and how much time they spent upstairs. How many girls they used, and so on."

"Right."

"When I present the bill, if Dempsey wants to dicker, maybe I'm amenable." Kilgore liked using big words now and then, to make him sound more educated than he was. "He tries to screw me, though, and it could go another way entirely."

"Understood."

"First chance you get, make sure that twelve-gauge underneath the bar is good to go."

"I check it at the start of every shift," Poe said.

"Check it again, Spence. Just don't let nobody see you doing it."

"Okay."

"And don't go waving it around unless I need you to. These boys ain't just some cowpokes off the trail."

"I know that."

"But if you have to use the scattergun, be goddamned sure you make it count."

S TERLING TIPPIT TIED up his blood bay mare outside the Red Dog, leaving slack enough for her to reach the water trough sitting below the hitching rail. He looked around once more at what there was of Devil's Crossing—precious little, even in the near dark—then unhooked the hammer thong that kept his Colt Dragoon revolver holstered and mounted the wooden sidewalk, stepping to the barroom's batwing doors.

Before he shouldered through them, Tippit had a look around inside. Four shifty-looking fellows playing cards out near the middle of the room, each wearing knives and pistols on their belts. They looked like he imagined Comancheros should, although Tippit had never seen one in the flesh before. Two of them Mexicans, the others scruffy whites who could have used a long hot bath.

Two other patrons stood together at the bar, neither with any weapons showing, and they didn't strike Tippit as outlaw types. Too old, for one thing, and their clothes, while threadbare, didn't have the ingrained dirt of someone living on the dodge. Behind the bar, a tall, broad, younger man was wiping whiskey glasses with a cloth that didn't offer much prospect of cleaning them.

Tippit went in and caught the four cardplayers eyeing

him while he tried not to let them catch him noticing. He passed their table without glancing down at anybody's cards or pile of coins, knowing how easy it could be to give offense in a strange town without intending to.

He stepped up to the bar, still feeling hostile eyes upon him, leaving two or three arm's lengths between himself and the two older fellows who were nursing beers. The bartender approached him, putting on a practiced smile, and asked Tippit, "Whiskey or beer?"

Scanning the backbar's row of bottles on display, he said, "Bourbon. The Old Grand-Dad."

"One Grand-dad coming up."

The barkeep poured his shot. Said, "I don't recollect you coming in before, mister."

"First time in town," Tippit replied. "I was supposed to meet somebody here, but I don't see him."

"Your friend got a name?"

Tippit tossed out the first that came to him. "Bliss Mossman. Claims to be a cattle buyer."

"Can't say I'm familiar with him, but we get all kinds."

"Slow night?" asked Tippit.

"Not too bad. We've got more guys up in the cribs, but they come in together. I can tell you none of 'em are livestock dealers."

"Guess I'll wait a spell and hope I didn't waste the trip," Tippit replied. He quaffed his bourbon down and tapped his empty shot glass on the bar. "Maybe I'd better have another one to keep that company."

L UBIE, YOU EVER seen that guy before?" Ardil McManus asked his fellow Comanchero, facing him across a table strewn with coins.

Grant stared a hole into the new arrival's back, then answered, "Not that I can recollect."

"How come you no ask either one of us?" asked José Calderón.

"Because he ain't a Mex," Ardil replied dismissively.

José sneered at him. "You think we couldn't know a gringo?"

"We know you, *cabrón*," Juanito said, making his brother laugh. "You gonna bet or check, *pendejo*?"

Peering at his cards through a whiskey haze, McManus said, "I'll see your dime and raise a nickel. How'd that be, *maricón*?"

"Is fine with me," Juanito said, and pushed five pennies out into the pot.

"That's fifteen cents to you, José," McManus said.

"I see you," José answered as he tossed a nickel out.

"Lubie?" McManus prodded. "Are you staying in or folding?"

"I'll stay for a nickel." Once he'd pushed that over, Grant pulled one card from his hand and dropped it facedown on the table. "And I'll take one card."

"Trying to fill a straight or flush?" McManus goaded him.

"Never you mind."

"One card it is," said Ardis, skimming one across the table.

Lubie Grant retrieved it, blinked at what it showed him. "Raise another dime," he said.

"I think you bluffing," said Juanito, on Grant's left, but then he folded anyway.

"Too rich for my blood," Ardil told the table. "Dealer folds."

"Chick-chick-chick," José taunted him.

"Keep chirping birdman," Ardis said. "I'd rather spend what I got left to get another poke upstairs."

"Do the girls charge you extra?" asked Juanito.

"Maybe puts a sack over his head," José chimed in.

"I'll have you know that little Margarita calls me 'raging bull.'"

Juanito blinked at him, feigning surprise, McManus thought. "She call you *toro furioso*?" he inquired.

"Naw," Ardil replied. "It sounded more like *culo gordo*."

Both brothers convulsed with laughter over that, and even Lubie Grant was smiling at him from across the poker table. "What?" Ardil demanded.

"*Culo gordo* means 'fat ass,'" Juanito told him. "You should learn more Spanish, eh?"

McManus bolted to his feet with fists clenched. "Goddamn sons of bitches!" he exploded.

"Whoa, now!" Lubie Grant protested. "Let's leave mothers outta this, Fat Ass."

Ardil was going for his pistol when he saw Grant's Colt Peacemaker—stolen off a dead man in Nogales eight months previously—pointed at his navel.

"Simmer down now, Ardil," Lubie urged him. "If you need a beer to cool you off, I'll stand you to it. Otherwise, I'll want to see how fast you are."

A RT CATLIN WAS in place behind the Red Dog by the time Ardil ordered his beer. There were no lamps out back to pierce the night's shadows on that side of Devil's Crossing, but he welcomed darkness as an aide to keeping him alive.

The moment anybody spotted him, Catlin and their entire mission would be at risk.

First thing upon arriving at his post, he'd tried the joint's back door and found it wasn't locked. Various sounds were audible inside, male voices for the most part, but a woman's conversation came from an open window on the Red Dog's second floor. Art couldn't make out any details, but took it for the reassuring patter that a working girl learned early on in her career, to keep her patrons satisfied and coming back for more.

From where he stood, holding his Henry rifle at the ready, Catlin couldn't say who was inside the Red Dog or how many of them there might be. The place was large enough to host a dozen men and more downstairs, but he had no idea about the second-story cribs, how many hookers were in residence, or whether they had customers lined up, waiting to take a turn.

One problem Art saw: there was an outhouse about twenty paces from the Red Dog's back door, meaning that anyone inside might have a hurry call at any time, skedaddling to get their business done without being caught short. Nothing that Art could do about it but stand pat and be prepared for trouble if a runner spotted him.

And in that case . . . what?

Another complication was the dry-goods shop next door to the saloon. It was a single-story building with the store in front and living quarters in the rear, where pale lamplight beamed through a windowpane of rippled glass. Catlin had tried to peer inside but couldn't manage it, though he had smelled food cooking, its aroma wafting from a kitchen stovepipe.

Listening outside the shop's back door, he'd tried to learn if the proprietor had family or not, but all was silent from within, except faint scraping sounds that might have been a spatula stirring the contents of a skillet.

Add that unknown person to potential users of the Red Dog's outhouse, and it doubled Catlin's risk. There was a narrow walkway between the store and the saloon, which would require pedestrians to move in single file, and that was yet another problem. Anyone could cross the street out front and wind up facing open prairie land behind the Red Dog and its neighbor.

Every passing minute made Art like the setup less.

And there was nothing he could do about it now but stand and wait for trouble, or a signal from his foreman to abort the hunt.

Melvin halstead was drunk. Not falling-down drunk, but his mind was hazy from the booze he'd put away downstairs.

That was a state Halstead preferred to facing life cold sober, when his temper often got the better of him and he wound up doing stupid things that got him into trouble—sometimes even into jail.

That was one good thing about riding with Oren Dempsey's Comancheros, as he'd done for going on two years now. There was usually liquor within easy reach, either from dives like the Red Dog, or lifted from the stock they sold to redskins on the sly, along with guns and ammunition, mirrors, bolts of brightly colored cloth, and any kind of worthless gewgaws they could lay hands on and peddle to the natives on their reservations.

Halstead didn't think about what happened once the braves got liquored up and started looting homesteads, killing as they went. That wasn't his fault, any more than bartenders in his world took responsibility for patrons stumbling around and suffering an injury because they couldn't walk or see straight.

That was life, and if their outfit wasn't selling to the Indians, somebody else would move in, taking up the slack. Mel Halstead thought it might as well be him.

Tonight—their last night for a while in Devil's Crossing, till they managed to accumulate more loot—Halstead sat watching dreamily while redheaded Lurleen finished undressing by lamplight. Downstairs in the bar, she'd worn a narrow skirt and ruffled bodice, lace around its low-cut neckline, but it didn't take her long to shed those garments once their talk of business was concluded. Halstead was relieved that Lurleen didn't wear a bustle, common among fancy ladies in the larger Kansas towns, but something Melvin personally couldn't understand.

Why would a woman strap on a device under her clothes that made her look deformed?

Beneath her outer garments, Lurleen wore a corset meant to emphasize her narrow waist, with knee-length pantaloons below. Now, posing for him, she stopped half-way through a pirouette and said, "Untie me, Mallard?"

Jesus, Melvin thought, but tipsy as he was, he didn't bother to correct her.

Hell, it wasn't like they'd ever meet again.

And there were times when having others garble up your name might even come in handy, if the law dogs started snuffling on their trail—which just might happen, after how they'd left that Nordski family when they were finished with them.

Rising on unsteady legs, Halstead put those stark images out of his mind and smiled.

"My pleasure, honeybunch," he said.

ZEB STEINMEIER PACED up and down behind the livery, burning off restless energy, holding his Volcanic rifle cocked and ready for whatever challenge might confront him on the dark outskirts of Devil's Crossing.

It was no coincidence that Steinmeier's rifle bore a close resemblance to Winchester's Model 1866, the famous "Yellow Boy." Designed in 1855 by Horace Smith and Daniel Wesson, when they'd started their Volcanic Repeating Arms Company, it was a lever-action model with the same alloy receiver as the later Winchester. In fact, Oliver Winchester had bought into Volcanic, forcing its insolvency in 1856 and moving its facility some sixty miles from Norwich to New Haven, in Connecticut, where he had changed the name to Winchester Repeating Arms and started cashing in big-time.

Zeb's vintage rifle had a sixteen-inch barrel and held ten rounds of .44-caliber ammunition. His sidearm—also a Volcanic—sported a six-inch barrel and held six rounds of the same in a tubular magazine under its barrel, with a lever-action trigger guard that would have made it awkward in a stand-up fight, although it was all right for snakes and other pests encountered on a cattle drive.

Tonight, Steinmeier hoped it wouldn't slow him down so much it got him killed.

He'd had a look inside the livery upon arrival, after first confirming that the hostler had gone home. Confirming twelve horses in stalls dozing or munching oats increased the odds that Sterling Tippit had it right about the Comancheros stopping off in town.

And where else would they be tonight, besides the Red Dog, with its red-eye and its soiled doves ripe for plucking?

Steinmeier's job, aside from counting horses with their mismatched brands, involved waiting within earshot of the saloon until a ruckus started, at which time he was expected to pitch in. Exactly how that was supposed to work eluded him, but Tippit couldn't pin the details down until he'd verified that they had found the Comancheros they were tracking.

Now all Zeb had to do was make his way across the street and pray he wasn't spotted in the process, touching off a fight before the other members of his makeshift posse were in place and ready to respond.

It was shaping up to be the worst night of his life.

And maybe the last.

* * *

STERLING TIPPIT HALF turned from the Red Dog's bar to face the poker table where an argument was swiftly heating up.

One of the players, on his feet now, got it started, shouting at the others, "Goddamn sons of bitches!"

"Whoa, now!" said the Comanchero facing him. "Let's leave mothers outta this, Fat Ass."

The first man who had shouted reached for his six-gun, then froze, finding the other had him covered, pistol barely visible over the poker table's edge.

The faster of them warned his comrade, "Simmer down now, Ardil. If you need a beer to cool you off, I'll stand you to it. Otherwise, I'll want to see how fast you are."

Tippit eased a hand down toward his Colt Dragoon, then heard the barkeep cursing as he hauled a sawed-off shotgun out and held it braced against his hip, twin muzzles angled toward the ceiling overhead.

"Enough of that!" the bartender called out. "This ain't that kind of place!"

That sounded like an outright lie to Tippit's ears—what frontier bar and whorehouse hadn't seen its share of brawls and shooting scrapes—but he was busy sliding to his left, giving the bartender an open field of fire.

Across the room from where he stood, the other drinkers at the bar were backing away as well, Tippit saw a couple of the cardplayers—the Mexicans—swivel in his direction, eyeballing the barkeep and his scattergun.

"You got no call to act like that, amigo," one of them advised.

"Best not to interfere," the other said, smiling as if the incident was just business as usual.

And maybe, Tippit thought, it was exactly that.

The one who'd sounded off first—called Ardil by

the Comanchero holding him at gunpoint—faced the bar now, glaring at the man behind it with the shotgun in his hands. "Be careful what you wish for," he advised.

"The only thing I want is for your friend to put his gun away," the bartender replied. "You wanna fight, take it outside."

"You sprout a badge that I can't see under that apron?" Ardil challenged him.

"I speak for Mr. Kilgore," the barkeep responded. "And this twelve-gauge speaks for me."

Behind Tippit, the drinkers that he took for locals were retreating, keeping to the barroom's north wall as they hightailed for the exit. Tippit tried to make himself a little smaller, knowing that it was a waste of time.

Instead, he took a chance and asked all four of them together, "Any chance you fellas might be Comancheros?"

All four pairs of eyes were locked on Tippit now. The one called Ardil answered back, "The hell is that to you?"

Glancing beyond them, where he'd noted movement at one of the Red Dog's windows facing toward the street, Tippit saw someone standing on the sidewalk.

Was that Zeb Steinmeier?"

"Mister!" barked the standing poker player. "I asked you—"

"I heard you," Tippit interrupted him. "We spotted something on the trail a while back. Thought it might be Comancheros' handiwork."

"And who in hell is 'we'?" Ardil inquired.

"Me and a couple friends," Tippit replied, in the split second left before chaos erupted in the Red Dog's gaming room.

CHAPTER ELEVEN

THE SOUND OF rapid-fire gunshots drew Catlin through the Red Dog's back door. He noted kitchen smells first thing, immediately followed by the reek of burned black powder.

He was standing in a narrow hallway, facing toward the barroom twenty-five or thirty feet ahead, beyond a dangling screen of beaded strings. A shotgun blast nearly eclipsed the pop-pop sound of pistols, two or three at least.

Somewhere upstairs, a woman squealed, cut off by a man's voice telling her to shut her pie hole. Other men were cursing, and a bottle shattered, likely toppling from a nightstand, while the sound of running footsteps—bare and shod alike—evoked the mental image of a small stampede.

Catlin had his Henry cocked and shouldered as he eased along the hallway, anxious to see what was happening in the saloon, but not in any hurry to catch lead himself.

As if in answer to his thought, a stray slug clipped one of the beaded strings suspended at the far end of the corridor, and Catlin ducked instinctively before it tore into the right-hand wall and burrowed deep.

A sweaty-looking character, wearing a dirty apron over long johns, stuck his head out of a doorway on Art's left and blinked twice as he saw the Henry pointed at his face. He squawked, reminding Catlin of a parrot he had seen two years before, at the Chicago Zoo in Lincoln Park. He looked to be a cook, and while his hands were empty, Catlin couldn't take the chance that he'd recover from his shock and come back with a cleaver or a butcher's knife.

Art pushed in through the kitchen door and found the peeper cowering beside a stove that could have used a thorough cleaning months ago. Wide-eyed and quaking, the cook showed him empty hands and whined, "I got nothing to do with that shit goin' on out front."

"Be smart, then," Catlin said. "Skin out the back and stay well clear until you don't hear shooting anymore."

"Yes, sir! And thank you, sir!"

Art stepped aside to let him pass, confirmed that he was loping toward the back door, then went back to check the kitchen, just in case the cook had a helper hiding out.

Nothing.

Art reckoned that he'd stalled his entry to the barroom long enough. Tippit was in the thick of it, presumably, and Catlin went to see if he was even still alive.

A FUMING STRING OF curses poured from Oren Dempsey's sour-tasting mouth as he scrambled around the little bedroom, pulling on his trousers, letting the suspenders droop until he found out that his gun belt wouldn't buckle properly around them. He'd already dropped the whiskey bottle that he'd brought upstairs and had to dodge barefoot around its broken glass, stepping in wasted alcohol.

Jasmine was mewling underneath the bed—a tight fit for her, but she'd managed it, after the shooting started up downstairs. Dempsey snapped at her to shut the hell up, but she kept on crying like a little kid who'd reached inside her Christmas stocking and produced only a lump of coal.

Once he had fastened on his pistol belt, Dempsey unholstered his LeMat revolver, spun its nine-shot cylinder, confirmed a shotgun shell was loaded in its second barrel, and prepared to head downstairs. He thought of picking up the trapdoor Springfield propped upright beside the sagging bed but left it there, deciding that if ten shots couldn't end the barroom battle, one more likely wouldn't do him any good.

His first thought, when the shooting started, was of trouble where he'd left four of his riders playing poker with two whiskey bottles on their table. Dempsey knew the Calderón brothers liked picking fights when they were drunk, and Lubie Grant had trouble hiding his disdain for Mexicans, although you'd think he might have grown accustomed to them after pulling jobs together for the past couple of years.

As for McManus, well . . .

Before he cleared the bedroom doorway, though, another thought hit Dempsey. What if this was more than just a dustup between rowdy Comancheros?

What if some dirt they had done was catching up with them at last?

More worried now than angry, Dempsey stopped short in the second-story corridor and doubled back to Jasmine's crib. He holstered his LeMat and moved directly to the bed, stooped down to grip its wooden

frame, then heaved it up and over, and stopped from falling by the offside wall.

Beneath the bed, Jasmine was squirming like a bug
will when the stone concealing it is suddenly removed.
She yelped and tried to roll away from him, but Dempsey
caught her tangled hair in one hand, hauled her naked
to her feet, and wrapped his left arm tight around her,
underneath her breasts.

His right hand drew the big LeMat again, its muzzle
grinding hard into her back, below one shoulder blade.

"Let's take a walk, darlin'," he hissed into her ear,
"and see what's goin' on downstairs."

S TERLING TIPPIT HADN'T been expecting all-out chaos
when he walked into the Red Dog, much less that
the Comancheros he was tracking would go wild and
light the fuse themselves.

Of course, the barkeep hadn't helped, pulling his
shotgun when a couple of the poker players started
squabbling at their table, halfway drunk and thinking
they could settle it with shooting irons.

And it had gone to hell from there, the moment that
the bartender produced his sawed-off coach gun, hoping it would calm the Comancheros down. Of course,
it had the opposite effect, and by the time Tippit cleared
leather with his Colt Dragoon, the barroom's smoky
air was full of flying lead.

It didn't seem that any of the cardplayers were bent
on shooting him, particularly. Once they all had guns
in hand and the bartender had fired off one barrel of
his Greener, it had turned into a loco free-for-all. The
Comancheros started firing at the bartender, whose
first round sprayed buckshot over their heads, not even
grazing anyone, and Tippit hit the floor, trying to make
himself invisible.

That didn't work, either.

While random bullets pocked the Red Dog's back-bar window and smashed whiskey bottles on the shelves below, one of the Mexicans saw Tippit with his Colt in hand and winged a shot in his direction, gouging splinters from the wooden facing of the bar near Tippit's head.

The Colt Dragoon bucked in Tippit's hand, his instinctive reaction sending a slug downrange without taking time to aim it precisely. He got lucky. A gout of blood spurted from the Comanchero's shoulder, impact spinning him around to hit the floor facedown.

Not dead but hurting at the very least—and that left three within the Bar X foreman's field of vision.

From the racket he could hear upstairs, he supposed that reinforcements would arrive in seconds flat. And when that happened, Tippit didn't want to be curled up against the bar in plain view.

Vaulting to his feet, he lunged across the bar and landed in a crouch beside the bartender, who stood hunched over, fumbling to reload his double-barreled shotgun. Glancing over at Tippit, he said, "You ain't supposed to be back here."

Before he could do anything about it, though, a bullet drilled the right side of his neck and came out on the left, blood spewing from its ragged exit wound. His head dropped over at an ugly angle, like a hanged man's, and his knees folded, the bulk of him almost collapsing onto Sterling Tippit's outstretched legs.

Reaching across the fallen body, Tippit grabbed the barkeep's twelve-gauge, double-checked its load before he snapped it shut and thumbed both hammers back. Wedging his legs beneath him, waiting for a lull in pistol fire, he counted down until his moment came, then sprang up like an oversized jack-in-the-box.

He caught three of the former poker players starting

to spread out and rush the bar. The fourth was still down, smearing blood across the floorboards as he tried to stand, without much visible success.

No time to hesitate, as three guns rose and tried to target him.

Tippit fired off both barrels of the Greener—left, then right—riding the weapon's recoil, sweeping its twin muzzles sideways between shots. The shotgun's sixteen-inch barrels sprayed buckshot across a wide front, striking two of the three Comancheros he'd hoped to bring down.

One took it squarely in his face, features erased by blood as his sombrero took flight with a portion of his scalp inside it. When he hit the barroom floor, limbs splayed, he shivered like a hooked trout drowning in fresh air.

The other moving Comanchero caught a charge beneath his upraised gun arm. He spun through three quarters of a circle with his buckskin shirt flapping around him, losing balance as he came out of the turn and dropping to all fours. He tried to rise again, palms sliding on the blood-slick floor, but Tippit dropped his borrowed scattergun, now empty, and reverted to his Colt, drilling a .44 round through the outlaw's right armpit to put him down.

That left one on the run and headed for the stairs to Tippit's right, fanning two shots off from his gun in rapid fire. Neither came close to Tippit, though he flinched involuntarily before he found his mark, leading the runner by a foot or so, triggering a fourth shot from his big Dragoon.

The Comanchero seemed to stumble on his own feet, pitching headlong toward another table, where his forehead struck wood with a solid whack as he went down. He was recoiling from that impact when Zeb

Steinmeier barged in through the Red Dog's batwing doors, Volcanic rifle raised, and punched a fresh hole through the Comanchero's back.

The gunman finally collapsed, blood pooling underneath him, pumping from a ruptured lung in jets until the gunman's life was finished draining out.

No other threats were presently in sight, but Tippit heard more men evacuating upstairs bedrooms, hastening to the relief of their comrades. Willing himself to focus, he began reloading the Dragoon one fat round at a time and wondered where the other members of his posse were right now.

S TAY UP HERE and out of sight," Mel Halstead warned Lurleen. "At least until the shooting stops."

"What's going on?" she asked him, in a whiny little-girl voice, sounding close to tears.

"How 'n hell would I know, woman?" Halstead answered back. "I'm goin' down to find that out right now."

"I don't think that's a good idea," she said, half sounding like she gave a damn about him. "It's not safe."

"Christ on a crutch," he snapped at her, drawing his Schofield six-gun with a showy flourish. "If it was safe, I wouldn't need this smoke wagon, would I?"

"I only meant—"

"You want a *good* idea?" he interrupted, mocking her. "Stay right here like I told you, till your boss comes by to fetch you." And he went out, muttering under his breath, "Supposing that he ever does, the fool."

Outside the bedroom doorway, Zachary Bodine nearly ran into Halstead running toward the Red Dog's stairs himself. The barrel of his Springfield rifle glanced off Melvin's shoulder with sufficient force to bruise him.

"Well, excuse hell outta me," Halstead jeered at Zach as he ran on, oblivious.

"Excuse this!" Bodine answered back, his left hand raised, its middle finger spiked.

Some people. If there wasn't gunplay going on downstairs . . .

Halstead refocused his attention on the clamor rising from the barroom, picking up his pace, eager to find out who was killing whom, and why.

ZEB STEINMEIER HAD hesitated entering the Red Dog's barroom when the shooting started up. He'd spotted Sterling Tippit at the bar, turning to watch some kind of hubbub at one of the poker tables, while the barkeep pulled a shotgun out from hiding and the whole scene went to hell in nothing flat.

Once bullets started flying back and forth, it seemed like suicide to walk in on the middle of it, with the bartender and Zeb's own foreman taking fire, unloading back in Steinmeier's direction, so he'd flattened up against the outer wall and started counting backward from one hundred in his head.

When he was halfway done with that, the firing slackened and he peered in through the window, saw one of the Comancheros—Christ, he hoped it was, at least—running in the direction of some stairs off to the left. Tippit had slipped behind the bar somehow, and he was lining up a pistol shot to drop the runner.

Thinking that the Bar X foreman ought to know what he was doing, Zeb pushed through the swinging doors with his Volcanic rifle braced against his shoulder, squeezing off his shot a split second after Tippit's Dragoon spat lead across the Red Dog's bar.

Between the two of them, they'd put the final poker player down.

When Tippit greeted him with a tight nod, Steinmeier tried to figure out if he'd hung back too long and come off looking like a coward, but the foreman didn't chastise him. Instead, he started moving down the bar's length, drawing closer to the stairs and whoever was storming down them, coming even later to the party than Steinmeier.

He passed the poker table with its scattered cards and coins, to reach another one nearby. Its placement granted Zeb a more direct view of the stairs, and so he flipped the table over on its edge, crouching behind it with his rifle aimed and braced.

Maybe five seconds now.

And four . . .

Three . . .

L ONNIE KILGORE COCKED his shotgun first the left-hand barrel, then the right—wishing he had a drink ready at hand to steel his nerves. Too bad Lonnie had drained the bottle he kept hidden in his desk while washing down the supper Cletus Robard had prepared for him.

Now he was going into battle nearly sober, and the Red Dog's owner didn't like it one damned bit.

For starters, Kilgore wished he had more guns around the place. Between the shotgun in his hands and the Apache six-gun in his pocket, it was all or nothing. It was hard to miss a man-sized target with the double-barrel, but he only had two shots before he had to reload, which meant fumbling with the spare shells in his pocket, and it didn't sound as if the shooters in his barroom would allow him any extra time.

With the Apache, by comparison, he'd have to move in kissing-close before he opened fire, and even then, he couldn't gain a hit, much less a kill with its small

caliber. On balance, Lonnie thought he might do better with the knuckle-duster or the two-inch dagger's
blade. But whether anyone would let him get in close
enough for that was doubtful.

More likely, they'd just cut him down on sight.

"To hell with that!" he said aloud as he trudged along
a not-so-secret passage from his office to the Red Dog's
barroom battleground, with access through a door behind the bar that he kept locked from the inside.

The Dog was *his* joint, and he wouldn't have it taken
from him by a gang of unwashed Comancheros who
committed God knew what crimes to accumulate the
cash they spent on Lonnie's booze and women two,
maybe three times a year.

He might be nothing but a small frog in a smaller
pond, all things considered, but he had to take a stand
sometime, somewhere.

And if he didn't . . . well, what was the point in even
drawing breath?

A RT CATLIN REACHED the beaded curtain separating
the saloon from various back rooms and paused
there for a moment, checking out the carnage on display
beyond it.

Straight ahead of him, four gunmen who he guessed
were Comancheros—or had been—lay sprawled in
blood, their pistols lying just beyond the reach of outflung hands. Off to his left, a good-sized man he'd never
seen before lay on his side behind the bar, shot through
the neck, head lolling from a severed spine.

Above that corpse stood Sterling Tippit, busily reloading his big Colt Dragoon. His chosen weapon was
the gun's Third Model, recently converted from black
powder to accept metallic cartridges, but still requiring

Tippit to remove the cylinder instead of dumping empties and replacing them through a convenient loading
gate.

As Tippit spotted Catlin, nodding curt acknowledg-
ment, Art heard a clatter on the stairs and spun in that
direction, shouldering his Henry, sighting down its barrel toward a clutch of five men rapidly descending from
the second floor. One of them was naked, none entirely
dressed; Catlin presumed that gunfire had drawn them
from their pleasure in the upstairs cribs.

But all of them were armed and on alert, spotting
their downed comrades, then cutting loose on Art and
Sterling Tippit, judged to be their enemies. Crouching
to clear the Bar X foreman's line of fire when he was
done reloading, Catlin framed the group's nude point
man in his rifle's sights and put his first round through
the gunman's hairy chest.

J ULIUS PRYOR RACED across the dusty street that
seemed to mark the county line bisecting Devil's
Crossing, Remington revolver in his hand. He reached
the Red Dog just as lamps were being lit in humble living quarters up and down the thoroughfare, the occupants alarmed by gunfire echoing from the saloon.

Last to arrive for the Bar X contingent, Pryor glanced
through the saloon's front window and saw a group of
men descending from the second floor and pegging
shots toward others at the bar. He recognized Art Catlin
crouching there and firing back at his assailants on the
stairs, while Sterling Tippit leaned across the bar, joining the melee with his Colt Dragoon. Zeb Steinmeier
was halfway across the barroom, kneeling under cover
of a capsized poker table, also blasting at the stairs
with his Volcanic rifle.

Get on with it, thought Pryor as he shoved in through the Red Dog's swinging doors and joined the battle with his Remington, winging one of the Comancheros with his first .46-caliber slug and pitching the gunman off balance, making him tumble head over heels down the staircase.

That first shot brought Steinmeier's head and rifle pivoting toward Pryor, but Zeb recognized his fellow drover instantly and swung his full attention back to the remaining enemies that Julius could see so far.

Four down, one wounded, four more rushing down the Red Dog's stairs, but Tippit's posse had been tracking twelve raiders from where they'd massacred the hapless Bjorlin family.

Where were the other three?

Julius pushed that question out of mind and focused on the gunmen he could see, who were intent on killing him and his companions if they got the chance.

The one he'd winged had landed in a heap but lurched upright immediately, still holding his pistol. Pryor had his six-gun leveled for a second shot, when someone to his right—Tippit or Catlin—dropped the wounded Comanchero with a head shot.

Cursing, Pryor sought another target while the four staircase survivors blazed away at anyone still standing in the barroom, and thinking, *Christ! Why won't they just hold still?*

O N PRECEDING VISITS to the Red Dog, Oren Dempsey had become acquainted with its layout, mapping entrances and exits in his mind against a day like this, when he might have to flee in an emergency. He'd also stumbled on the narrow hallway that connected Lonnie Kilgore's private office to the bar, and used it now in hopes he could surprise his unknown enemies and turn the tables on them to his own advantage.

It was something of an edge—but, then again, not much of one.

No sooner had he eased into the murky corridor than Dempsey realized someone was passing through ahead of him. He recognized the slump of Kilgore's shoulders and the bald spot on his crown that had increased in size a bit since Dempsey last stopped off in Devil's Crossing, roughly five months earlier.

He reckoned going bald was an embarrassment, but nothing that Kilgore would have to suffer with much longer.

Dempsey suspected that his host had put tonight's ambush in motion. As to why, the Comanchero leader neither knew nor cared. To his mind, it was normal for a businessman to be corrupt, scheming to offer Dempsey's men a place to drink and get their bell ropes pulled for pay, while setting up a massacre that would eliminate them, letting Kilgore loot their corpses afterward.

In fact, it was the kind of plan Dempsey himself might have devised, if he were a more settled type, amenable to staying put and managing a tavern-cum-bordello rather than ranging at will and hunting victims on the plains.

He understood betrayal, sometimes practiced it himself, but deemed it unforgivable when he wound up on the receiving end.

With that in mind, he shouted out to Kilgore from behind, making his presence known.

"Hey, Lonnie! What's your goddamn hurry?"

Kilgore spun around to face him, letting Dempsey see the coach gun in his hands.

"Are you deaf, Oren?" Lonnie answered. "Can't you hear what's going on out front?"

"I hear just fine," Dempsey replied. "And the next thing I wanna hear is why in hell you pulled this crap on us."

Kilgore blinked at him, frowning as he feigned confusion. "What? Have you been sucking locoweed? You think I want my own damned place shot up?"

"I reckon that depends on what you hope to get from it," Dempsey replied, and fired the shotgun barrel of his big LeMat revolver without bothering to aim. The pellets staggered Kilgore, dropped him to his knees, gaping in wonderment at how his night had gone so suddenly, disastrously awry.

Gasping through his pain, Kilgore began to curse Dempsey. "You dumb son of a—"

"Dumb, am I?" The Comanchero leader cut him off. "Which one of us is gutshot, on his knees, you rotten piece of—"

In his outrage, Dempsey barely saw the sawed-off coach gun's muzzled rising, had no time to cock his pistol for another shot before both barrels roared at him and he was airborne, tumbling backward into black oblivion.

ART CATLIN FIRED his fourth shot at the Comancheros on the Red Dog's stairs, by which time all of them were down and either thrashing on the floor or lying deathly still.

Counting the bodies, he called out to his companions from the cattle drive, "There's three still unaccounted for."

"I heard a couple shots back here somewhere," Tippit advised, moving behind the bar until he stood before a door that wouldn't open when he tried its knob. "Locked from the other side," he said.

While Catlin went around to join him, Zeb Steinmeier and Julius Pryor covering their backs, Tippit picked up what must have been the barkeep's scatter-gun. He found fresh shells in a box under the bar, then ditched the shotgun's empties and reloaded it.

"Fire in the hole!" their foreman warned the rest of them, before he fired one barrel, shattering the door's lock, then proceeded through it with the Greener raised and ready.

"Two more down!" Tippit called out, then backed out of the hallway set behind the door, while Catlin peered inside.

"I doubt the heavyset one was a Comanchero," he told Tippit.

From the far side of the bar, Steinmeier asked him, "Does he have a mustache and bald spot? Wearing little wire-rimmed spectacles?"

"He does," Catlin confirmed.

"That's Lonnie Something, I forget his last name," Zeb replied. "He owns this place."

"Not anymore," Tippit advised.

"The other one must be a Comanchero, then," said Catlin. "Guess we'll never know what made the two of 'em draw down on one another."

"Doesn't matter now," said Tippit. "We're still missing two more raiders by my count."

"That matches horses at the livery," Steinmeier said.

Julius Pryor put his two cents in, saying, "We need to find 'em, then."

"Fan out," Tippit ordered, "but watch yourselves. Unless they got away somehow, don't count on them to fold without a fight."

While Zeb and Pryor made their way upstairs, Catlin trailed Tippit down the corridor obstructed by two bloody corpses, finally emerging in a cluttered office where Art guessed the bar's proprietor had been disturbed while going over paperwork. From there, a left turn took them to the hallway Catlin had traversed between the back door of the Red Dog and its barroom, now a slaughter pen.

They checked the kitchen—no sign of the cook Catlin had braced before—and tried a closet filled with mops and brooms, but not a fugitive in sight. Relaxing just a smidgen, Tippit said, "They must still be upstairs."

"Unless they jumped out of a window," Art replied.

"Or that."

Before they could retreat to mount the stairs, a crackle of gunfire resounded from the Red Dog's second floor. A woman screamed, immediately followed by more shots, and then a wail of pain that could have been produced by either sex, depending on the injury.

They clambered up the stairs and reached the upper story just as Pryor and Steinmeier left one of the bedrooms, Pryor looking slightly green around the gills.

"You two all right?" asked Tippit.

"If you want to call it that," Julius said.

"We found the last two," Steinmeier elaborated, "holed up with a couple of the whores. Held pistols on 'em, threatening to kill 'em if we wouldn't let the Comancheros go."

"And then?" Art asked.

"I reckon they got tired of waiting," Zeb replied. "Shot both of 'em like it was nothing, then pulled down on us. That didn't go the way they'd hoped."

Tippit went down to check the crib while Art hung back. He'd seen enough blood for one night and didn't need two ventilated women added to the butcher's bill.

"Well, damn it!" Tippit growled, retreating from the small bedroom. "At least that makes a dozen."

"So, we're finished, then?" asked Pryor staring at their foreman.

"Done with this, at least," Tippit replied. "Now all we have to do is catch up with the herd."

CHAPTER TWELVE

Wednesday, May 21

Wabaunsee County, Kansas

IT HAD TAKEN Sterling Tippit's manhunters two days to track and overtake the Bar X herd. During that time, they'd talked a bit about the firefight they'd engaged in with the Comancheros and the women who'd been killed, besides.

Of all the raiders they had killed, only the leader of the pack had been identified by name. The hooker he'd monopolized while they were staying at the Red Dog heard the owner—Lonnie Kilgore, also dead now—call the man in charge "Oren" on one occasion, "Mr. Dempsey" on another, but the rest, all white or Mexican except one Chinaman, were being planted without markers to identify them.

That is, if the residents of Devil's Crossing felt like

digging thirteen graves, instead of dragging them a mile or so from town and letting nature take its course.

Whatever, Catlin thought. The dead, in his opinion, neither knew nor cared what might become of their abandoned bodies once they'd ceased to serve a purpose.

On the ride back to resume their paying jobs, there'd naturally been some talk about the killings, Catlin staying out of it as much as possible. Before dropping his bounty hunter's trade, he had collected twenty-seven fugitives, eleven of them still alive when he'd delivered them to lawmen scattered from Wyoming Territory to Nevada, Southern California, then back around through Arizona and New Mexico.

Another way to say it: he'd killed sixteen men, counting the Grimes brothers, who'd brought his years of hunting wayward humans to an end.

Or so he'd thought when he joined the Bar X drive.

Since then, six weeks and four days gone, he'd taken part in killing more men than he had gunned down altogether in the previous five years. That said, Art couldn't claim the simpler life of punching cows had worked out very well for him so far.

Still, it had come as a relief to join up with the herd again, get back into the old routine that he'd become accustomed to since setting out from Santa Fe on the first Saturday in April. There had been a rain squall on May 9 that left the drovers soaking wet before they had a chance to don their slickers, but it hadn't been a cold rain, and there'd been no claims of illness afterward.

The week after that storm, they'd passed through territory rife with timber rattlers, losing three steers on successive days to bites around their throats and muzzles while they grazed by night—a waste of money and of meat, since Piney Rollins claimed he couldn't

serve the beef without a risk of poisoning whoever ate
it. Catlin reckoned that was false—he'd heard of people drinking rattler's venom without injury, unless they
had a cut or open sore somewhere between their lips
and stomach—but he'd kept that to himself in case
those tales were wrong.

Now that they were past the snaky district, there
had been no other predators to fret about except coyotes, who were prone to following the longhorns from
a distance, sneaking closer after dark to see if they
could spot a lame or ailing steer to savage, fleeing with
whatever morsels they could claim before the drovers
came at them with guns.

So far, the stalk had been in vain.

And rustlers?

They would be a constant threat, preying on Mr.
Mossman's mind until his cattle were secure inside
corrals at Independence, still roughly a hundred and
twenty miles away, to the northeast. That meant another ten days on the trail if no other calamities surprised them on the meantime.

Which would suit Art Catlin fine.

If he could pass the last ten days of their excursion
without drawing down on anybody else, he would be
satisfied. Hearing the boss talk to his foreman over
meals, it seemed the problems on this drive so far had
been unusual—which didn't mean that Catlin planned
to turn around and do it all again.

But if he did . . .

Well, he would have to wait and see about that, ten
days, maybe two weeks down the road.

B LISS MOSSMAN SAW his foreman drawing nearer as
he sat astride his flea-bitten gray gelding, watching
as his herd passed by. Slightly diminished since they'd

started out from Santa Fe, the stock that still survived should turn a handsome profit in Missouri.

But until they reached that terminus, he couldn't count on anything.

Wabaunsee County had been formally created back in 1859, nearly four decades after statehood was achieved, named for a chief of the Potawatomi tribe. Five years before that, while Kansans and Missourians were at each other's throats on slavery, famed abolitionist Reverend Henry Ward Beecher had endowed a local congregation of his Free Soil church, shipping rifles to the faithful in crates labeled "Beecher's Bibles," used to defend cover waystations along the Underground Railroad.

The net result, of course, had been more bloodshed, though the Show Me state had no monopoly on that during those years before the Civil War. John Brown's raiders had started out in "Bleeding Kansas," executing slave owners before they marched on Harpers Ferry in Virginia and their grim messiah finally stretched rope for "treason" against Dixie.

There was irony in that, Mossman supposed, since barely one year after Brown was hanged, South Carolina had seceded from the Union, followed in the next six months by ten more states that cast themselves as traitors to the USA. Four years of bloody conflict later, all the states were reunited, but old hatreds simmered just below the surface, and not only in the so-called Solid South.

On balance, Mossman was relieved that he had spent the war and misnamed "Reconstruction" in the West, where every individual was free to come and go, provided he or she had ample cash in hand.

Tippit was close enough to speak now without shouting as he said, "We're in the home stretch now, boss."

Mossman nodded, still watching the longhorns passing in review. "Don't want to count those chickens yet, though."

"No, sir," Tippit granted, then felt moved to follow up. "You smell more trouble coming?"

"I'm no psychic, if that's what you mean," Mossman replied.

He read a couple of the eastern papers, mostly keeping up with beef prices, but Mossman knew about the "seers" and table-tappers, also known as "mediums," who claimed they could foretell the future and commune with ghosts. Until he saw a ghost himself and couldn't blame it on mescal, Mossman dismissed all that as bunkum.

"Want to clue me in, then?" Tippit asked.

"Just life and herding steers," Mossman replied. "On any morning when the sun comes up, I look for problems down the trail."

"Makes sense, I guess," his foreman said.

"Expect the worst," said Mossman. "In my personal experience, you won't often be wrong, but when you're disappointed, take it as a nice surprise."

"One way to look at it," Sterling granted.

"The only one I've found so far that doesn't let me down," Mossman replied.

"No towns so far, at least."

"They come and go," the boss reminded him.

At the last census, three years earlier, Wabaunsee County claimed some thirty-three hundred inhabitants, most of them clumped around the county seat at Alma. Smaller settlements sprang up and died away from year to year, at wide spots in the road like Newbury and Volland. When their people packed it in, the tiny towns soon blew away as if they'd been a mere mirage.

And maybe it was just as well.

The fewer people he encountered on a drive, the easier things seemed to go.

* * *

J ED FINDLAY DIDN'T know Bliss Mossman or his foreman, much less any of the Bar X drovers. If they'd
passed him on a city street, he guessed that few would
notice him. None would perceive him as a threat.

He had that kind of face, not hideous or handsome,
nothing to get lodged in any stranger's memory. If
Findlay had been called on to describe himself, he would
have said that he was average: five eight in cowboy boots,
a trifle on the slender side, with mousy-colored hair
under his flat-brimmed hat. His clothing was trail-worn
and verging on threadbare. Even his horse was average, a dun with no distinctive markings anywhere, no
brand to signal where he had acquired it, or from whom.

A stranger's interest in Findlay wouldn't perk except where weapons were concerned. He wore twin
Colt Single Action Army revolvers—the "Peacemaker,"
Colt's newest six-gun—and the rifle in his saddle boot
was another newcomer on the market, Winchester's
Model 1873, chambered for the same .44-40 Winchester
rounds as his sidearms. In a boot sheath, on his right-
hand side, Jed also packed an Arkansas toothpick, its
double-edged blade fourteen inches long.

The hardware marked Jared as a killer to discerning eyes, and the observer would have been correct in
thinking so.

Findlay wasn't the sort to keep a score, much less to
notch his guns, but if required to guess—say, on a bet—
he would have estimated twenty-five to thirty-odd. He
wasn't known for it, like others he could name, except
in certain circles where such skill was valued and re-
warded properly.

Like now.

This month, Jed Findlay was a scout of sorts. His job
was to patrol Wabaunsee and adjoining Morris County,

to the southwest, watching out for travelers worth stopping and relieving of their goods, whether the loot was
livestock, cash, or personal belongings that could easily
be sold—or "fenced," as top professionals preferred—
for legal tender on illegal spoils.

Jed sometimes scouted westbound travelers along
the Cimarron, but never recommended raiding wagon
trains, with their inherent risk of trigger-happy yokels
on the move and large numbers of witnesses who'd have
to be eliminated in the process. Cattle drives were better, all depending on how many drovers were involved,
along with stagecoaches that might be bearing mail or
a Wells Fargo strongbox carrying a treasure trove of
bank deposits.

R AILROADS WERE OUTSIDE Jed's line. He left them
to wild-eyed former Confederates like the James-
Younger gang, still fighting a war that they'd lost
years ago.

Today, Jed was covering cattle drive, using a telescope to track its progress overland. He didn't recognize the outfit's brand, nor did that matter to him.
Findlay had his orders—to observe, assess, and then
report—providing only certain basic information to
the men who paid his salary.

He counted sixteen riders, each packing at least one
firearm, plus two men—make that a man and boy—
aboard the chuck wagon. There might well be more guns
in among the pots and pans, tin plates and bedrolls,
dried goods, and smoked meats the wagon hauled, its
stores diminishing each day it traveled farther from
wherever home might be.

Again, Findlay had no idea and didn't give a damn.

Counting the stock was trickier, the way those longhorns jostled one another without doing any damage, stretching from southwest to northeast nearly as far as he could see. Jed knew he couldn't calculate their numbers with any precision, but an estimate would satisfy his bosses.

Say two thousand, give or take a few. Figure most of them would be two or three years old, bringing four or five dollars per hundredweight in Independence. Round it off somewhere between $150,000 to $190,000 on the hoof, while beef in stores back east would sell between ten cents and thirty cents per pound, depending on the cut.

But none of that meant much to Findlay or his paymasters. The men he worked for didn't deal in fencing stolen cattle as they might have done with jewels, for instance, if a stash of them had ever come to hand. No, they preferred to ransom stolen livestock for a fraction of its going rate, without incurring any costs for care, feeding, or transportation to the nearest slaughterhouse.

A wise trail boss, confronted with the loss of half a herd or more, would pay the ransom in lieu of going home with light pockets that wouldn't get him through next winter to another spring. And Jed's fee was static, 5 percent of what his bosses made from any scheme he organized—in this case, possibly as much as fifteen hundred bucks.

And if he had to get his hands dirty while earning that much, well, Findlay was used to it.

For now, he'd seen enough. Later, he'd make another run to reconnoiter their nighttime security, and that would tell him all he had to know about their strengths and weaknesses.

From there on in, the men who'd hired him would be carrying the weight themselves.

* * *

SUPPER WAS PORK and beans with rice, to make a change from the potatoes they were used to eating cubed and fried. Art Catlin found the food a bit monotonous, but tasty overall, and filling, which would get him through his night watch once he'd washed it down with strong black coffee.

Sitting next to him, Julius Pryor had been picking at his food, clearly preoccupied with something far behind them now. Catlin had seen some gunfight virgins in his time—had once been one of them himself, if he could dredge up dusty memories—and now he recognized the signs.

Four weeks and change had passed since they rode out of Devil's Crossing, but Catlin still recognized the signs.

"You know there's no point feeling guilty, right?" he said.

Pryor looked over at him, not quite startled. Said, "I don't know what you mean."

"The Comancheros we put down," Art said. "We both know what they'd done, and you can guess about what all the hurt they caused before the Bjorlins came along. Nobody's missing them we shot—or, if they are, it's no one I'm inclined to give a damn about."

Pryor nodded without conviction, answered back, "I know all that. But I keep seeing 'em, you know?"

"That's not uncommon, on your first time out," Catlin replied.

"Don't tell me it gets easier, okay? Fact is, I don't think I could stand it getting any easier."

"Just means you're human," Art said. "Chances are, you could live out your life and never have to make that call again in thirty, forty years."

"But you have, right?" Julius seemed to have forgotten that he had a plate of food in front of him, his eyes locked onto Catlin's now. "How do you deal with it?"

Art made believe that he was delving for deep thoughts, then said, "It really *does* get easier—for some, at least. I couldn't tell you how the Comancheros make their peace with killing. Maybe there was something left out of the mix when they were growing up. But if you're in a fight for something that resembles justice, it's no different than soldiers in a war."

"Except we choose the war," said Pryor, in a hopeless tone of voice.

Art took a long shot. Asked, "Are you a praying man?"

"Not much. My folks took me to church on Sunday as a kid, o' course, but I grew out of it."

"Same here," said Catlin. "When I started hunting fugitives—not saying you should try that, mind you—I decided that the people I was after made their choices as they went along. They robbed, raped, killed, whatever, and it suited them. They didn't let it get under their skins or keep them up at night, except to celebrate their latest crime, so why should I be agonizing over it on their behalf?"

"Like mad dogs, I suppose," Julius said.

"I'd say they're worse. A dog with rabies is infected from outside. It can't control what happens next, no more than fire can stop itself from burning things. But people make a choice—to drink or gamble, rob or kill, whatever. No one else has forced it on 'em, and they all know where the road ends—prison or a graveyard—when they take that first small step."

"I guess that's right."

Art frowned. Told Julius, "I won't pretend that I can tell you how to feel, what you should think, much less how to shake loose of dreams. I *will* say that for most

of us, time helps. Not saying that the memories will
ever go away, unless you lose your mind, but they do
fade and lose most of their sting."

"I hope so," Pryor said. He didn't sound convinced.

"You're on first watch tonight?" Art asked.

"I am."

"Same here. You feel like talking any more, just flag
me down. Or you can tell the steers," Art said, half-
joking. "One thing that I'll say for cattle; they're good
listeners."

"And so are you. Appreciated it, Art."

Pryor was rising when Catlin reached out and caught
him by the sleeve.

"You plan on eating that?"

J ULIUS PRYOR WASN'T lying when he'd told Catlin that
  talking to him helped a bit.

It simply hadn't helped *enough*, and now he was
convinced that nothing would.

At least, not while he kept on riding for the Bar X,
seeing the same faces morning, noon, and night, imagining what they were thinking of him when his back
was turned.

There goes a killer. Stay the hell out of his way.

Of course, nobody said that to his face, and other
drovers would deny the thought had even crossed their
minds. But still . . .

Before he'd signed on for the drive, Pryor had never
shot a man and had no reason to believe he ever would.
His last fight had been sometime in the fifth or sixth
grade, and he'd lost that one when Tommy Guthrie
gave him a fat lip.

Then came the renegade Apaches, and Julius hadn't
begged off when he was selected for the group pursuing them. He'd shot one of the raiders he was certain

of, but that felt *different* somehow, the dead man being both a rustler and a "redskin," as his father always called the native tribes, suggesting they were somehow less than human.

Even so, Julius had suffered through some uneasiness that time, but thought the killing was behind him, something filed away like old tax records or forgotten correspondence with a distant relative, fading away with time.

But no.

The Comancheros changed all that.

First, Pryor was a witness to the carnage they had wreaked upon a helpless family of immigrants, then he was tasked once more to run the killers down and punish them. Could he have passed that duty off to someone else, without wearing a coward's brand of shame to show for it?

Doubtful. At least, Julius hadn't dared to take that chance.

Now, more than two weeks later, and he couldn't close his eyes at night without imagining grim scenes inside the Red Dog. Red with blood, that was—not only from the guilty Comancheros but from the saloon's proprietor, its barkeep, and two of its working girls. Call it a massacre, and no mistake—a massacre that never would have happened if four drovers with no stake in what had happened to the Swedes had simply kept on driving longhorns to the auction house in Independence.

If they'd only let it go.

And how would Julius have felt in that case? How would he have lived with doing nothing after all?

Too many goddamned questions.

Pryor only knew he couldn't stand it any longer and remaining with the drive—surrounded by his fellow killers—was a surefire way to make things worse. He had to get away, was taking off tonight, in fact.

He'd planned ahead, leaving his bedroll by the campfire with a terse note tucked inside it. When he disappeared while riding herd tonight, someone would check sooner or later and report his parting comments to the rest. They would revile him, naturally, as a coward and a quitter. There would be no payout for the weeks he'd worked since riding out from Santa Fe in April. That was understood and Julius wouldn't complain.

Where would he go from there?

He didn't have a clue, and for the first time since the shooting stopped at Devil's Crossing, that felt good.

J ED FINDLAY MOVED in closer to the herd once night had fallen, taking full advantage of a dim third-quarter moon with scudding clouds.

He'd counted three drovers on watch for the first shift and charted their lazy circuits around the long-horns, talking softly to the grazing, dozing steers. Monotony like that dulled human senses, even during wartime at a post that witnessed little action. Men let down their guard and made mistakes.

Which made them vulnerable to surprise attacks.

The men his bosses sent to raid the herd, based on Findlay's reconnaissance, had all committed murders in their time, but killing cowboys would not be their goal this time. Sure, they would fire if fired upon, but their intent would be to get the longhorns running, headed for a destination that their owner hadn't planned, and pen them up securely there until a ransom was negotiated and procured.

How much?

The rub was striking at the herd before it got to Independence and was sold. Trail bosses carried cash to help out with emergencies, but nothing like the sum Findlay's employers would be hoping for.

And that was where the law came into play.

Findlay's employers had a justice of the peace and an attorney on their payroll, contracts more or less complete, with only certain numbers, dates, and signatures to be applied and notarized. When that was done, the trail boss—call him Mr. X—would be obliged on paper to remit a predetermined sum for services rendered, and he would be accompanied by two sworn lawmen to ensure that he paid up at point of sale.

Would Mr. X complain to anybody in Missouri?

Probably, but few would care to act in contravention of a contract certified in Kansas by lawful authorities. Whining that he had been robbed, his arm twisted around behind his back, likely would not accomplish much for Mr. X—whereas if he clammed up and kept the deal he had agreed to, he'd go home with money in his pocket.

Less than he'd expected, granted, but money, nonetheless.

And gold beat hot lead any day.

Jed was watching when one of the drovers on the first watch started riding off into the night, not rushing, but not looking back to see if anyone had seen him, either.

And he had to ask himself, *Now, what the hell is this about?*

A RT CATLIN RAISED a hand as Danny Underwood approached, preparing to relieve him for the second shift. Job Hooper had already met Bryce Zimmerman and sent him back to camp. Now only Nehemiah Wolford still remained, trotting his grulla mare over to ask Catlin, "Where's Julius got off to?"

Catlin swiveled in his saddle, scanned the herd, but couldn't catch a glimpse of Pryor anywhere. "Damned if I know," he said. "You want me to, I'll help you look around for him."

"Already looked," Wolford replied. "No sign of 'im."

"Did you try calling him?" Art asked.

"Loud as I could without spooking the herd."

"Okay. I'll pass the word to Tippit."

"Fair enough," said Wolford, and moved on.

Most of the drovers not on watch were tucked up in their bedrolls by that time, dawn coming early on the trail, but Catlin found the Bar X foreman sipping coffee with their boss. Approaching them on foot, Art tried to keep his voice low-key, saying, "Sorry to interrupt, but we might have a problem on our hands."

"Such as?" Bliss Mossman asked.

"Julius Pryor, boss. His shift relief can't find him anywhere."

Both men were frowning at him now. "Say that again," Tippit instructed.

"Seems like he's just gone," Art said.

"'Just gone,'" Mossman echoed his words. "What does that even mean?"

Catlin restrained himself from shrugging. "Beats me, boss. Wolford's been looking for him but he's not around."

"You were on watch with him and Zimmerman," said Tippit.

"Yes, sir. Zimmerman came in on time, but Pryor . . . well . . ."

Both men were on their feet now, their coffee dregs dumped on the ground. Mossman called out across the campfire, "Bryce? Bryce Zimmerman! We need you over here, pronto!"

"Right with you, boss," the answer came.

The third drover on watch appeared but had no more to add as to Pryor's whereabouts. He couldn't say exactly when he'd last seen Julius, but guessed it was a half hour or more before he was relieved.

"Thought nothing of it, boss," Zimmerman said. "I thought he might have answered nature's call, you know?"

Catlin spoke up, suggesting, "If he left his bedroll, maybe someone ought to take a look at it."

That set a couple of the other hands to muttering, but Mr. Mossman hushed them. "That's the best idea I've heard so far," he said. "Beats standing here and jawboning, at least."

Five minutes later, Tippit had the missing man's blanket unrolled surrounded by a growing crowd of nervous-looking hands. The first thing anybody noticed was a sheet of paper, folded over into quarters. Mossman picked it up, scanned it, then read the note aloud.

"'Sorry to everyone for leaving in the lurk'—he must mean 'lurch'—'but I can't take it anymore. Don't mean to leave you short but I'm just in the way, no good to anybody. Sorry.' And he's signed it with initials."

Focusing on Catlin, Tippit said, "I recollect you eating supper with him, Art. Did he say anything that helps explain this?"

"Told me that the shooting back at Devil's Crossing had been preying on his mind. Made out like it was interfering with his sleep, and from the little that he ate, it seemed like he was off his feed."

"Enough to harm himself?" Mossman inquired.

Catlin could only shrug. "He didn't mention anything like that, or else I would've told you straightaway, boss. Asked me how he was supposed to live with killing men. I told him getting over it takes time."

"Well, shit." Mossman balled up the note and let it drop into the campfire, curling into ash a moment later.

"Now we're two men down since leaving Santa Fe, with better than a week to go before we cross into Missouri. Anybody else feel like they can't go on, or does a contract still mean something to the rest of you?"

The others mostly shook their heads, a few responding verbally, "No, sir."

Shaking his head, Mossman told, them, "All right. The schedule for tonight's watch stands. We'll change it up tomorrow. Thank Julius, if you ever see 'im, for the extra work you'll have to shoulder now."

CHAPTER THIRTEEN

Tuesday, May 27

Longwood, Kansas

I T'S CLEAR WE have our work cut out for us." Cyrus Harding, the elected mayor of Longwood in Wabaunsee County, eyed the other four men seated in his smallish office as he spoke. "But if we pull it off, we'll be set for the winter, anyway, and might have cash enough to relocate before we start over."

Harding was a portly fellow who believed in living well and sometimes took advantage of his size to literally throw his weight around. The others, occupying chairs set up around his desk, included Justice of the Peace Odell Butler; Bert Whitesell, the town's marshal; the Honorable Tilman Crull, attorney; and their scout, Jed Findlay.

In Crull's case, "Honorable" was a title that accom-

panied his law degree by custom rather than a testi-
mony to his character.

In fact, the game they played was Crull's idea, facilitated and refined by Harding, Butler, Whitesell, and
the other residents of Longwood—one hundred and
four at last count—who had signed off on the scheme
once promised their small slices of the pie.

"We owe another vote of thanks to Jed, here,"
Harding pressed on, "for scouting our next target. Jed,
as you-all know, is our front-line soldier, and his compensation, as per usual, will be commensurate."

Unless, thought Harding, *we can come up with a
way to cut him out and split his share among ourselves.*

Gunmen and scouts were plentiful in Kansas, welcomed to the Union on the eve of Civil War, after
seven grim years of bloodshed between Free Soilers
and advocates of slavery. Some twenty thousand Kansas men wore blue during the war, against one thousand who had signed up with Confederate units, and
loyal Kansas units lost more men per thousand under
arms than any other state, in combat and from virulent
disease.

For many who'd survived, there was no coming
home per se, no turning back the calendar to placid
times of yesteryear. For many veterans—and even
those who had not served—life was revealed as fragile,
fleeting, and a time for doing anything a man might
please.

Whatever he could get away with in the end.

Odell Butler cleared his throat, then said, "We all
appreciate the hard work Jed's done so far, of course.
I might point out, however, that he counted eighteen
men with guns minding the herd."

"I'd call it seventeen, Your Honor. One is just a kid
who helps around the chuck wagon."

"Perhaps a marksman in his own right," Butler answered him, "but for the sake of argument, let's call it *seven*teen. Considering the population of Longwood—"

"We still have them outnumbered six to one," said Marshal Whitesell, butting in. "I have to say I like those odds."

"And then subtract the number of our womenfolk and children, if you please," Butler replied, a tinge of color rising in his flaccid jowls.

"Still makes it four to one," Whitesell replied.

"We're getting off the point here," Harding said, trying to bring them back on track. "Our plan is not to fight the drovers and annihilate them, but to carry out negotiations satisfying to both sides."

"Imagining that they'll be 'satisfied' to ransom their own cattle," Butler said.

Butler was frowning at the jurist now. "What's on your mind, Odell?" he asked. "Unless it was a dream I had, you were in favor of the plan on Tuesday week. What's giving you these second thoughts?"

"Our other . . . operations, shall we say . . . were on a more reserved and modest scale. At most, we dealt with half a dozen individuals, or with some company back east that could absorb the loss."

It was the lawyer's turn, Crull leaning in toward Butler as he said, "You've already signed off on this, Your Honor"—maybe stressing that for irony—"and if you pull out now, there could be . . . repercussions."

Glowering, their justice of the peace replied, "I don't take kindly to your threats, Tilman."

"What threats, Odell? If you've been stricken with a bout of conscience, maybe you should think about refunding all the cash you've pocketed on other deals before today."

"Now listen here!" the judge began to bluster.

"No," Mayor Harding intervened. "We've said and heard enough. The plan's in operation and we'll see it through. If anybody wants to cut loose afterward, they're free to go their own way—with the understanding that their lips stay sealed for good."

Three pairs of eyes bored into Butler, Jed Findlay staying out of it, until the judge nodded and softly said, "All right. We go ahead."

LOSING JULIUS PRYOR had played havoc with the night watch, shaving down the number of free evenings that any given drover could expect. Beyond that, though, Art Catlin didn't find the workload that much heavier than when they'd had one extra hand to help.

He still wondered about where Julius had gone, of course, hoping the guilt he carried had not broken him. When Catlin had been six or seven years of age, one of his schoolmates' fathers had committed suicide, sticking a shotgun's muzzle underneath his chin to blow away his money troubles. From later talk Catlin had overheard, that buckshot blast had wrecked a bedroom ceiling but did nothing to relieve the dead man's widow or their children from the debts that burdened them. They'd disappeared from town without a word to anyone after their house and other property were repossessed by an unsympathetic bank.

It was six days now since Pryor had pulled his disappearing act, and Catlin had begun to phase him out of short-term memory. Why cling to mental images of someone he would likely never see again—or, if he did, would have no clue on how to deal with?

Catlin had never made friends easily, and once out on his own had seen no pressing need to try. When he'd begun collecting bounties, mention of the way he made his living was enough to put most people off, besides a few who pestered him with morbid questions till Art put them in their place. Since riding out of

Santa Fe, he had been cordial with the other Bar X drovers, but he couldn't see them being lifelong pals who stayed in touch no matter how their paths diverged. He felt no need for that and reckoned that the others shared his view.

Granted, that attitude might need adjustment if he hung around the Bar X once the drive was over, but he wouldn't have to ponder that decision till they got the herd to Independence and were paid off for their labors on the trail. Another week at least, and likely more, before he had to face that choice.

Until then, he would take it one day at a time and wait to see what happened next.

B LISS MOSSMAN DIDN'T like to think he was a superstitious man. He'd never seen a ghost or feared a black cat passing by, had walked beneath some ladders on occasion, didn't put off doing anything on Friday the thirteenth, and never suffered bad luck—much less seven years of it—after he'd dropped a mirror.

Even so, he had begun to wonder if this cattle drive was somehow cursed.

A dozen times, he'd driven herds to market and had always suffered some mishaps along the way. Steers came up lame or died along the way from sundry causes, and he took the loss in stride. Julius Pryor wasn't the first drover who'd deserted Mossman, though he'd vanished with less warning than the others—mostly drunks, plus one sneak thief who might have caught a beating from the other cowboy's if he'd stuck around.

And yes, he'd seen employees killed before, not only on trail drives, but at the Bar X spread itself. Things happened sometimes when you worked around large animals, men packing guns, working with cutting tools and branding irons. Mortality was part of life. Each

birth carried a death sentence along with it before the
newborn even had a chance to sin.

But this time out, between the sandstorm, the
Apaches, and the Comancheros, Mossman almost had
to wonder if he'd crossed some *bruja* that he didn't
even know about. The present drive to Independence
had already seen more dangers than the last three seasons he could think of put together.

Mossman would be glad to see the end of it, and no
mistake.

And yet, watching his drovers go about their jobs
this morning, Mossman never would have guessed that
they had been through hell and back again.

Well, most of them.

Roughly one hundred miles to go, and if they met
no further obstacles before the time came for crossing
the Missouri River—

"Damn it!" Mossman muttered to himself.

He'd likely jinxed it now by picturing their final ten
days or so being trouble-free.

And there it was again, the silly superstition that
made some folks who'd spilled salt at supper toss a few
grains over their left shoulders, hang a horseshoe over
their front doors, or drop a penny in a wishing well to
grant their hearts' desires.

Ridiculous.

No one who Mossman knew was out to get him, and
the ones who'd tried before were mostly underground.
As far as risks from nature went, no one could claim
immunity from rain, wind, lightning, or the rest of it.

A man did what he had to do and soldiered through
it—until one day he did not.

The good news on that score was this: when Mossman's time ran out at last, he had a sneaking hunch he
wouldn't know the difference.

* * *

BACK ON THE road again, and Jed Findlay reckoned it was just as well. Most times, he'd rather be out in the open air than cooped up in stuffy room with men who paid his salary while looking down their noses at him.

Jed wasn't happy with the way Odell Butler had tried to weasel out of their agreement when he started having second thoughts. It wasn't like the others counted on their justice of the peace to wield a gun if anything went wrong. He only had to witness, sign, and notarize a simple contract binding under Kansas law, as long as no one raised the sticky question of coercion later on.

What was the worst thing that could happen? Findlay frowned, thinking of two in turn.

If the trail boss and his drovers made their minds up to play rough, reject the bargain offered to them, and decide to shoot it out. In that case, Findlay didn't know who would come out on top or even manage to survive the clash.

The second possibility involved Judge Butler backing out again, once livestock from the herd had been sequestered prior to ransoming. In that event, Findlay supposed it might be necessary to remove Butler and have somebody else replace him, sworn in by the mayor as Longwood's new, more amiable justice of the peace.

If that occurred, would Bert Whitesell get rid of Butler on his own, or pass the grunt work to his deputy, Alonzo Markland? Might the two of them together even try to foist the job off onto Jed, knowing that he didn't mind pulling a trigger now and then?

Findlay decided not to think about that now. Butler

controlled his own fate, and Jed had other, more impor-
tant work to do. Tracking the herd for starters, making
sure it stayed on course for Longwood's designated team
to intercept.

And his toughest job was a last-minute thing, requiring him to infiltrate the trail drive's camp, present himself as just another drifter—maybe even one in search of
work—and be on hand to help out when the raid went
down.

The more he studied on it, the more Jed thought asking for work might be the way to go. He knew such things
occurred from time to time—he'd cadged a three-week
job that way himself, some four years back—and Findlay reckoned he could sell his story easily enough.

But if the drive had ample hands already, and the
trail boss wasn't feeling charitable . . . well, Findlay
knew he could come up with something else. Even a
supper with the crew could be enough to let him get a
sense of them and carry word back to his bosses as to
what they might be facing in a showdown.

In which case, he would have to reconsider standing
in the line of fire.

B ERT WHITESELL LIT a thin, gnarly cheroot and drew
its bitter smoke into his lungs. If asked, he could
not have explained why he still smoked the rancid
things, but since no one appeared to care—or else kept
their objections under wraps—no excuse for his bad
habit was required.

Seated across from Whitesell, studying the marshal's boot soles where Whitesell had propped them on
the corner of his desk, Chief Deputy Alonzo Markland chewed a toothpick, frowning as he tried to frame
some comment that he seemed to think his boss might
not appreciate.

"Chief deputy" was overstating Markland's rank—he was the Longwood marshal's *only* deputy, in fact—but it was stamped onto the tin star that was Whitesell's only other badge, which narrowed down their options. On occasion, Whitesell swore in other part-time backup as required, and he was running through a mental list of names while waiting for Alonzo to make up his mind and speak.

The best part of a minute later, Markland asked, "You think we might be going overboard this time, Bert?"

If they hadn't been alone, Whitesell would have reminded his subordinate to call him "Marshal," but it hardly mattered with nobody else around.

"It stands to be a big payday," Whitesell reminded Markland.

"If we live to spend it," said his second-in-command.

"You got cold feet, Alonzo?"

"Not this child," Markland replied, making a face to sell his point. "But on the other hand . . ."

"Just spit it out."

"I'd rather not get kilt unless there's no avoiding it."

The marshal took another drag on his cheroot and fouled the office air.

"I got no reason to believe the plan won't go the way Mayor Harding and them others got it all laid out," Whitesell replied.

"You call that tub o' guts the mayor, even when he ain't around?"

"I make a habit of it," Whitesell granted. "Helps me not to make any mistakes."

"We both know he only got elected 'cause he gave out shots o' whiskey at the polls. Same thing with Butler."

"And same thing for me," the marshal said, "in case it slipped your mind. You, on the other hand, just owe your job to me alone."

"I ain't forgetting that," Markland assured him. "I don't wanna see you getting ventilated, neither."

"That's mighty white o' you, Alonzo."

"I'm just saying—"

"I know what you're saying, and you'd best not let them others hear you."

"Yeah, all right."

"And don't go getting snippy with me, neither. You want someone else to wear that badge, just leave it when you head off to the livery."

"Okay! I hear you, boss." Laying it on a tad too thick.

"Before you break out in a sweat," Whitesell went on, "I've got some other boys lined up to help us if the drovers want to play it tough."

"What are they gonna use for badges?" asked Alonzo.

"I was thinking armbands, like that other time with the sheepherders."

Markland had to grin at that. "I reckon that could do it," he conceded.

"So, I've put your mind at ease?"

"At least until the lead starts flying."

"Shouldn't come to that, supposing that the trail boss is a reasonable man. But if it *does*, I'd best not catch you trying to run out on me, Alonzo."

"Hell, you know me, Bert!"

"That's why I mentioned it. You show up for the party, I'll expect you to be dancing like the rest of us."

"You know I will."

"I know you'd *better*." Whitesell drove it home. "Or else, you just might have a nasty accident."

ART CATLIN FINISHED mopping up the last dregs of his sausage gravy with a biscuit, stuffed that in his mouth, and chewed it slowly while he watched steam rising from his coffee cup.

"Breakfast for supper," Piney Rollins called it, and it hadn't been half-bad. Fried eggs, with gravy on potatoes—also fried, of course—and Catlin wondered if tomorrow morning Piney wouldn't stand the whole thing on its head, serving them supper to begin their day.

At least, he thought, it was a change of pace.

The past couple of days, he'd half expected that Julius Pryor might return to join them, but by now Catlin guessed that ship had well and truly sailed. He didn't miss Julius in the way he might have felt a true friend's passing, but of late Art found himself watching the other cowboys, checking them for subtle signs of getting weary, standing on the verge of giving up.

Maybe that happened all the time on cattle drives. Art couldn't say, this trip being his first, but he could see how certain men might tire of the routine and call it quits instead of playing out the string.

He rose from where he'd been sitting with Linton McCormick and Job Hooper, saying, "See you out there in a little bit."

The others, on first watch with Catlin, nodded without speaking, both men concentrating on the task of finishing their meals. The best thing about drawing first shift—and the only good thing Art could think of—was getting that extra work out of the way and sleeping through the night uninterrupted until dawn broke in the east.

Catlin had no reason to think that either of his fellow watchmen would desert their posts during the night, but he would doubtless still be watching them as time allowed, alert to any deviation from the circuits they'd be following around the herd. And why not? With the longhorns resting peacefully, no sign of troublesome coyotes in a week or more, how else was he supposed to pass the time?

And if one of them *did* try sneaking off into the

night, what should he do about it? Fire a warning shot and rouse the camp to hot pursuit of the defector? Was it his role to control the other Bar X hands, rather than riding herd on livestock?

No.

But if another drover disappeared on Catlin's watch, he knew it would reflect on him as well, whether that blame was justified or not.

So, he would keep his eyes open, remain alert, and determine his response when something happened, *if* it happened.

And in that event, he'd let the chips fall where they might.

STERLING TIPPIT TRIED to duck the restless feeling that had troubled him since sundown, but he couldn't seem to shake it. There was nothing he could put a finger on, as far as what was making him uneasy, but it seemed to go beyond the extra weight of caution that he felt near the conclusion of a drive.

They were so close to Independence, relatively speaking, but he knew that anything might still go wrong and cost the Bar X everything.

As midnight neared, the foreman knew he had to get some sleep and leave the outfit's posted guards to do their job without him hovering around them like a mother hen. His watchful presence, riding herd on them, was likely to distract them from their tasks at hand and prod them toward careless mistakes.

At least Tippit had satisfied himself, to the extent that it was possible, that no human intruders had the herd under surveillance, waiting for a chance to strike and make off with whatever they could steal. Granted, he had no ironclad guarantee that someone wasn't watching from a distance, laying plans, but he could only do so much staying awake all night, running his blood bay to a frazzle so that it was worn-out come the dawn and their departure from the campsite.

Turning in was one thing, though, while drifting off to sleep was something else entirely.

As he lay down on one blanket, with another on top, Sterling was fully dressed except for boots, prepared within his limits for whatever rude surprise might interrupt his night. His Sharps carbine rested at his left-hand side; his Colt Dragoon—still holstered, with its hammer thong unfastened—covered by his right hand as he tried to make himself relax.

The sound of someone walking by alerted Tippit, made him crack an eyelid, recognizing Bliss Mossman by firelight. He supposed the boss felt even more vague worries weighing on his mind and hoped they both could manage a few hours' rest before another long day overtook them.

Waiting for unconsciousness to find him in the darkness, Tippit listened to familiar sounds that he was long accustomed to: the longhorns dozing, softly snoring, while a few of them still grazed; one of the first shift's watchmen speaking softly to the steers, as if to reassure them that their long trek led to peaceful pastures rather than a slaughterhouse; spare mounts in the remuda snorting now and then, responding to some new scent on the breeze.

All calm and quiet as it should be—for the moment, anyway.

Tippit had no reason to brood on trouble waiting in the wings, but there it was, as in years past. He started worrying as soon as the Bar X was out of sight, and never really stopped until the steers were crammed into their pens, awaiting transformation into steaks, roasts, brisket, ribs, and all the rest of it.

Tippit's whole life was based on death, but that was

true of everything in nature, from the wild's great predators to scuttling insects. Nothing changed as populations shifted from the countryside to cities, faced with crime across the board, many living in poverty, pursuing thankless jobs that wore them down in factories and offices.

No one cashed out of life alive, but with a bit of luck and perseverance, they could still enjoy some bits and pieces of the game.

And wake at dawn to start it all over again.

CHAPTER FOURTEEN

Monday, June 2

PINEY ROLLINS HAD pork chops and beans on the fire for supper, the mixture of aromas stirring appetites in camp. Art Catlin needed no reminder of his growling appetite, but lined up with the rest, tin plate in hand, to claim his share.

It takes a serious distraction to divert cowhands from sizzling meat, and that was what confronted Catlin now, ears perking at a lookout's call of "Rider coming in!"

All eyes turned toward the stranger on his dun mount, drawing closer slowly, cautiously, backlit by sundown in the west. More than a few hands drifted into touch with holstered six-guns, measuring the distance as the man they'd never seen before approached.

The rider's left hand held his horse's reins. His right was raised to shoulder height with fingers splayed, revealing no intent to draw his holstered pistol.

Make that *two* pistols, Art realized, a matching set

of Colts, backed up by what appeared to be a Winchester secured inside a saddle boot. Nothing to make the Bar X hands draw down on him.

At least, not yet.

Bliss Mossman left his place in line to meet the rider, Sterling Tippit following a yard or so behind him, offset to his right in case the stranger tried something and they both required quick access to their sidearms. They stood waiting while the horseman reined in, leaned over his saddle horn, and introduced himself.

Art couldn't make out what was being said from twenty yards away, the back-and-forth of it, but he saw nothing to excite alarm offhand. Piney had started dishing out more food, urging the hands to move along while they were eyeballing the stranger and remarking on his unexpected visitation to the camp.

"Some drifter," Nehemiah Wolford said.

"Maybe looking for work," Bryce Zimmerman opined.

"Could use another hand," Zeb Steinmeier allowed. "Lighten the load some."

"Wouldn't hurt," Linton McCormick granted.

"Maybe not," Job Hooper said. Adding, "If we could trust him."

"People out of work all over," Danny Underwood reminded Job.

"And outlaws hunting, too," Jerome Guenther advised, putting his two cents in.

"The boss won't take him on if he has any doubts," said Mike Limbaugh, taking the plate Tim Berryman had loaded up with food, putting Art Catlin next in line for service.

Once Berryman had piled his plate, Art went to find a seat beside the campfire, still watching the stranger chat with Mossman and Tippit. By the time Catlin sat down, the rider had dismounted and was shaking hands with both men, Tippit leading him away toward the remuda with his dun trailing.

Apparently, the men in charge were satisfied with what they'd heard so far. Art didn't doubt their judgment necessarily, knowing they'd put the Bar X and its livestock first, sidestepping any risk they could identify and thus avoid, but he would wait to hear what they'd decided—if the new arrival had been cleared to spend one night in camp or was about to join the team—and then make up his own mind when he'd had a chance to meet the man.

There would be time enough to learn his habits on the trail, assuming he'd signed on.

And if he hadn't, Art supposed it wouldn't matter anyhow.

B LISS MOSSMAN'S APPETITE was gnawing at him, but he thought he'd taken time enough to give the stranger a once-over, feel him out a bit, and offer him a job for their remaining days out on the trail to Independence.

There had been no readily apparent warning signs to put him off the rider at a glance or after speaking with him long enough to glean the information that the new arrival wanted to reveal. Whatever lay behind that affable façade, Mossman supposed he would discover it in time, and he would not relax his guard entirely until they had reached trail's end.

The horseman gave his name as Jay Fielding, though Mossman had no means of proving that. In his experience, outlaws were not the only travelers who hid behind false names. Others that came to mind were men with broken marriages behind them, certain grieving widowers, and those with hungry creditors pursuing them. He didn't care so much about the stranger's

given name, as long as Fielding or whoever played it
straight at work, carried his weight, and stirred up no
dissension in the Bar X ranks.

In that case, as explained to him already, he would
have to leave the crew and forfeit any pay earned in the
meantime for his violation of the standing rules.

Fielding claimed that he hailed from Iowa, someplace called Ackley that Mossman hadn't heard of previously. He was thirty-two years old and looked it,
seeming healthy overall, and said he was experienced
with ranching, though he'd never ridden on a cattle
drive before. Beyond that, he was well armed and had
once possessed enough cash to equip himself in style.
Colt Peacemakers sold new for seventeen dollars
apiece, and his Winchester '73 would have cost him
another twenty.

Whether he was any good with them or simply packed
the guns for show would only be revealed if trouble
overtook them on the trail.

Beyond that, Fielding vowed he wasn't wanted by
the law, and Mossman could not contradict him in the
absence of a valid "Wanted" flyer. At a glance, he didn't
have the jailhouse pallor many ex-convicts displayed,
nor did a first impression of him mark Fielding as someone who'd spent any length of time locked down or
digging ditches with a road gang's shackles on.

After assessing him, getting a nod from Sterling
Tippit on the side, Mossman had offered Fielding fifteen bucks and found to work their last few days on the
approach to Independence. Fielding had agreed to sign
a standard Bar X contract after supper and to take a
turn at riding herd over the stock that very night.

So far, so good. And if it Mossman's first impression
of the man was faulty, it would be no problem firing him.

Even with three guns, what could one man do against
sixteen?

Not much.

That was another benefit of being boss. Bliss Mossman trusted his ability at judging other men, but if he got it wrong from time to time, as any mortal might, employees were disposable. Fielding could hit the lonely road again and see what lay in store for him tomorrow or the next day, with no harm done to the Bart X herd.

SELLING HIMSELF TO Bliss Mossman, the trail boss, had been easier than Jed Findlay was expecting. He'd made up the "Fielding" alias, using his own initials as a hedge against forgetfulness, and told the truth on other points—his birth in Iowa (shaving a year off of his age), and his experience with ranching, although that had ended when he left home at sixteen. He'd left out sundry brushes with the law across four states, knowing that Mossman couldn't check his record for arrests or jailbreaks, and would hardly come across one of his Indiana "Wanted" posters while the herd was traveling.

Granted, he might catch wind of something if he started asking questions in Missouri, but by that time, it would be too late.

The Bar X foreman, Sterling Tippit, led Findlay to the remuda, where his dun had food and water, leaving Jed to go off and find his own supper before they met again for night watch duty. That was fine with Findlay, giving him a better close-up look at the security precautions Mossman had in place to fend off raiders after dark.

Not that a plan would do him any good.

Findlay's design, now that he'd managed to insert himself among the trail drive's other hands, was to remain in place until they'd closed the gap to Longwood, whereupon he'd signal watchers waiting for the herd's approach and set their end game into play.

The signal that he had in mind, facilitated by his presence in the bosom of the camp, would also pay a dividend in chaos that would hamper Mossman's plan for self-defense. With eight or ten good gunmen riding for the town, Jed believed that victory should be within their grasp.

And win or lose, once that played out, he would be moving on.

The lords of Longwood were becoming more ambitious than was good for them. Success encouraged arrogance, and arrogance, more times than not, resulted in a sudden fall from grace. Before their house of cards came crashing down on Harding, Butler, and the rest, Jed planned to collect his pay and put long miles between himself and whatever came next.

The key to gambling successfully, regardless of the stakes involved, was knowing when to quit. Failure to heed that golden rule could land him in a prison cell or even take him to the gallows.

But if that happened, he damned sure wasn't going down alone.

Findlay knew who'd given orders for the banditry that kept Longwood afloat, and who had carried out those criminal instructions. He could dictate chapter and verse as to guilt, and in several cases, he literally knew where the bodies were buried.

To ensure his silence, Harding and the rest could either pay him off or try to kill him. If they went in that direction, Findlay would make sure that they regretted it—that is, the ones who managed to survive.

Fighting a whole town that existed solely for corruption would not be an easy task, but neither did he view it as impossible. Alone, he'd put more men to sleep than any other two or three hired guns on Longwood's payroll, and he'd made no secret of that fact.

Whoever tried to take him out should come prepared for the fight of his life, prepared to go all in and trust his future to a turn of the last card.

Sterling Tippit wasn't absolutely sold on their new hired hand, but he'd seen nothing to contradict his boss's first impression of Jay Fielding. In the circumstances, it was better not to make a fuss and start off on the wrong foot with a man who might be with them all the way to Independence.

And if not, should Fielding do something that got him fired by Mr. Mossman, then the problem solved itself.

Assuming there was any problem to be solved.

A week, maybe ten days if all went well, and Fielding either would have proved his worth or washed out with his walking papers. If he made the cut, then Mr. Mossman might decide to offer him a permanent position at the Bar X, which Fielding could accept or tell the boss, "No, thanks."

By that time, Tippit would have better cause for judging him than just a vague feeling something, somehow, wasn't ringing true.

And how could he prove that until the guy fell short somehow or proved he wasn't to be trusted.

Minor pilferage was rare on cattle drives, the pool of suspects limited to start with, no man ever truly on his own unless he had to answer one of nature's calls— and even then, with no females around, there was a minimum of privacy.

In all his time with the Bar X—and at the Slim Chance spread before that, outside Tucson in the Arizona Territory—he had only seen two thieves at work. One had been caught rifling another cowboy's saddle-bags and caught a beating for his trouble, prior to being fired. The other, four years back, had robbed some of his coworkers and slipped away by night, fleeing to God knew where. By now, Tippit supposed he might have gone straight—or, more likely, been picked off by someone who had caught him in the act.

Good riddance, either way.

Tippit got back to the chuck wagon for his supper and found Fielding waiting in the lineup, jabbering in Spanish with Luis Chávez and Jaime Reyes. They seemed to be getting on all right, and Sterling put his niggling doubts aside for now.

Fielding's arrival would permit adjustment of the night watch schedule, more or less restoring the time off from losing sleep each hand enjoyed. It still wasn't precisely as they'd started out from Santa Fe, since Merritt Dietz was killed, but Fielding could take up the slack for Julius Pryor's taking off without a by-your-leave. More to the point, he seemed happy to help—or did a decent imitation of it, anyway.

And Tippit didn't care if he was really overjoyed to pull the extra duty, or if that was just an act, playing obsequious to land a job, so long as he fulfilled his obligation and was not discovered sleeping on the job.

And if that happened, Tippit wouldn't need his boss's vote to cut the new man loose.

ART CATLIN'S UNEVENTFUL turn on night watch ran its course at ten o'clock. The new man came to spell him, smiling in the dark as he approached.

"I didn't meet you earlier," the stranger said, and leaned across his saddle to shake hands. "Jay Fielding."

Catlin shook with him and introduced himself, feeling no need for any questions that were bound to come off sounding rude and pushy. One thing he had learned during his years of traveling the West in search of fugitives: most people made the move to change their luck, the lives "back home" that left them unfulfilled, sometimes even their names. And Art believed in granting most of them a second chance.

Except for those who simply used the great wide-open as a cover for ongoing crimes.

"Got any tips for riding herd on longhorns overnight?" Fielding inquired.

"I'm fairly new to it, myself," Catlin replied. "Best thing I can suggest is that you stay awake and count on something unexpected happening. It's hard to be surprised that way; you can be relieved if nothing comes along."

"Alrighty, then."

Art left him to it, spotted Underwood and Guenther taking over for Gallardo and Wolford. As Catlin joined the others riding back to camp Wolford asked him, "How does the new man seem to you?"

"Just met him," Art replied. "I wouldn't claim to know him yet."

"He seems all right to me," Gallardo offered, without being asked.

"Don't know for sure," Wolford replied. "It's like I seen him somewhere, back a year or two, but can't remember when or where it was."

Francisco prodded Nehemiah. "Was he up to something?"

"That's the hell of it," said Wolford. "I can't pin it down so far."

Approaching the remuda, Catlin said, "Best thing I can suggest, sing out to Tippit or the boss if you remember what it was, the circumstances. Failing that, it's likely best to let it go."

"Maybe," said Wolford, plainly not convinced. "I'm gonna keep my eyes skinned, just in case."

"Never a bad idea," Catlin allowed, dismounting and preparing to unsaddle his strawberry roan. He missed his bedroll, never doubting that he'd fall asleep without a hitch tonight.

But Art was wrong. Instead of dropping off first thing, he spent the better part of half an hour trying to accommodate the ground beneath him. It was no more hard or lumpy than the soil he'd slept on nightly since the drive rode out of Santa Fe eight weeks before— softer than some places, in fact. Still, Catlin couldn't switch his mind off, going back over the things he'd seen and heard that day.

It always circled back around to Fielding, new man on the team.

So, what if Wolford *had* seen him before? The circumstances being hazy indicated that the incident—if it occurred at all and wasn't just a conjured fantasy— must have been trivial, forgettable. The odds of Nehemiah blanking out a crime, a brawl, or anything like that were slim to none.

Forget about it, Catlin told himself.

And just about the time midnight arrived, he did exactly that.

J ED FINDLAY DID his best to question Danny Underwood without appearing to, keeping it casual, asking the kinds of things a new man coming late to join the drive would naturally want to know.

"Is this your first time out with Mr. Mossman?" he inquired.

"Me? Nope," said Underwood. "It's my third year with the Bar X."

"Out of New Mexico, I think somebody told me?"

"Right. A couple miles from Santa Fe."

"I just met him," Findlay offered, "but he seems okay to work for."

"I've got no complaints," Danny replied. "He runs a tight ship; now, don't get me wrong, but he won't blame the hands for something ain't their fault."

"A fair man, then."

"I'd have to say so. Like this one time . . ."

Danny launched into a convoluted story of two cowboys on the Bar X spread who'd started feuding over something trivial—the details didn't interest Jed—until their boss stepped in and settled things between them without any fisticuffs or worse. The whole time Underwood was talking, Findlay sized him up and heard the third night watchman, Jerry Guenther, quieting the steers with snatches of a song that sounded like a hymn, "Tell Me the Old, Old Story."

Did that mean he was a praying man, or was his chosen song the only one he knew offhand?

Who even cared?

"Well, that beats all," Findlay allowed as Underwood concluded his dull narrative at last.

"And no more ever came of it," Danny said, nodding. "That's the kind of boss he is."

"I'm hoping he might take me on full-time, if I fit in all right."

That was a total crock, of course, but Findlay was adept at selling lies to gullible strangers.

"Don't do him wrong," Danny advised, "and you should have a decent shot."

"That's good to know. Speaking of which, I'd better get back on my rounds."

"Same here."

"I'll see you later," Jed allowed. "And thanks for the advice."

Turning from Wolford, Jed rode on toward Guenther,

hoping he'd wrap up the hymn before Findlay was close enough to speak without raising his voice. In fact, the song concluded prematurely, as if Guenther had forgotten the last stanza and refrain.

Guenther heard Jed approaching, half turned in his saddle, raised a hand in greeting. "How's it going?" he inquired.

"Beats working as a whorehouse bouncer," Findlay said.

Another job he'd never done, although he'd visited some brothels in his time. He watched Guenther, alert for any signs of being put off by Jed's humor, but nothing surfaced.

"Takes all kinds, I guess," Jerome replied.

"It does that," Findlay said, then launched into the spiel he'd used with Danny Underwood, probing for any weakness in the herd's security or lapse in loyalty to Mossman from his drovers.

Any weak link was an edge over his prey, something to use against them when the time was ripe.

While they were talking underneath the stars, casting about to watch for straying steers, Findlay was judging Guenther, from his height and heft to the man's choice of weapons: a Springfield Model 1868 rifle inside a saddle boot, a Colt Pocket Police revolver holstered on his left hip for a cross-hand draw.

The weapons gave Guenther six shots in all before reloading, and that chore would take some time, particularly if the drover's hands went shaky under fire. Jed likely wouldn't get to pass that information on before the raiders struck, but every observation might be of value later.

When they had passed a quarter of an hour talking quietly, Findlay rode on, circling the drowsy longhorns, counting horses in the camp's remuda. He was passing the chuck wagon when someone on the inside—either

Piney Rollins or his "Little Mary"—killed the only lamp still showing. After that, by campfire light, Jed scanned the drovers sleeping under blankets, hats over their faces. And imagined them roused out of dreamland by night riders whooping, hollering, and firing guns.

Nothing Jed hadn't seen before, but every time was still unique in some small way, human responses being unpredictable until you saw them acted out.

By which time it was normally too late.

Findlay had no intention of participating in the raid himself. He'd been employed to scout and infiltrate the trail drive, which was enough dirty work for what he stood to earn. Granted, he would not hesitate to kill, either in self-defense or if he'd been retained for an assassination, but participating in a free-for-all with thirty-odd armed men wasn't Jed Findlay's stock-in-trade.

Another thing he did not plan to do was make any friends among the Bar X drovers, from their boss on down the line. Jed could be amiable, even charming, when it served his purpose, but he wasn't cultivating any soft spots for the cowboys who would hate him—maybe even seek to kill him—once his lies and motives were revealed.

He had a few days yet before that fuse burned down to detonation, and beyond that . . .

What?

Likely another settlement, another game, either a solo fraud or outright robbery, depending on what he discovered on arrival and his judgment of potential allies.

But he wouldn't think about that now, with one job still a week or more from playing out. Distraction of the Bar X team was crucial, but it could prove fatal if Findlay became embroiled in it himself.

After a while, he'd found, the pigeons all seemed to resemble one another—not in race, or even sex, but through inherent weakness and a willingness to be deceived. Most of them couldn't see a trap closing around them until it was sprung, and then, sometimes, a crucial difference might be revealed.

Some folks rolled over, blamed themselves for being duped, and paid up without any argument, but others . . . well, you never could reliably predict what anyone might do. A person previously judged as weak, even defenseless, might turn fighting mad when cornered, throwing caution to the winds.

And anything could happen then, unless a fellow was prepared. A rough-and-tumble childhood had taught Findlay to strike first if it was required, and to keep his guard up at all times.

Failure to keep that lesson foremost in his mind was tantamount to suicide.

CHAPTER FIFTEEN

Wednesday, June 4

ART CATLIN SAT across the campfire from Jay Fielding, eating scrambled eggs and sausage on the
morning of the new hand's second full day with the
Bar X herd. From what he saw and heard, Fielding was
getting along well with other drovers, seeming anxious
to fit in with them and pull his weight.

The sole exception was Nehemiah Wolford, who
looked askance at Fielding when the new man wasn't
watching, clearly trying to remember where and when
he'd seen Fielding before, if it was true their paths had
even crossed.

Art wasn't horning in on that, had no desire to stir
up dissension in the Bar X ranks. If Wolford got his
thinking sorted out, Catlin assumed he'd do the right
thing and report any potential problem to the foreman
or to Mr. Mossman. That would be the only reasonable
play, and Catlin couldn't see himself precipitating any

heat between the two men when he didn't have a clue what Nehemiah might be fishing for.

When they were thrown together on the job, by day or night, Catlin had seen no evidence of any ancient feud between them, nothing to suggest that Fielding viewed Wolford with anything but cordiality. Art had observed them talking now and then, mostly at meals, when Wolford masked whatever feelings of uneasiness were dogging him. He'd even seen them laughing once, over some comment Fielding made, and Catlin wondered whether Wolford had decided just to let his fragment of a fading memory evaporate.

It didn't look that way this morning, though.

As Wolford finished off his eggs, he cast a final sidelong look at Fielding, frowned, then rose and took his plate and silverware back to the chuck wagon. Without a backward glance, he moved toward the remuda and prepared to saddle up his grulla mare.

Business as usual . . . except, not quite.

Reluctantly, although the last thing that he needed was an extra job, Catlin decided that he'd have to keep an eye on both men for a while, in case whatever Wolford was attempting to recover from his memory broke free and prompted him to act somehow.

And what would happen if that came to pass?

It might be nothing. Then again, it could be hell on wheels.

Art's only other choice, as far as he could see, would be to have a word with Mr. Mossman or his foreman. But to say exactly *what*?

If pressed, he couldn't say. In fact, Art didn't have the ghost of an idea.

Stay out of it, a small voice in his head cautioned. *Mind your own business*.

Words to live by, normally . . . but there were times when doing nothing might result in injury or worse.

So, he would wait and watch as best he could, hoping that he was wrong, that Wolford drew a mental blank and ultimately gave up rummaging around a lifetime made of memories.

Again, Art told himself if it was something serious, remembering what happened shouldn't be a problem. He would just let nature take its course, without a prod from anybody else, much less himself.

Catlin had seen enough trouble, brought much of it upon himself by going into harm's way voluntarily, and working for the Bar X was supposed to be a change of pace, maybe the start of a new life.

Out with the old, in with the new, and no distractions, please.

He was a cowboy now, at least in the short term, and if he never had to fire another shot in anger that would be ideal.

Longwood, Kansas

"Too early for a shot of whiskey?" Murray Glatman asked.

"Never," Marshal Bert Whitesell replied.

The men sat facing one another across Murray's desk, inside his second-story office at the Badger's Tail, Longwood's saloon and brothel. It was Glatman's place, featuring poker, dice, and a roulette wheel in addition to the girls and liquor. Other men might hold official titles in Longwood—the marshal, Mayor Harding, Justice of the Peace Butler—but no one who had spent more than a couple days in town doubted that Murray Glatman called the shots.

And lately, he'd been branching out.

"You have the men lined up?" Glatman inquired.

"All set, ready to go," Whitesell replied. "Has Findlay figured out his signal yet?"

Their scout had grudgingly agreed to infiltrate the cattle drive if possible. No word from him since Sunday told Glatman that Jed had pulled it off and planned to stay in character until he judged the time was ripe to move against the herd.

"He couldn't work that out until he had a closer look," Glatman advised the town's marshal. "Says whatever he decided on should be unmistakable. The boys are ready when that happens?"

"Only overnight," Whitesell reminded him. "They can't risk being spotted in the daytime."

"Night it is," Glatman confirmed, sipping his whiskey from a coffee mug. "How many guns lined up?"

"I handpicked eight. They'll be outnumbered two to one," the lawman said, anticipating Glatman's question, "but with Findlay on their side and night to cover them, it ought to be all right."

The town's boss gave him hard eyes. "'Ought to be' sounds wishy-washy, Bert. It doesn't reassure me."

"Mr. G, you know the score. I can't go with 'em. Same thing with Alonzo, just in case it falls apart at the last minute."

"And again, I'm losing confidence."

"Hold on, now. I ain't saying something *will* go wrong, you understand. I passed around those extra armbands that you gave me, so the men are covered if they need 'em."

"And their story is . . . ?"

"Just like you laid it out. Trespassing onto private land, and I—well, *we*—help bargain down the charge. Arrange for payment of a fine in lieu of outright confiscation or a trial that ties 'em up until they miss delivering on time."

"That's if one of your men gets caught alive."

"Exactly. One of 'em gets kilt, he can't do any talking, can he?"

"I sure as hell hope not," Glatman replied, half smiling.

"And if they get clean away—which I intend—the other story plays out smooth as silk."

That story put the blame on rustlers who'd allegedly been plaguing Longwood and its environs for a while now, but the lazy kind who'd rather ransom back a herd than try to sell the steers themselves, either at Independence or in Mexico, with all the risks that might entail.

"You've dealt with that as well?"

"Sure did. Monty McCauley and his kin sit on the herd. Mayor Harding claims he's carried out negotiations, fronting Longwood's money as a favor, since it's more than what the trail boss should be carrying. Judge Butler calls on Mr. Crull to draw up an agreement that will reimburse the town. Trail boss signs off on it, and either me or Markland rides to Independence with 'em, making sure the townsfolk get paid back in full for their good deed."

Whitesell ran through the tale as Murray Glatman had conceived it, laying down chapter and verse. It might appear transparent to outsiders, but it was the kind of thing that *could* happen, particularly in a small town where the founders wanted to protect their reputations as men of integrity. Good Christian men who'd help a stranger out when he was down and asked no more in compensation than their rightful due.

And after paying off the stooges he'd manipulated, pocketing the lion's share himself, Glatman imagined he could use a long vacation. He was thinking San Francisco, confident his skills could make him richer still on the Barbary Coast, with its dance halls, casinos, saloons, and brothels. Although he'd never been there, Glatman liked the sound of it, imagined it would feel like coming home.

"More whiskey for the road, Marshal?" he asked.

* * *

JED FINDLAY WAS already tired of cow-punching.

He didn't let that show, of course, by any word or gesture, any wry expression on his face that would bctray ingratitude for being hired with sunshine promises of meager pay on some uncertain future date.

Findlay had mastered feigning patience as an adolescent, from a master who'd recruited him as an apprentice and a part-time whipping boy. His tutor's name was Ezra Wright, a confidence man from St. Louis who'd alternated between lectures and beatings until the day when Findlay wouldn't take it anymore and left him with his throat slit, minus his bankroll.

From there, Jed's life had been a roller-coaster ride of holdups, swindles, and the like that kept him hopping and left other bodies in his wake, but he had no complaints.

Nobody ever claimed that life outside the law would be a cakewalk, but it suited him.

Today, as they were drawing near to Longwood and the climax of his latest operation, Findlay wondered if the whole thing was about to fall apart on him and vanish like the contents of a newfangled flush toilet—what some people called a "monkey closet"—that he'd read about in luxury hotels back east.

And in particular, he was worried about one Bar X cowboy whose name and face he couldn't manage to recall.

That wasn't like Findlay. Over the years he'd honed his memory for names and faces that might come around to haunt him somewhere down the road. Rich men he'd cheated out of money, bank tellers he'd left alive, the relatives of people he had murdered for one reason or another, be it contract killing or simple expedience.

But now . . .

He couldn't place Wolford, despite their relatively close association since Findlay had joined the cattle drive. The drover's face evoked no memory, nor did his voice.

Still, he'd caught the bent-nosed cowboy watching him—no, make that *staring* at him—more than once, frowning as if he thought he should remember Findlay but he couldn't pin it down in terms of time and place.

At first, Findlay had tried to let it go, hoping that Nehcmiah would get over it, but now the clock was ticking on his biggest payday ever, and damn it, he had to know.

Except he couldn't bring it up himself, in case . . .

In case of what?

Veering off course to stop a pair of longhorns straying from their charted course, Jed reckoned he would have to wait and see.

N o troubles so far?" Sterling Tippit asked.

"No, sir," Jay Fielding answered. "Not a one."

"The other men are treating you okay?"

The new man bobbed his head in the affirmative. "I've got me no complaints."

Wish I could say the same and mean it, Tippit thought, but kept that to himself. Instead, he said, "So, you won't mind the second shift tonight, with Wolford and Chávez."

Not really asking, making it an order, but without the snap to it.

"Suits me, sir," Fielding said.

"Good man."

Riding away from him, Tippit was pleased with how their new hire had been working out so far. They shouldn't be much longer on the trail, in case the work was getting under Findlay's skin, but if he wasn't lying, if he was as content and easygoing as he seemed, Tippit would not have been surprised if Mr. Mossman tried to keep him on.

Whichever way that went, it was no skin off Tippit's nose.

If things ran smoothly over the duration of the cattle drive, he would be satisfied.

But if they didn't . . .

It was Tippit's job as foreman to make sure the drovers stayed in line and carried out the tasks assigned to them, on time and as required. Some might complain from time to time, but that was only natural, especially for workingmen denied venal pleasures of the flesh for weeks on end. Sterling wasn't required to serve as their confessor or their nanny, only as a ramrod keeping them in line.

Passing the chuck wagon, he called to Piney Rollins, "What's up for tonight?"

"Mulligan stew," the cook replied, "using some rabbits that we caught over the past couple of nights."

"Those cottontails that I keep seeing since we hit this stretch of prairie?"

"Maybe not the same ones, but their kin," said Rollins. "And I'm thinking maybe apple pie for after."

Tippit smiled. "Vents in the crust," he said, "to let off steam."

"The way your momma used to do it," Piney said.

"Better, I hope," the foreman answered back. "She couldn't make a decent pie to save her life."

"Sorry to hear that." Piney's grin said otherwise.

"My grandma, now," Sterling went on, "*she* knew her way around an oven, no two ways about it."

"So, you still came out all right."

"Can't rightly answer that," Tippit replied. "I'm not done yet."

With that, he turned his blood bay mare away and went in search of strays or drovers who were slacking off.

If he was lucky, Tippit would find neither, and the day could finish winding down in peace.

How many more, until they reached the reeking Independence stockyards? Six or seven if their luck held out.

And if it didn't . . . well, then, who could say?

IT CAME TO Nehemiah Wolford over supper, reaching nearly four years back through time to where and when he'd seen the new man in their midst.

It was in St. George, Utah, named for one of twelve apostles in the Mormon Church and its first counselor to "President" Brigham Young at the time. Wolford had been working on a spread outside of town, dispatched one market day to help retrieve supplies and see them safely back to what his boss called Deseret Acres. Mormons were down on alcohol, but there were still saloons around, equipped with "Zion curtains" screening bartenders from customers who ordered drinks.

The theory, as Wolford understood it, was to cut down heavy drinking by concealing alcohol in kegs and bottles from the people who were swilling it a few feet away, bellied up against the bar. That didn't stop them getting drunk but made church elders feel like they were "doing something" to combat the scourge of Demon Rum.

That afternoon, a Saturday, two men had started quarreling while Wolford sipped the one whiskey per week that he allowed himself, standing some twenty feet away from them. One of the men was larger by a head or more and grabbed his adversary by the neck before he stiffened, cried aloud with pain, and slumped against the bar. That was the first time Wolford saw the other fellow's face, a glimpse before he fled the barroom, and the main impression Nehemiah had of him was bright blood dripping from the long blade of his knife.

He'd never learned the stabber's name, but now, allowing for the forty-odd months lying in between that day and this, he made it sixty–forty that the stranger with the pigsticker had been none other than Jay Fielding in the flesh.

And so what, if it was?

The man he'd cut survived, as Wolford later heard it told, while Fielding—nameless at the time—escaped across the border to Nevada and was never seen again in Mormon Land, as far as Nehemiah knew.

Now that he'd worked it out, or *thought* he had, what should he do?

The first and likely best idea was nothing. Knifing someone in a fight four years ago, and some eleven hundred miles from where the Bar X herd was bedding down tonight, was hardly news, particularly when the fellow being sliced had seemed to start the trouble and he hadn't even died.

But how would Wolford's conscience handle that, withholding it from Mr. Mossman and the rest of them?

Or would he make things worse by spilling what Jay Fielding might prefer to keep a secret, maybe costing him his short-term job with the Bar X? In that case, would it mark him—Wolford—as a tattler, undeserving of his fellow cowhands' trust?

That left a third option, namely, to speak with Fielding privately, disclose his knowledge where nobody else could overhear, and tell the new man that he didn't plan to tell tales out of school.

On balance, that seemed best to Wolford, and he had the perfect time in mind for doing it.

Tonight, when they shared second watch with Luis Chávez.

That, he thought, should get it done and off his mind at last.

JED FINDLAY DRIFTED past the camp's chuck wagon on his dun, taking his time. The light from a full moon let him consult his stolen pocket watch—the one with "Happy Anniversary, David" engraved across the inside of its hinged cover—confirming that his shift still had two hours more to run.

Tonight, he'd made his mind up as to how he'd signal Longwood's rustling crew when it was time. Once he had worked that out, he saw no obstacles to handling it.

Just then, he spotted Nehemiah Wolford riding toward him from the north, approaching at an angle that would briefly put them side by side.

Speaking of obstacles, Jed thought, and plastered on a smile with just the right proportion of affability and weariness combined.

"Slow night," Wolford observed, when he was near enough to speak without raising his voice.

"The way I like it," Findlay said.

"I hear that." Wolford cleared his throat, then asked, "You holding up all right so far, with the Bar X?"

"You make the second man tonight who's asked me that. The foreman send you over here?"

"Tippit? I lost track of him after supper."

"He's around here somewhere," Fielding answered. "Checking up."

"I'll keep an eye out, then." A moment's hesitation, then, "There's something that I need to ask you."

"Need to? That's a cut above 'want to,' I guess."

Ignoring that, Wolford came out with it. "You ever been to Utah, Jay?"

And there it was, the start of it at least.

"I might have," Findlay answered, noncommittal. "Maybe more than once."

"This would've been four years ago, the early spring. St. George, to pin it down more."

Nodding slowly, Findlay said, "That rings a bell."

"Place called the Seagull, a saloon, named for the birds some Mormons claim rescued their crops from grasshoppers in '47, sent by God."

"I would've just turned six years old," Findlay replied. "And I'm not Mormon."

Wolford swallowed. Replied, "I think you take my meaning."

"Do I?" Findlay eased his dun closer to Nehemiah's grulla mare, sliding his right hand slowly toward the knife handle protruding from his boot.

Ignoring Jed's response, Wolford said, "I just want to tell you I remember where I saw you, four years back. It's your business and I don't aim to tell a soul."

"I can appreciate that," said Findlay. "And you're right."

"Right about what?"

Jed knew where Chávez was, nearly a hundred yards away, and didn't have to think about it twice. He drew his Arkansas toothpick and jammed its blade up under Wolford's chin, keeping the pressure on until its tip butted against the inside of his fellow drover's skull.

One twist, and Findlay saw the light go out of Wolford's eyes, his body going slack. He might have toppled from the saddle as Findlay withdrew his dripping blade, but Jed used his left hand to brace the corpse, keep it astride his mount.

That wouldn't last, but he could keep the body balanced long enough to lead the grulla mare away, trailing his dun, until they'd reached a point two hundred fifty yards beyond the nearest longhorns, say three hundred from the camp and chuck wagon. A gentle shove, then toppled Nehemiah to the ground and let his animal roam free.

Now all Jed had to do was go about his normal rounds and wait.

ART CATLIN HAD the graveyard shift, with Job Hooper and Mike Limbaugh. That meant he'd slept the better part of six hours and would be riding herd until the first pale light of dawn before breakfast.

Not all that bad, once you got used to it.

Tonight, though—or call it this morning—he was looking at another problem from the start.

Three men rode out to the relief of three coworkers, same as always, but this time, as on the night when Julius Pryor disappeared, they came up one man short.

Art saw Hooper hook up with Jay Fielding, and Limbaugh with Chávez—but where in hell was Wolford?

Nowhere to be seen.

"This shit again?" Hooper called out to Art, across a group of longhorns acting grumpy as their sleep was interrupted.

"I'll start looking for him," Catlin said. "You'd better tell the boss."

And what he thought was, *Damn. At least it wasn't on my watch this time.*

It took twenty minutes, while more drovers were turned out, before Art spotted Wolford's grulla by moonlight. The mare was cropping grass, no rider on her back or anywhere nearby that Catlin could detect.

A cowboy answering a midnight call of nature

should be near his horse, maybe holding its reins, depending on what kind of hurry call it was. In this case, though . . .

His roan caught up to Nehemiah's mount, which didn't shy away or seem at all skittish. When he was near enough to lean across and take the grulla's reins, Art spotted dark smears on the empty saddle, nearly black under the moon, that looked and smelled like blood.

Catlin cursed, then put two fingers in his mouth and whistled for the other cowboys who were circling around the herd, trying to find their missing coworker. Wherever Wolford was, it looked to Art as if he was beyond saving by now.

"Tell me," Bliss Mossman ordered as he rode up to the scene, with Sterling Tippit trailing him a few yards back.

With nothing much to tell, Art let the men in charge examine Wolford's animal, circling around it slowly on their own.

"This how you found her, then?" asked Mossman.

"Yes, sir. Still no sign of Nehemiah but the blood. I didn't want to leave it standing here or lead it off before you had a chance to check the ground for signs."

"Good thinking," Mossman granted. Then, to Tippit, "Better fetch back Fielding and Chávez. We need to question them, first thing."

At least, Art thought, *we know he didn't run away.*

But this was even worse.

Unless he missed his guess, this meant murder.

CHAPTER SIXTEEN

Thursday, June 5

D URING THE SEARCH that followed, Catlin hoped he
   wouldn't be the one to find Wolford, and as it
turned out, he was not.

That fell to Jaime Reyes, whom they found sitting
astride a dapple gray from the remuda rather than his
own usual mare, and pointing to a body on the ground
when others rallied to his shout. Bliss Mossman told the
rest to stay aboard their animals while he dismounted,
circling all around the corpse, making a futile search
for clues.

"Murder," he said at last, confirming what his men
could plainly see by lantern light.

Someone had stabbed Wolford beneath his chin, a
straight thrust through his soft palate into his brain,
which had released the blood discovered on his grulla's
saddle and a lot more besides, turning his checkered

shirt and denim pants a crusty brown from neck to thighs as it dried out.

As Mr. Mossman straightened up from bending over Nehemiah, everyone around the ring of mounted spectators was peering at the other Bar X hands with quick, suspicious eyes. It didn't take a genius to see that most of them wore knives sheathed on their belts or in their boot tops, where they could be reached in haste to cope with an emergency. Catlin was one of three or four who didn't, but he kept a folder in his pocket, even its blade long enough to be responsible for Wolford's fatal wound.

Off to Art's left, halfway around the circle, Mike Limbaugh muttered, "Damn! It must be one of us."

"Hold on, now," Sterling Tippit interjected. "We don't know that. There could be another explanation."

"So, what is it?" asked Linton McCormick.

"Someone from outside," Tippit answered. "It wouldn't be the first time we were snuck up on."

No doubt he meant to help, calming things down, but Mr. Mossman soon established that the other men on watch admitted seeing no one, and the same was true for their replacements. Group suspicion naturally zeroed in from there on Catlin and Fielding, presumed to be the nearest hands to Wolford when he'd died.

Art understood that natural impulse. He knew damned well that *he* had played no part in Nehemiah's death, nor could he think of any reason why the new man on their team, only three nights in camp so far, would have a killing grudge against a victim he had never met before.

"I hate this, boys," said Mossman. "But I need to see your knives and hands. We'll start with Art and Jay, then check the rest of you."

That raised a growling round of protest, most drovers insisting that they'd been asleep, but all that proved was that no individual could vouch for anybody else. Sleepers could describe whose bedrolls had been close to theirs but couldn't swear that someone hadn't lain and feigned snoring until he had a chance to rise and slip away.

"Let's get this done," said Catlin, digging in a pocket for his folding knife, a lock-back model with a four-inch blade, and passed it down to Sterling Tippit's waiting hand. Piney Rollins stepped up and held his lantern close while Tippit and Mossman examined it, first opening the blade, then peering closely at the wooden handle and its groove in search of bloodstains. Finally, they did the same for Catlin's hands and gave him back the knife.

Fielding in turn produced his wicked-looking Arkansas toothpick, provoking whispers from a couple of the other cowboys, but once again, their foreman found no telltale stains on blade or hands.

From there, it went around the circle, no one daring to protest the search for fear of seeming guilty. Only Linton McCormick had no knife at all, claiming he'd never owned one, and none of the other Bar X men remembered seeing him with one in hand except at mealtimes. Finally, to keep things on the up-and-up, Mossman and Tippit checked each other's hands and knives under close scrutiny from thirteen other pairs of eyes.

"All right, now," Mossman said, when they were done. "We found nothing, which *proves* nothing. I won't be pointing any fingers, but I need to hear from anyone who wants to stop the drive here while we fetch the county sheriff to investigate."

"Who'd go to get him?" Guenther asked.

"I'd pick someone," Mossman replied, "or we could choose by casting lots."

"It makes no difference," Bryce Zimmerman chimed in. "Suppose we pick the killer and he just rides off without bringing the law? We could sit here till doomsday waiting for 'em."

"Could happen," Mossman granted. "The alternative is planting Wolford at first light and moving on ourselves."

"But what about the killer?" asked Job Hooper.

"All that I can say is keep your eyes peeled," Mossman answered back. "Be on your guard, but not so jumpy that you shoot whatever moves before you know what's happening."

More muttering at that, but no one had a viable alternative. After he'd let a minute pass, Mossman said, "Okay, then. You men on watch, stick to your schedules for the time that's left tonight. Wrap Wolford in a tarp for now. We'll bury him soon as the sun comes up."

A ND SO IT WAS.
    Catlin managed an hour's troubled sleep and rose weary at daybreak with the other Bar X hands. Their funeral for Nehemiah Wolford took the best part of an hour, from turning the first spade full of sod to covering the hole and tamping down the turf that covered it.

Bliss Mossman kept his reading from the Good Book short and to the point, a verse from Genesis: "Whoso sheddeth man's blood, by man shall his blood be shed: for in the image of God made He man."

The gist of that was clear enough, but Catlin wound up wondering if that made God a murderer, Himself. In fact, according to Scripture, who else had killed as many men, women, and children throughout human history— the whole at one sitting, back in ancient times, except for Noah and his brood, who'd turned out to be sinners just like those whom the Almighty didn't spare?

That was too much for Art to think about with little sleep and worry on his mind. He managed to eat breakfast without really tasting it, and then got saddled up to face another day out on the trail.

A brooding aura of suspicion hung over the drive as it proceeded, with the longhorns seeming slower than the men in charge of them had grown accustomed to over the seven weeks and counting since they'd started out from Santa Fe. It was ridiculous, Art realized, but if you watched the steers closely this morning, some of them seemed to be rolling anxious eyes to watch the mounted drovers, as if fearful one of them would snap and run amok.

But if that feeling came directly from Catlin's imagination, such was not the case among his fellow cowboys. Few shared any conversation as the day wore on, and what cross talk there was centered around who might have murdered Nehemiah Wolford, what the killer's motive was, and if he might decide to strike again.

Art wondered when the small cracks in their unified façade would start to widen, drovers dropping out, preferring to forgo their pay rather than be the next man on the unknown slayer's chopping block.

And worse yet, when would mounting fear provoke a violent outburst in their ranks?

B LISS MOSSMAN HAD moved on from wondering if this year's drive was somehow jinxed. With last night's murder added to the list of things that had gone badly wrong so far, how could he doubt it?

In his years of herding cattle—first for other ranchers, then on his own account for the Bar X—he'd never seen or heard of anybody being murdered by a fellow ranch hand on a cattle drive. The closest he had ever come to something similar, going on sixteen years ago, had been a quarrel between drunken cowboys that ended with gunplay, both men wounded, neither of them fatally.

But this was something else entirely, Mossman realized. Someone—more than likely one of his own men—

had gotten close enough by means of guile that he could plunge a blade through Nehemiah Wolford's throat into his skull. It was a sly and treacherous attack that reeked of enmity that Mossman couldn't understand.

Wolford had worked at the Bar X for going on four years. In all that time, Mossman had never seen him quarrel with anyone among the other hands or when they rode to Santa Fe. He'd made no enemies during the present drive, as far as Mossman knew, and had participated in no squabbles, even of the minor, soon forgotten kind.

That said, his murder had been calculated, cold, *deliberate*. It could not have been accidental, nor an act committed in the heat of passion spawned by argument, since someone else in camp would have been roused by shouting or a cry of mortal pain.

But, wait. Could Wolford even make a sound once his assassin plunged a blade under his chin and stilled his tongue forever? Did the killer's method speak to a desire for secrecy? And if that were the case, why was the body dumped where anyone might find it, once they started scouring the prairie for a missing drover?

Mossman couldn't make sense of the evidence, such as it was. Right now he only knew that everyone who served him on the drive—and maybe all that he'd been working toward for years on end—was in potential danger.

And there wasn't a damned thing that he could do about it.

Longwood, Kansas

"They're getting close," Murray Glatman advised the other four men gathered in his office at the Badger's Tail Saloon.

He didn't have to tell them *who* was getting close. Between them, they had thought of little else since Jed Findlay had warned them of the cattle drive's approach and plans were hatched to seize the golden opportunity. Watching their faces now, Glatman saw that three out of the four appeared committed to proceeding with their scheme.

The odd man out was the aged justice of the peace, Odell Butler.

"We've got the men in place?" Mayor Harding asked.

"All set to go," Marshal Whitesell replied. "As soon as Findlay gives the signal, they'll move in."

"Can you remind us what that signal is?" asked lawyer Tilman Crull.

"Sorry, but no," said Whitesell. "Jed still wasn't sure when he hooked up with them, and we've had no chance to communicate since then."

"Something dramatic, I'd assume," the mayor said.

Glatman swallowed a desire to tell them what he thought about assumptions, but said, "Jed knows his business. We can trust him to be obvious without putting himself in too much danger."

"Can we, though?" Judge Butler asked the room at large. "Trust him, I mean?"

Glatman answered with a question of his own. "Why not, Your Honor?"

"Why not?" Butler's cheeks were coloring beneath his normal pallid white. "First off, we don't know him from Adam, Murray. You're the one who recommended him and sang his praises till we cut him in for ten percent. Nobody else here in this room today can vouch for him at all."

"I see," Glatman replied. "So, it's not Jed you're doubting now, but me. Is that it?"

"Well . . ."

"Nobody's saying that, Murray," Harding pitched in.

"They're not?" Glatman showed them his reptile's grin. "It sounds to me like one of you just did exactly that."

"I'm sure that Odell didn't mean—"

"Don't speak for me, Cyrus," their justice of the peace cut in. "Murray's not wrong. None of us ever heard of Findlay until Murray brought him in, singing his praises to high heaven. Now we hear that Bert's men still don't know how Findlay plans to signal them for their attack, their raid, whatever you call it."

Glatman refreshed his whiskey glass but offered no more to his guests. He sipped it thoughtfully, then said, "You're right, Odell. I recommended him. I stand by that, and you-all went along with it. I didn't hear you bitch about it earlier. So, what's the problem now, *Your Honor*?"

Making Butler's title sound more like a sneer.

"I only think we should be cautious, Murray. And I've come to think your man is overpriced."

"Again, you-all signed off on what he should receive."

"I only meant—"

But Glatman interrupted Butler. Said, "If you want out of this, Odell, you need to say so, and I mean right now. Mayor Harding can appoint another JP in your place, and you can leave. You've got nothing to keep you here. No family, except that daughter and grandson I've heard you talk about. They still live in St. Louis, don't they? I recall it as Ward Six, on Compton Street."

"Murray—"

"I see no reason why you couldn't go and stay with them awhile. See how they're getting on."

"I fear that you've misunderstood me," Butler said, not quite whining.

Glatman allowed himself a shrug. "That's possible, I guess."

"I have no wish and no plan to abandon our agreement."

"Ah. Well, that's a load off all our minds, I'm sure, Odell." Glatman quaffed off his whiskey, smacked his lips, and said, "Now, if there's nothing else, we all have work to do."

SUPPER IN CAMP that night was quiet, talk subdued among the Bar X drovers. None of them had slept well after finding Nehemiah Wolford's corpse, and all seemed anxious to turn in once they had finished eating, even if it meant keeping their guns closer than normal once they'd bedded down.

As for the hands on first night watch—Steinmeier, Underwood, and Guenther—they were dragging as they dropped their empty plates and coffee cups at the chuck wagon, taking guns and saddles off to start their shift. They looked as if it were a toss-up as to whether raw fatigue or a knife-wielding lunatic would catch up to them first.

Catlin was off tonight, as luck would have it, and certain that he'd spend the hours with his Colt Navy revolver and his Henry rifle close at hand. As to whether he'd sleep or not, despite how tired he was . . . well, he would have to wait and see.

One thing they had no shortage of in camp tonight was nerves strung tightly as piano wire, each cowboy wondering if he would wake up in the morning or be wrapped in tarp and slated for an early grave.

If anyone had asked Catlin just then whether he would prefer a cowboy's life over that of a bounty hunter, he could not have answered honestly.

At least in his former profession there'd been few nights when he'd feared to close his eye.

SEEN ANYTHING?" CLYDE Byers asked.
    "You think we'd still be sitting here?" Vern Killian replied.

"Guess not."

Dumb shit, Killian thought, but didn't speak the words aloud. He'd been appointed leader of the team tonight, with vague instructions to await a signal from their inside man and act accordingly. Bert Whitesell hadn't told him what that signal might consist of—gunshots, hollering, somebody beating on a cook's triangle, shouting, "Come and get it!"—but there'd been nothing so far, and the other members of his raiding party were on edge.

That said, they were as primed and ready as a group of mismatched ne'er-do-wells could ever be, bracing themselves to steal a herd of cattle—or a goodly number of them, anyway—from armed men who outnumbered them by nearly two to one.

Against that, Killian and his eight men were well armed, each of them a killer in his own right, with deputy marshal's badges tucked away for use at need. Killian still wasn't sure how that would work. It was a "last resort" according to Marshal Whitesell—but how would flashing badges help after they tried to raid the herd? Would anybody on the other side even take time to look at them or listen to the lie before they blew the phony deputies to hell and gone?

"So, how's this guy supposed to call us in?" Doc Quigley asked. Killian didn't know how Quigley got his nickname, but he'd never been a doctor, clearly never even went to school trying to be one.

"All of you stop asking me to tell the future," Killian commanded. "I was told we couldn't miss the signal, and that's all I know, damn it!"

Carl Ragsdale griped, "If he waits any longer, this outfit will be in Longwood or beyond it."

Killian ignored him. Told the group at large, "If any of you haven't checked your guns by now, you'd best get to it."

"How many times we gotta check 'em?" Tony Good-enough inquired.

"As often as it takes to keep your ass from getting kilt by carelessness," Killian said. "Now, all of you shut up and let me think!"

And what he thought was, *Come on, Findlay. What's the goddamn holdup?*

J ED FINDLAY WAS no telepath and didn't need to be. He could imagine Marshal Whitesell's raiders huddled in the darkness, waiting for a sign to make their move, and knew that he was running perilously short on time to call them in.

The good news: Findlay was excused from riding herd tonight and had decided that there'd never be a better time than now.

He had considered half a dozen ways of tipping off the Longwood crew, deciding that the easiest—and safest, for himself—would cause a panic in the Bar X camp while drawing the three men on night watch from their rounds.

And how better to get that done than with the chuck wagon?

Findlay had looked around inside the wagon when the cook served up breakfast and supper, acting casual about it, and had gained a better view inside while complimenting Piney Rollins on a stew that Jed considered mediocre. He knew where the lamps were kept when Piney doused them for the night and figured he could reach one easily enough by climbing on the wagon's tailgate, taking care to make a minimum of racket in the process.

After that . . .

The trick, he realized, was rising from his bedroll, slipping past the sleeping drovers ranged around the campfire without waking anyone. Jay knew that everyone was edgy since he'd skewered Nehemiah Wolford, and he'd caught a couple of them staring at him, likely whispering behind his back, but no one had accused him yet, and now they'd missed their chance.

Jay didn't bother with his blankets as he rose, just left them lying rumpled where they were. He hadn't taken off his gun belt when he went to bed, so didn't have to wrestle with that now, and his Winchester nestled in its scabbard as he raised the saddle to his shoulder, not quite tiptoeing around the fire, moving toward the remuda.

Anxious moments there, while he was saddling his dun and trying not to rouse the wrangler, Jared Olney, stretched out near the horses. Findlay had considered knifing him, but he didn't want to risk a scuffle that might rouse the camp, surrounding him with eager guns before he signaled out for help from Whitesell's men.

Instead of mounting up when he was finished with the saddle, Jay led his mount slowly and cautiously to reach the chuck wagon. Once there, he struck a match to verify the lanterns were in place and lifted one outside. It took a second match to light the wick, and Findlay cursed the tiny scraping sounds its chimney made as he removed it, gaining access to the burner.

Nearly trembling with excitement, Jed knew that if anything went wrong, it would most likely happen now.

But nothing did.

He turned the wick up, got it lit, and stepped back far enough that he could hurl the lamp without a backsplash that would set his clothes on fire. He heard the lamp's font shatter on impact, then flames were leaping up inside, climbing the wagon's canvas bonnet in a flash as Findlay mounted up and lashed his animal into an all-out gallop.

Art Catlin woke to chaos—men running around and shouting, "Fire!"—before he fully realized that he had drifted off to sleep.

How long? It didn't matter now. There was a new emergency to occupy his mind.

Before Catlin was even on his feet, he saw the chuck wagon in flames. Someone was howling from the heart of that inferno, with a voice that sounded vaguely like Tim Berryman's.

Art tugged his boots on and retrieved his guns. They wouldn't help him fight the blaze, but something told him that the drive had bigger problems now than having its supplies go up in smoke.

As if responding to his silent thought, gunfire rang out along the herd's perimeter. Jogging around the chuck wagon, shielding his eyes from firelight for a better view, Art saw a line of muzzle flashes in the darkness, drawing closer as a skirmish line of horsemen charged the camp.

He called a warning out to anybody who might listen, even though the raging fire half blinded them, its roar serving to muffle gunshots at a hundred yards and closing. Seconds later, Art heard Mr. Mossman shouting for his hands to arm themselves and do it now.

The blazing wagon, its expanding pall of smoke, and crackling gunfire all combined to spook the longhorns, rousing them to panic. On the outskirts of the herd, armed horsemen had begun to circle wide around the herd's main body, coming at the steers from a southwesterly direction, whipping up a stampede frenzy with their rebel yells and gunfire.

Facing them on foot was madness.

Cursing, Catlin broke for the remuda and his stallion at an all-out run.

JOLTED FROM SLEEP by shouts of "Fire!" and someone crying out in pain, it seemed to Sterling Tippit that he'd woken from a nightmare to discover he was trapped in hell on earth. It took a moment for his mind to clear and recognize reality, but even then what he was seeing made no sense.

The chuck wagon on fire, men beating at the flames with blankets, then discarding them as they caught fire in turn—how was this happening? If Piney Rollins or his teenage helper had done something foolish, Tippit meant to have their hides.

But, no.

Beyond the fire that ruined his night vision, Sterling heard gunfire and drew his Colt Dragoon revolver, making ready to respond in kind. If he could only find out who was shooting and determine why . . .

Another hectic moment passed before he spotted riders circling around the Bar X herd, firing their guns into the air. It didn't seem as if they'd marked a human target yet, preoccupied with stirring up the longhorns, trying to stampede them.

Rustlers?

What else could it be?

Art Catlin sprinted past him, bound for the remuda if he didn't veer off course before arriving there. Tippit pursued him, knowing that the best way to oppose armed riders was on horseback, fighting as their equal, rather than a grounded target they could pick off as they pleased.

He fell in behind Catlin, burdened by his saddle as he ran for his flea-bitten gray.

VERN KILLIAN HAD given up on strategy the moment that his raiders started shooting. It was no good shouting at them to cease fire, since few of them would hear him and they likely wouldn't follow his instructions anyhow.

That was the way of any battle, as he'd learned during the War Between the States, serving with the 2nd Arkansas Infantry Regiment. He'd been wounded twice, at Shiloh and again at Perryville, lucky to be alive and make it home with nothing but a slight limp in cold weather to remind him of the hell he'd managed to survive.

The Golden Rule of combat was "No plan survives the first contact." And if he'd needed any further proof of that, Killian had it now.

At least the longhorns were behaving reasonably true to form, half of them or more charging away to the northeast, toward Longwood. Townsmen, mounted and afoot, were waiting for them there, to halt their charge and steer them into holding pens prepared for just that purpose.

Killian's riders were meant to guide the herd, but some of them were dueling with the drovers now, distracted from their main task by the exigency of survival in the moment. It would be a minor miracle, he thought, if none of them were killed or captured on the battlefield.

To think that he had volunteered for this. Killian knew he wasn't drunk when Whitesell pitched the proposition to him, but he wondered now if he had lost his ever-loving mind.

One of his raiders, Mason Hedges, galloped past Killian's red taffy mare on his rabicano gelding, hunched over the saddle horn and calling out, "I'm hit! To hell with this! I'm getting out of here!"

Killian let him go and wished him luck. The other members of his party were approximately following instructions, whooping at the longhorns, driving them in Longwood's general direction by the light of a three-quarters moon. Behind them, most on foot, the trail drive's cowboys were unloading with their firearms, having little luck beyond one of them winging Hedges with a lucky shot.

"To hell with this is right!" Killian muttered to himself, and spurred his mount to greater speed, ducking his head as if a change in posture would prevent him being cut down from behind.

He couldn't say for sure how many cattle they were running with, but it appeared to be somewhere between one third and one half of the herd. Enough to make the trail boss track them, anyhow, and wind up in negotiations with the men in charge of Longwood.

And if that wasn't a risky scheme, Killian didn't know what was.

"To hell with it!" he said again, his horse blithely ignoring him.

As long as he got paid for this night's outing, that was all he cared about.

Well, that and living to enjoy his newfound wealth.

CHAPTER SEVENTEEN

Thursday, June 5

WE'VE LOST TIM Berryman," Bliss Mossman told the Bar X team. "The burns were just too much for him."

Art Catlin noted Piney Rollins, standing near their boss, using a dingy handkerchief to dab his eyes. He wasted no time wondering if smoke had stung his eyes or he'd been moved to tears by losing his apprentice.

The chuck wagon had burned down to its axles once the shooting started and no drovers could be spared to douse its flames. That meant their food was gone, together with a brace of water barrels and assorted tools. The only upside was survival of the dray horses that pulled the wagon daily, now put out of work.

Mossman and Sterling Tippit had begun to count the drive's remaining longhorns at first light, Tippit reporting to the men that roughly half of their two thousand steers were missing since the night's pell-mell stampede.

With that in mind, it was a wonder that they'd suffered no more human losses. Berryman turned out to be their sole fatality, trapped when the wagon's blazing bonnet fell on top of him while he was scrambling to salvage anything he could. Jerome Guenther was the only drover wounded in the gunfight, suffering a shallow graze—more than a rash than anything more serious—across his left thigh when a bullet came too close for comfort.

And then, there was Jay Fielding. Or, rather, there wasn't.

Somehow, in the midst of conflict, he had disappeared, together with his dun, saddle and all. Only a fool would bet he'd fled in panic from the shooting, rather than precipitating it himself.

While a couple of the Bar X hands prepared a grave for Berryman, his life snuffed out at age sixteen, Mossman addressed the drovers who weren't tied up riding herd on the remainder of their stock.

"You-all know me. I can't and won't sit still for this. I aim to get those steers back and to settle up for Tim, or else die trying. If I can't do that, it ain't worth going back to Santa Fe."

Some of the drovers started muttering at that, and Mossman left them to it for a minute, maybe two, before he spoke again.

"I figure that my odds of doing it alone are slim and then some, but I won't ask anyone to come along and join me after all you've been through up to now."

The mutters faded out to whispers then, Catlin ignoring them and waiting for the boss to finish up. He had a fair idea of what was coming, but he'd never claimed to be a mind reader. In fact, he was surprised when Guenther raised his lightly bandaged arm and said, "I'll go along, boss, if you'll have me."

"What about your arm, Jerry?" Mossman inquired.

"I shoot right-handed, boss," Guenther replied. "It shouldn't slow me down none."

That raised scattered laughter and it seemed to crack the mournful mood.

And thus encouraged, others started sounding off.

"I'm in," said Mike Limbaugh.

"*Yo también,*" said Francisco Gallardo.

"I missed out on the Comancheros," Job Hooper pitched in. "I may as well try this bunch on for size."

"Thanks, all of you," their boss said. "I was hoping to ride out with five and leave the rest on guard, but four should be all right."

"I'll make it six," Art Catlin said, already wondering what made him volunteer for his third shooting match since they'd left Santa Fe. Because he had no doubt that there'd be shooting, bloodletting, however it turned out.

The very thing he'd sought to get away from when he joined the Bar X drive.

Maybe I'm just a fool, he thought as Mossman smiled at him and said, "All right, then. Six it is. You volunteers arm up and we'll get going soon as we're finished with Tim."

Longwood, Kansas

Jed Findlay's head was achy and his dry throat burned as he rode into Longwood from the south and hitched his dun outside the Badger's Tail. He went inside, ordered a shot of whiskey and a beer back from the sleepy-looking bartender, sipped a little of the brew to soothe his gullet, then tossed down the amber liquid fire.

Better, although no one could have told that from looking at him.

Findlay was bedraggled, unwashed from the trail, smelling of smoke and dust. Dark circles underneath his eyes bespoke a lack of sleep he hoped to remedy before much longer.

Just as soon as he got paid.

He had not ridden back to Longwood with the raiders but skedaddled out of camp before they struck in answer to the bonfire he had started. Galloping away, he'd heard gunfire and high-pitched screaming from the chuck wagon. That made him grimace as he thought of someone trapped inside that conflagration, but he knew it wouldn't worry him for long.

Whoever fried, his pain was likely over now, eclipsed by death—and when Jed thought about it, he decided there was no good way to die.

Well, maybe short of checking out at the climactic moment with a pretty girl.

Not likely in Jed's case, if he were honest with himself.

The second item on his list of things to do was getting clear of Longwood, pronto. But since Murray Glatman owed him money for a job now done, Findlay was staying put until he had the cash in hand.

And if the town's boss tried to cheat him out of it, there would be hell to pay.

BLISS MOSSMAN AND his riders had no difficulty following the stampede's trail from camp in a northeasterly direction. It occurred to Mossman that wherever his longhorns had dashed off to, at least they'd started moving in a rough beeline toward Independence, where he'd meant to take them in the first place.

On the other hand, that knowledge didn't help a bit.

The good news about a stampede was how it flattened and disrupted turf, making the errant livestock relatively easy to pursue.

The bad news: these steers hadn't simply run away from lightning or a burst of thunder. They'd been stolen from him, and the youngest member of his trail drive cooked inside the chuck wagon by men heedless of who was slain or injured in the course of acting out their crime.

And Mossman felt the same lack of concern for them.

His first thought had been Comancheros, maybe even friends of those his men had dealt with back at Devil's Crossing, but that didn't quite add up. For one thing, rustling a thousand steers wasn't the normal Comanchero stock-in-trade. And for another, even if they knew the thugs who'd died at Devil's Crossing, how could they select the Bar X drive for vengeance, even if they cared enough to try?

No, he'd decided. This was something else, beyond his personal experience.

The nearest town in the direction they were headed, Longwood, hadn't yet been settled when Mossman's first herd had made its one-way trip along the Cimarron five years ago. It was a new addition to the landscape, barely two years old, from what he'd heard, and last year Mossman had deliberately bypassed it, thinking the herd would cause unnecessary problems for a small crossroads community.

But now it seemed his missing steers were on their way directly toward that settlement, being guided by the men who'd stolen them. What that meant, only time would tell, and Mossman saw no point in making bets against himself as to the way it would play out.

Expect the worst, he thought, *and life will rarely let you down.*

Bᴀᴄᴋ ᴀᴛ ᴛʜᴇ Bar X campsite, Sterling Tippit wasn't thrilled with being left in charge of eight cowboys and half a herd of steers.

Granted, as foreman of the spread and on the yearly

trail drives, he would typically stand in between the
boss and working hands, making decisions without
running back to Mr. Mossman for permission, but today, looking around, that job felt more like punishment
than a promotion.

What, for instance, was he meant to do if Mossman
and the men he'd taken with him never made it back?
Should Tippit carry on with the surviving steers and
drovers to the Independence stockyards? Did he even
have legal authority to sell the longhorns that remained?

Worse yet, what would he tell Gayle Mossman and
her son?

Tippit was not the kind of man who panicked under
pressure, and had not reached his breaking point as
yet, but he knew well the risks of traveling uncharted
territory, taking on responsibility that normally be-
longed to his superiors. In war, that might result in
decorations or a battlefield promotion, but he wasn't in
the military, just a cowboy who was butting up against
the limits of his personal experience and duty.

Everyone Mossman had left behind in camp was
glum this morning, nerves on edge and tempers frayed.
Hands lingered close to guns as the remaining drovers
went about their normal tasks, watching for strays and
minimizing any further stress upon the stock. No one
could say what obstacle they might encounter next, assuming they moved on, or what would happen if they
turned the herd around to go back home.

Maybe financial ruin, for a start.

Tippit had seen the bank in Santa Fe where Mr.
Mossman kept his savings, but he'd never passed its
doors, knew nothing of how much money his boss had
gathered over time. They talked about buying supplies
as needed, and the market price of steers, but nothing
beyond that. Tippit knew how the ranch worked, under-

stood that one bad year could leave it hanging by a thread, but that was never meant to be his personal responsibility.

But now, if Mr. M was riding into trouble that he couldn't solve with five guns at his back, there would be misery enough to go around, and then some.

When the drovers came to him with questions now—when would their boss return? where had he gone? How long were they supposed to wait for news?—Tippit could only say that he had no idea.

And how much longer could he get away with that, before the drovers started to desert, as Julius Pryor had done?

They had no stake in the Bar X beyond the wages they'd been promised once the herd was sold in Independence. None of them were boss material or cared to be. If it became apparent that their leader wasn't coming back, why would they wait around indefinitely to protect his property?

In the short term, with the chuck wagon in ashes and no coffee served that morning, much less breakfast, Mossman's drovers could not be expected to remain on watch and starve, or do their best against another raid while stomachs growled and their strength failed.

Long term . . . well, Tippit didn't even care to think about that now.

The hell of it was that he didn't have a choice.

Longwood, Kansas

The town was nothing special from a distance, and Art Catlin found that drawing closer to it didn't change that first impression. It wasn't the smallest burg he'd seen—say twice the size of Devil's Crossing on the border between Ford and Hodgeman counties—but it was drab and weary-looking, likely nothing its inhabitants had any cause to celebrate.

As they approached it in midmorning, Catlin counted half a dozen shops, a livery, and a saloon. There was no church and nothing that he thought might be a school for any children living thereabouts. Art reckoned, from the look of it, that Longwood's citizens had slim hopes of prosperity and likely focused more on living hand to mouth.

Arriving at the town's outskirts, Art saw that he'd been wrong about one of the structures he'd mistaken for a store. It housed a marshal's office on the ground floor and what looked to be an office overhead. A sign out front identified it as the Longwood Justice Center, telling Catlin that its occupants were prone to ostentation.

Opposite that building stood the Badger's Tail Saloon and bawdy house, positioned as if staring down the local law.

Or were the two sides working in cahoots, perhaps?

The one thing that he didn't see was any further sign of longhorns in the neighborhood.

"No sign of any cattle," said Job Hooper as they passed a sign that read WELCOME TO LONGWOOD.

"Couldn't say for sure," Bliss Mossman answered. "With the state their main street's in, a herd could pass right through and out the other side without leaving a trace."

Eyeing the unpaved thoroughfare, such as it was, Catlin had to agree. The dirt was weathered, beaten flat by wagon wheels and horses' hooves, baked in the early summer sun. In autumn, he supposed that rain would make a swamp of it, the town prepared to freeze in winter under snow and ice.

"Reckon we'll have to ask around," Mike Limbaugh said.

"Or not," Catlin replied as two men wearing badges stepped out of the marshal's office, studying the new arrivals. One of them, the apparent man in charge, waved them across the street to join him where he stood, his deputy beside him, on a sidewalk made of wooden planks.

"You look like cattlemen to me," the marshal said.

"And you have a discerning eye," Mossman replied.

"Climb down and come inside, why don't you?" said the town's mouthpiece. Then, to his deputy, "Alonzo, go and fetch the judge, the mayor, and Mr. Crull."

Before dismounting, Mossman asked, "You always call the big guns in before receiving a complaint, Marshal?"

"Whitesell's the name. And answering your question, no, not as a rule. Thing is, I know what you've come looking for. We need to have a talk."

M AYOR HARDING CLEARED his throat and looked around Bert Whitesell's crowded office. Nine men exceeded any number that he'd seen inside that room before, five of the drovers short on chairs, with Deputy Alonzo Markland stationed outside the front door.

"I guess you wonder why I've called you here," said Harding, after they had all been introduced to one another.

"I might be," Bliss Mossman replied, "except you didn't call us here. We came to ask about some cattle stolen from my herd last night, a few miles out of town."

"A point well-taken," Harding said, feeling a tinge of blush rise in his cheeks. "Let's start by pardoning each other for misspeaking, shall we?"

"Come again?" the trail boss said.

"Granting that you weren't summoned here, but

would have been in time, it's my task to inform you that your steers were not stolen."

The drover's shifted nervously, and Harding felt tense beads of sweat accumulating under the stiff collar of his dress shirt.

"You-all may have another name for it around here," Mossman said. "But when a bunch of men with guns show up at midnight, stampede half my herd while throwing shots around and burning my chuck wagon, that's theft to me."

Harding cleared his throat again, felt foolish doing it, before he said, "In fact, we call it confiscation."

"You had best explain that, Mr. Harding," Mossman said.

"Landowners hereabouts have suffered damage from herds crossing private property, mistaking it for open range."

"Nothing was posted," Mossman told him.

"Be that as it may, the land *is* held in private hands. Its owners have complained to Marshal Whitesell more than once."

"About my herd?" Mossman challenged.

"And herds in general," Harding replied. "Last night, a confiscation was performed, pending a legal resolution of the trespass, and a special deputy was wounded in performance of his duty. That offense, all by itself, could lead to prison time."

"What deputy?" Mossman demanded. "All we saw was men on horseback, firing in the air around midnight, stampeding half of my longhorns. None of the raiders bothered to identify themselves as lawmen, and they wounded one of my men, too. You want to see Francisco's leg? He's standing right behind me."

"The deputies complain of being fired upon before they had a chance to speak," said Harding. "Am I right about that, Marshal?"

"Right as rain," Bert Whitesell said.

"I don't accept that," Bliss Mossman replied.

"Unfortunately, your acceptance of the law is neither here nor there." Turning to Odell Butler, Harding said, "Judge, if you don't mind weighing in on this?"

BUTLER UNDERSTOOD WHAT Harding and the other town officials were expecting him to say. He also realized that if he failed to play his part in the charade, the consequences might be dire. That said, it still required a nearly Herculean effort for him to respond as Longwood's justice of the peace.

"I understand our visitor's confusion," he began, "but as the law now stands, his violations are clear-cut. We have trespassing for a start, which calls for reparations at the very least. Concerning Marshal Whitesell's injured deputy, that matter is more serious."

"I'm not a lawyer," Bliss Mossman replied, "but I *do* know that seizure of a person's property requires an order from a court with legal jurisdiction."

"Which I serve as justice of the peace," Butler replied, drawing a folded piece of paper from an inside pocket of his frock coat. "And this is my order for seizure of the property at issue, to wit, livestock."

Butler saw no need to mention that he'd finished writing out the order over breakfast that morning, backdating it to make it seem legitimate.

Mossman perused the writ and slid it back across the table toward its author. "Am I right in thinking that you're Longwood's justice of the peace?" he asked.

"Yes. As I have just explained, sir."

"Then I take it that your jurisdiction is restricted to the town itself?"

Butler resisted grimacing despite a sudden clenching

of his ample stomach. "I'm afraid that I don't take your meaning, Mr. Moth . . . er, that is, Mossman."

"Well, you have a county seat at Alma, forty miles or so northwest of here. Wabaunsee County has a sheriff and a district court as usual?"

"I'm not sure—"

"And *they* would have proper jurisdiction over matters such as this." He made a careless flicking motion toward Butler's court order with two fingers of his left hand. "And since these so-called deputies came out ten miles or so from town to grab my cattle, it appears to me that neither you nor Marshal Whitesell has a whit of jurisdiction over anything that may have happened well beyond the town's limits."

At that, attorney Tilman Crull chimed in, giving Butler a chance to breathe. "That question *might* be in dispute," he said, "but a petition to the district court would mean an average delay of—what's your best guess, Marshal? Ten days, more or less?"

"Could be a couple weeks," Whitesell replied. "Of course, we'd have to hold the cattle till it all got sorted out."

Mossman was silent for a long moment, eyes shifting from one adversary to the next, his anger palpable. At last, he said, "But let me guess, now. You-all have a plan to make the problem go away?"

"That's most perceptive of you," Harding said. "And yes, we do."

ART CATLIN HAD one hand resting on the curved butt of his Colt Dragoon, prepared for anything, as Mr. Mossman said, "All right, I'm listening."

"As an alternative to costly and protracted litigation," said the man identified as Crull, "a civil judgment could be entered on the town's behalf, settled by you, to see the case resolved and put to bed."

"Ransom, you mean," the Bar X boss replied.

"No, sir!" Marshal Whitesell objected. "That term indicates a criminal extortion. Under law, as ordered by Judge Butler, you would pay a fine for trespassing and injuring the deputy, at which time any confiscated property would be yours to take away as you see fit."

"A fine," Mossman repeated, with a wry expression on his face as if the word itself was steeped in vinegar.

"Precisely," Crull agreed.

"And how much might that come to?"

The mayor turned to his judge. "Your Honor?"

"Um, yes. By my careful calculation, the longhorns would be three dollars each, and another fifty for the deputy. He's gutshot, by the way."

"Three thousand fifty, then," said Mossman.

"That would be correct, sir," Butler said. He sounded vaguely breathless as if nearly choking on the words.

"You understand that I don't carry that amount of money with me on the trail," Mossman replied. "It draws thieves in like crap lures flies."

"That *is* a problem," lawyer Crull put in. "But I can solve it for you, Mr. Mossman."

"Oh? How's that?"

"Your herd is bound for Independence, is it?"

"Should we ever get there," Mossman said.

"If you agree to pay the fine—in writing, duly notarized—perhaps Marshal Whitesell would ride along with you, collect the payment after sale, and bring it back."

"You'd trust him?" Mossman challenged. "I mean, with a roll of cash like that?"

Whitesell bristled at that. "I ain't the one who broke the law here," he protested.

"If a law *was* broken," Mossman countered, rising from the straight-backed wooden chair he occupied in front of Butler's desk. "As it stands, I'll need to think on this a bit, and maybe even sleep on it. Meanwhile, I need to see my cattle and make sure they're being taken care of properly."

"They've been secured on a ranch outside of town," said Marshall Whitesell. "As to any drop-in visits, I'd consider that unwise."

Mossman pinned the marshal with a gimlet gaze. "You want me to redeem them sight unseen, without even a head count? That ain't happening. Once I confirm what state they're in, I'll give your offer due consideration."

"If it solves the problem," Mayor Harding said, "why not?"

"Suppose he tries to pull a fast one?" Whitesell groused.

"I ain't the one who's got *your* stock penned up and maybe starving," Mossman said.

"Well . . ."

"Bert," the mayor responded. "Give an inch, will you?"

"All right, then," Whitesell granted. "I can have Alonzo take 'em by the Sutton spread before they sign off on the settlement."

"That's all I'm asking for," Mossman averred. "Just put my mind at ease."

"Okay," the marshal said, then shouted through the office door, "Alonzo! Get in here!"

CHAPTER EIGHTEEN

T HEIR RIDE OUT to the Sutton ranch took up the best
part of an hour, with Alonzo Markland rambling
on for most of that time, drawing no response from any
member of the Bar X posse. As the spread came into
view at last, Markland rode on ahead to "warn the owners," as he put it, of some unexpected company arriving.

Art Catlin was busy eyeballing the run-down house
and barn as Mossman's party followed up, searching
for any indications of an ambush, finding none. From
fifty yards, they glimpsed the first few longhorns wan-
dering around a fenced-in field behind the ranch
house, Mossman urging his flea-bitten gray gelding to
greater speed, his drovers keeping pace.

"I want you watching out for any signs of injury," he
told them as they neared the fence. "After the run they
had last night, some of 'em could be lame."

Which, Catlin realized, would mean a loss for the
Bar X. If steers could not proceed to market in a timely
fashion, they would have to be put down without

reaching the point of sale, putting a crimp in Mossman's pocketbook. Without a chuck wagon, they couldn't even save the beef for vittles on the portion of their journey that remained.

As they surveyed the stock, Alonzo Markland came back with an older man in overalls. Art couldn't guess his age beyond a range somewhere between forty and sixty years. The younger age would mean he'd led a hard life on the prairie, while the latter might have chalked him up as well preserved.

"Joe Sutter," the landowner introduced himself. "You come to bail your cattle out for trespassing?"

"Thinking about it," Mr. Mossman said. "I need to look them over first."

"You'll find 'em in the same condition they came in here," Sutter said. "I ain't been feeding 'em because I can't afford it."

"But you volunteered to take them in," Catlin observed.

"Well . . . sure. It were my civic duty, weren't it?"

"Or a paying job," Art said.

"Can't say I follow you," the rancher answered in a grumpy voice.

"Never mind that," Mossman interrupted. "Deputy, go back and tell your boss I've seen enough for now."

"Meaning what?"

"Meaning I'll speak to him in person if there's any more to say."

They left him standing there, against the paddock fence, and started back to camp. When they had ridden for a hundred yards or so, Job Hooper asked the boss, "What are we gonna do, sir?"

"Get those cattle back and settle up in Longwood," Mossman answered back.

"How do you see us doing that?" Catlin inquired.

Without a backward glance, the boss said, "I ain't

worked it out yet, but I guess something will come to me."

They rode on for another while before Mossman asked Catlin, "Art? Did you see any guards around the Sutter place?"

"Nobody showing in the house's windows or around the barn, boss. Doesn't mean they haven't got some people hiding out. I couldn't see inside the hayloft or the privy, nor around behind the house."

"Right, then," Mossman said. "I figure that they'd have to leave at least a couple men to keep the old man company while this plays out.

"And there were eight or nine of 'em, at least, that hit the camp last night," Guenther recalled.

"Plus Fielding," Mossman said. "Don't leave that tricky bastard out."

"He's likely miles away by now," said Mike Limbaugh.

"If he got paid," their boss amended. "If he's not, tonight I'm gonna make him wish he was."

"They claim one man was wounded," Catlin said. "If true, that makes at least fourteen we're up against, plus maybe old man Sutter."

"And another one in town," Mossman amended.

"Who is that, boss?" Francisco Gallardo asked.

"Whoever thought up the whole thing," their boss replied.

"How do you figure that, boss?" Guenther, bringing up the rear, inquired.

Mossman glanced back, half-smiling. "Because those four didn't have the brains between 'em," he said. "Nor the nerve to pull it off."

Longwood, Kansas

"So, how'd they take it?" Murray Glatman asked the men arrayed before him in his office at the Beaver's Tail.

There were four of them in attendance: Mayor Harding, Marshal Whitesell and his slouching deputy, plus Odell Butler. Tilman Crull was at his own place, finalizing paperwork, or so he'd claimed.

Deputy Markland knew the question had been meant for him, since he'd accompanied the drovers to Joe Sutter's spread and seen them off from there. He told Glatman, "Guy said he'd seen enough, sir."

"He'd seen enough?"

"Yes, sir."

"How did he say it?"

That one seemed to puzzle Markland. "I don't follow you," he answered back.

"Tell me *exactly* what he said. Pretend you're him, Alonzo."

"Well, Mr. G, the best I recollect, it was 'Go back and tell your boss I seen enough for now.' Something like that. I even asked 'im what be meant by that."

"And?" Glatman prodded him.

"Guy says, 'I'll speak to him in person if there's any more to say.'"

Glatman was frowning now, not quite a scowl but working up to one. "Who do you think he meant by 'him,' Alonzo?"

"Tell my boss, he said. I figured that must be the marshal, here."

"No," Glatman said emphatically.

Alonzo tried again. "Maybe the mayor, then?"

"I doubt that very much."

"What are you getting at, Murray?" Harding inquired.

"He's onto me."

Four blank stares greeted his announcement. After half a minute, give or take, Bert Whitesell asked, "How could that be?"

"He's thinking past you-all," Glatman replied. "He's looking for the man behind the plan."

From their expressions, Murray Glatman could imagine wheels turning inside their heads. Harding and Whitesell looked vaguely insulted. Butler sat back, seeming almost relieved. Alonzo Markland, as he often did, just seemed confused.

Harding recovered first, saying, "That isn't possible."

"I don't mean he's onto *me*, exactly. But he reckons someone put all this together and the rest of you are . . . helping out."

It was the kindest way of putting these four in their proper place that Glatman could come up with on short notice. Watching Butler, Whitesell, and the mayor exchange glances, he saw the pieces falling into place.

"You see it now," said Glatman, maybe giving them more credit than was due.

"Well, now," said Whitesell, "I don't see—"

"Just take my word for it," Glatman commanded. "When this Mossman character comes back to get his steers, he won't be signing any papers promising you half of what he gets from Independence. No. He's in a taking mood, not promising you anything."

"You seem to know a lot about some guy you've never seen," Whitesell retorted.

"Not the man, per se. I know his type," Glatman corrected the town marshal. "Yes, indeed. I've known them all my life."

"I must say," Butler offered, "that sounds . . . ominous."

Glatman reached out for the whiskey bottle on his desk and poured himself a shot, not offering to share. Only when it had scorched his throat and lit a fire around his heart did he see fit to speak again.

"Your Honor, I believe you're right," he said. "In

fact, I'll see your 'ominous' and raise you an 'alarming.' Bert, those deputies of yours?"

"Yes, sir?"

"Make sure they're ready for another shivaree come sundown."

B LISS MOSSMAN FINISHED sketching out a rough map in the dirt a few yards from their erstwhile chuck wagon's ashes. With his drovers standing in a ring around him, studying what he had drawn, he thought the layout was complete.

A small *X* marked their camp and the remainder of his herd. A blocked-out square stood in for Longwood, while a circle represented Sutter's ranch, where Mossman's rustled stock was penned and waiting for release.

On balance, Mossman thought it looked more like a game of tic-tac-toe drawn by an idiot than anything his men could use to navigate a strike on two points simultaneously.

"As you see," he told the hands, "I ain't no artist, but I hope you get the point. Here, at the Sutter spread"— he poked the circle with his drawing stick—"is where they've got the steers. They won't risk moving 'em to town, since there's no place to hold 'em there. Tonight, I mean to go and fetch 'em back."

"How many men watching the herd, *jefe*?" asked Jaime Reyes.

"None we saw," Mossman replied. "But it's a safe bet they won't leave the stock unguarded overnight."

"How many of us go to bring 'em back?" asked Danny Underwood.

Frowning at that, Mossman replied, "We've got the same problem they do. I need some of you here to watch the longhorns we've got left. That splits the rest between the Sutter place and Longwood."

"Why go back to town at all?" Bryce Zimmerman inquired.

"Two reasons," Mossman answered. "First, smart money says they'll keep some of their guns there, covering the men behind this thing, and I don't want them chasing after us when we collect the stolen stock."

"And second?" Jerome Guenther asked.

"I want to send a message to the seven sons of bitches putting us through this."

"*¿Siete?* How you figure that, *jefe*?" asked Luis Chávez.

"Five we saw and spoke to," Mossman said. "On top of them, Jay Fielding or whatever his real name is, and the man who set it up."

"The one none of us knows," Mike Limbaugh said. "Makes him a little hard to pin down, boss."

"Not necessarily," Mossman replied. "We know he lives in town and has the brains, together with the cash, to set this up. He's someone who the others look up to, or else they're scared to go against him."

Art Catlin spoke up then, saying, "Someone who fits that bill, figure he runs a business of his own, and probably the biggest one in town. Everybody knows him or knows *of* him, even if they don't trade with him regularly."

"That'll work," Mossman agreed. "I'm thinking the saloon and bawdy house, across the street from what they're pleased to call their 'Justice Center.' And he shouldn't be too hard to find."

"So, what's the play, then, boss?" their wrangler, Jared Olney, asked.

"First thing, I need to know who's in or out," Mossman replied. "You've seen and done enough on this trip for a dozen cattle drives. There'd be no shame in backing out while you still can. I'll take a show of hands."

When none were raised, he pressed ahead. "All

right, then. Doing this the right way means we have to split three ways. Some stay to watch the stock, the rest divide between the Sutter place and Longwood. Beyond that, I'm open to suggestions. Anyone?"

Alonzo Markland wasn't sure if he should be angry over his relegation to the Sutter spread, or if he ought to feel relieved.

On the one hand, Mr. Glatman and Bert Whitesell had assigned four men to help him guard the place, and they were bound to follow Markland's orders since he had the only badge among them that meant anything. He knew them all by reputation—Clyde Byers, Doc Quigley, Hebron Walsh, and Myron Jarvis—trusting Whitesell's word that they were handy in a fight.

But on the *other* hand, Alonzo reckoned that if Mossman and his drovers made a move tonight, some trick instead of simply signing off on Mr. Glatman's deal to get their longhorns back, they'd have to raid the Sutter place—and that meant Markland would be front and center on the firing line.

He could forget about Joe Sutter, blind in one eye and the other going hazy on him? So it would be five men counting Markland, ranged against however many hands Bliss Mossman reckoned he could spare while still guarding the livestock he had left.

Shading his eyes, Alonzo peered into the sky and estimated that some three hours remained until sundown. If he were back in Longwood, he'd be stopping by the Badger's Tail before too long, to wet his whistle with a beer or something stronger. Drinking while on duty was against the rules, of course, but in a small town where it seemed that nothing ever happened, Markland didn't see the harm in it.

As for tonight, though, he supposed the safest thing was staying on his toes.

Coffee might help, but he'd already tried a cup of Sutter's brew and found it tasted like dishwater passed through a rusty sieve. Before he tried that swill again, Alonzo thought he'd have a drink out of the farm's horse trough.

Joe Sutter lived alone, being a widower who'd never fathered any children Markland knew about. If some existed, Sutter never spoke of them and it was certain none were part of Longwood's mismatched population.

There was no denying that the town was . . . peculiar. It seemed to have an odd magnetic quality, attracting losers from all over Kansas and a few out of Missouri, too. Markland himself had traveled all the way from Texas before winding up in Longwood, passing by the marshal's office where a window sign announced NEED DEPUTY. Next thing Alonzo knew, he was the second lawman in a burg that barely needed one, but who was he to spurn four dollars weekly and a roof over his head year-round?

The change from what Longwood had been to what it was now set in when Murray Glatman turned up with a wagon full of whores and whiskey, plus another full of lumber, and hired shiftless local men to start construction on the Badger's Tail. When it was done and making money, Glatman found himself the town's top man, able to rig elections since the yokels didn't care who called the shots, as long as things ran smoothly and seemed relatively fair.

So why am I guarding a herd of stolen longhorns, waiting for the rightful owners to show up and take them back? Alonzo asked himself.

"For money, that's what," Markland answered, troubled at discovering he'd said the words aloud. At least nobody was around to overhear him talking to himself, but he would have to watch that all the same.

And that, in turn, meant he would have to make it through the coming night alive.

STERLING TIPPIT HAD his choice of men to leave behind, guarding the half herd that was verging on its second night camped in the same place, watching dusk descend.

Because he wasn't staying with them, Tippit had picked Jared Olney to protect the drive's remuda, Piney Rollins due to age and inexperience, Bryce Zimmerman for his Winchester Model 1866, and Francisco Gallardo since his wounded leg was acting up a bit following the rounds of Longwood and the Sutter ranch.

Tippit's assignment was to hit the ranch and bring back Mr. Mossman's steers at any cost. To that end, he'd be riding with five Bar X drovers: Danny Underwood, Linton McCormick, Zeb Steinmeier, Jerome Guenther, and Jaime Reyes. He had no idea what they'd be running into, but assumed resistance was a given.

That left Bliss Mossman riding into Longwood with four hands behind him. Art Catlin was probably the coolest head among them, with Job Hooper, Mike Limbaugh, and Luis Chávez backing him.

Splitting their forces was a bad idea, in Sterling's estimation, but he didn't call the shots and ultimately had the least to lose if Mr. M's plan fell apart. In that case, Mossman might lose everything he'd built up over time.

All Tippit stood to forfeit was his life.

And who would even give a damn when he was gone? Nobody he could think to name.

When he saw Piney Rollins headed his way, Tippit braced himself. He knew their cook was at loose ends, but finding a replacement for their chuck wagon and various supplies wasn't Sterling's priority just now. Aside from bringing back the stolen longhorns, Sterling was supposed to keep an eye out for a suitable wagon, prepared to offer Joe Sutter fair payment for it if the old man didn't try to fight them on the steers.

And if he *did*, Sutter stood to lose more than a wagon when the smoke cleared.

"Mr. Tippit!" Piney called out to him. "Can I have a word?"

"I'll try to find a wagon for you," Sterling told him, "but the stock comes first, you understand."

"Sure, sure." Piney waved that away and said, "It's something else."

"Go on, then. We're just getting ready to light out."

"That Fielding fella. You know he's the one that lit the wagon up and cooked young Berryman?"

"We figured that," Tippit replied.

"Well, if you see him—"

"I intend to put him down. It's on my list."

"I thought it might be. One thing, though, before you blow his candle out."

"What's that?"

"I wish you'd tell him it's for Tim."

A RT CATLIN WATCHED the sun set on Wabaunsee County while his strawberry roan stallion carried him toward Longwood and what waited for Bliss Mossman's riders there.

Whatever that might prove to be, he reckoned it would mean blood spilled and bodies ripe for burial.

As far as Catlin was concerned, their boss was probably correct in his surmise that whoever held sway over the Badger's Tail Saloon and brothel might well be the brains behind their current plight—but *probably* and *definitely* were two entirely different things. His own experience at hunting fugitives from justice taught Art that he was fallible and sometimes chased false trails to an unsatisfying end.

If that turned out to be the case tonight, his life was riding on the line along with Mossman's and the rest.

The flip side of that coin was that Longwood harbored at least five obvious extortionists: the mayor, its justice of the peace, the attorney, the marshal, and his deputy. If Jay Fielding was still hanging around, he bumped the total up to six and would outnumber Mossman's party.

On the other hand, Catlin wasn't as worried by the odds as he would have been if they were going up against that many skilled gunfighters. His first meeting with Cyrus Harding told Art that the mayor wasn't a fighting man at heart. Ditto the lawyer, who seemed used to winning quarrels with his mouth. Judge Butler, for his part, was obviously shaky, acting like a man with one foot in the grave.

If need be, he could get a shove in that direction soon enough.

Which left Marshal Whitesell, Whitesell's second-in-command, and maybe Fielding, if that was in fact his name. Those three were armed and possibly acquainted with killing, although Art doubted that they had much call for shooting in Longwood. Arresting the odd drunk or wife-beater was more likely their speed, and if they hadn't kept in practice on the killing side, there was a chance their nerve might fail them when it mattered most.

And Fielding?

That one was a puzzle Catlin hadn't yet resolved. The man had wormed his way into Bliss Mossman's confidence, seemed friendly to the other Bar X drovers, but he'd also graduated to the top of Catlin's suspect list for knifing Nehemiah Wolford while they were on watch together, two nights earlier.

Art couldn't work out why Fielding had murdered Wolford, and the motive wasn't preying on his mind. The possibility of it—established now as fact in Catlin's mind, along with the torching of the Bar X chuck wagon, frying Tim Berryman alive—was all he needed to square off against the infiltrator for a showdown.

That is, if the Judas who'd betrayed them hadn't pocketed his money and lit out as soon as he got back to Longwood, after setting up the midnight raid on Mossman's herd.

What kind of adversary would he prove to be? Again, Art couldn't say.

Fielding carried two Colts, but that could be a bit of ostentation on his part. Some of the two-gun outlaws Art had known and brought to book could barely handle one six-shooter when the chips were down. That would not be a safe assumption with a man who'd slain two people Catlin knew of personally, but the way Fielding had killed—stabbing one unsuspecting victim, setting a teenage boy on fire—was very different from facing down a man who'd buried sixteen wanted criminals and put eleven more behind steel bars.

Guess I'll just have to wait and see, Art thought, and part of him was hoping that he got the chance to do exactly that.

CHAPTER NINETEEN

The Sutter Ranch

STERLING TIPPIT SAT astride his blood bay mare, surrounded by the five men he'd selected and addressing them in whispers.

"You can see the layout pretty well from here," he said. "No sign of anybody stirring, but I'd bet a month's pay that we're bound to run into some guns. Watch out for shooters in the house or hiding in its shadow, likewise for the barn. If they cut loose on us, defend yourselves but spare the cattle. They're the main reason we're here."

"And what if we're outnumbered?" Zebulon Steinmeier asked.

"Same thing as back in Devil's Crossing, when the Comancheros had us two or three to one. We made it out; they didn't."

"And whoever runs the place, *jefe*?" Jaime Reyes inquired. "Will he be fighting?"

"I couldn't tell you, one way or another," Tippit said. "The boss says he's an old guy, didn't have a weapon when they met him earlier today, but who would stake a claim out here with nothing to protect him? Take for granted that whoever's firing at you has to be an enemy."

"And we're not taking prisoners?" Linton McCormick asked.

"We ain't lawmen," Sterling replied. "The only thing we're after here is property that Longwood's thieves already stole from us. If they decide to give it up without a fight, so much the better, but we'd be a bunch of idiots to count on that."

"My momma didn't raise no fools," said Danny Underwood.

"Remember that," said Tippit, "and you should come through all right. More questions?"

No one spoke, so Tippit cocked his head downrange, toward what appeared to be a sleeping ranch, and said, "Okay, let's go. And fan out so we don't make one big target."

The Bar X foreman's heart was in his throat as he rode toward the pen that held their stolen cattle, circling around the east side of the Sutter spread. He wished that they weren't backlit by a nearly full three-quarter moon, but all his men had donned the darkest shirts that they possessed before departing camp. It might not help them in the long run, but he figured anything was worth a try.

If they could only reach the paddock unobserved and start to drive the longhorns out before any lookouts dispatched from Longwood opened fire . . .

That hope went up in gun smoke seconds later, when they'd closed to roughly half their starting distance from the ranch proper. A rifle shot cracked out below them, Tippit glimpsing the suggestion of a muzzle flash along the east end of the ranch house, then two others opened up and set the night to echoing.

"That tears it!" he told anyone inclined to listen. "Keep your heads down, boys, and ride like hell!"

Longwood

Art Catlin sat beside Luis Chávez, both drovers mounted, pistols in their hands, staring along the settlement's main street from the north end of town.

Bliss Mossman had divided his combatants as they neared Longwood with night upon them, sending Catlin and Chávez around to block any opponents fleeing northward, while their boss closed from the south with Job Hooper and Mike Limbaugh. Catlin was undecided as to whether that was wise or foolish, but he hadn't questioned it up front, and now it was too late.

Their target was designated as the Longwood "Justice Center," though Art saw no reason to suppose the mayor, the marshal, or Judge Butler would still be there, now that suppertime had come and gone. There was a possibility, of course, but if he and Chávez missed any of the men they'd come to find, it meant they'd have to start searching the town from door to door.

And that, as Catlin knew, would just make matters worse.

His first choice for a secondary place to cover was the Badger's Tail saloon, but Mossman had reserved that for himself and his companions, still convinced they'd find the man behind their livestock loss somewhere inside. If he was wrong on that score, both groups might be homing in on targets that would turn out to be duds.

In which case, what should they do next?

Forget about it, Catlin thought. He would have kept

his fingers crossed for luck, but that would only interfere with shooting if the need arose.

Without streetlights of any kind, the shapes of
Mossman, Hooper, and Limbaugh were barely shadow
shapes as they approached the Badger's Tail, but Catlin took it as his cue to move.

"We're up," he told Chávez, and urged his strawberry roan stallion toward the marshal's office on the
ground floor of the Justice Center. Reining in before
he reached that destination, Art dismounted at a hitching rail outside the hardware shop next door and looped
his horse's reins over the rail without securing them.

If anything went wrong from that point on, he
hoped the animal, at least, would manage to escape.

Beside him, Chávez slid down from the saddle his cremello stallion wore and joined Art on the wooden sidewalk leading toward the marshal's door. A lamp inside
the office, turned down low, cast dim light through a window that had gone too long without a decent washing.

As they reached it, Catlin looked inside and saw
Bert Whitesell hunched over his desk, eating a sand-
wich that had dribbled leaky contents on a stack of
"Wanted" posters set in front of him.

"Stay here and cover me," he told Chávez, then
pushed in through the office door.

"Well, now," Whitesell remarked, setting his sand-
wich down while his right hand dipped out of sight,
below his desktop.

The Sutter Ranch

Alonzo Markland saw the riders coming and tried to
whistle through his teeth in warning, but the best that
he could manage was a hissing sound that made him
think of snakes crawling around his feet.

He thought of calling out instead, to rally his supporting gunmen, but Alonzo reckoned that would only tip off the horsemen that they'd been observed and might be coming under fire. Instead, he cocked his Colt New Line revolving rifle—not so new these days, since factory production of it had ceased in 1864—and braced its twenty-four-inch barrel on the top rail of a fence he'd chosen as his lookout post.

Now all he had to do was wait until his targets closed the gap between them and he had a chance to bring them under fire.

But someone beat Alonzo to it, with seconds to spare, the shot ringing out from behind him, its round flying over his head.

Cursing whoever fired that shot, Markland observed his targets scattering, three riders veering sharply to the left, three others jinking in the opposite direction. Following one trio with his Colt's iron sights, Alonzo fired and lost sight of all three behind a cloud of the long gun's black powder smoke.

Before he had another chance to aim and fire, the new arrivals opened up with everything they had, their muzzle flashes blinking at him, bullets sizzling on both sides of Alonzo and above his head. Behind him, his supporting gunmen—Quigley, Byers, Walsh, and Jarvis—were returning fire with more enthusiasm than good marksmanship, the hostile riders still advancing steadily.

Markland decided that the cedar split-rail fence in front of him made lousy cover against gunfire, and started running in an awkward crouch back toward the barn, trying to make himself as small as possible to hostile snipers. Pausing to return fire was a luxury Alonzo didn't think he could afford just now, so he increased his pace and started weaving in a serpentine pattern he hoped would spoil the aim of anyone intent on drilling him.

He had nearly reached his destination when a bullet found him, white-hot pain causing his hands to spasm and release his rifle. Worse, it fell directly into his path, tripped him, and pitched him face foremost into the rough siding of Sutter's barn.

On impact, Markland felt his nose splinter, then nothing as he slithered to the ground, his mouth and spurting nostrils leaving bloody tracks that looked jet-black under the moon's wan light.

Longwood

"All right, we're square now," Murray Glatman told the man standing before his desk and counting greenbacks in varied denominations, lips moving as he kept track.

Jed Findlay finished, rolled the bills, and stuffed them in the left-front pocket of his denim jeans. "All square," he granted as he turned to exit Glatman's office in the Badger's Tail.

Glatman craned forward in his swivel chair, stopped Fielding with his right hand on the doorknob, then asked, "But are you sure that you don't want to stick around a little longer?"

Findlay smiled at him, surprising Glatman. "Why would I do that?" he asked. "To get my head blown off by cowboys stewing over how I killed a couple of their own?"

"Maybe to take them out if they can't recognize a good deal when they're staring at it."

"Or they're riled at getting screwed," Findlay replied, still with that vaguely mocking smile.

"Look at it this way," Glatman urged him. "Say they

take me out and all the others. If you're not around, you think they'll just forget about what you've already done and let you get away with it?"

"If they pass on your offer," Findlay said, "I reckon you and yours will slow 'em down enough to let me have a fair head start. Once I clear out, they won't know where to look or even know my name."

"I didn't take you for a man who leaves unfinished business," Glatman said.

"Our business *is* finished," Findlay replied. "You just said so yourself."

Glatman allowed himself a shrug and tried to make it casual. "What's wrong with making a new deal, for higher stakes?"

"How much?" the gunman asked.

"What would you say to five percent?"

Fielding surprised Glatman by laughing that away. When he'd recovered from that first gale of hilarity, the younger man inquired, "That would be five percent of *what*, exactly, if the trail boss turns you down?"

"First thing to keep in mind," Glatman replied, "their boss has no idea of who I am or what I have to do with it."

"You sure of that?" asked Fielding. "Are you trusting any of your milquetoast partners to keep quiet once he sticks a pistol in their faces? Hell, first thing they'll do after wetting themselves is give you up."

"I'll take that as your final no, then, should I?"

"It's a no all right . . . at least, at five percent."

"Are we negotiating now?" Glatman inquired.

"Maybe." Fielding considered it, then said, "From here on in, I want a hundred bucks for any man I have to kill. The first two, you can say were on the house."

"Agreed," said Glatman, "but I'll limit that to gunmen from the cattle drive. I wouldn't want you dropping any decent townsfolk by mistake."

Instead of laughing this time, Fielding answered, "Decent townsfolk? Where would I find one of those?"

"I'm done sparring with you," Glatman told him. "Do we have a deal or not?"

"We do," said Fielding. "Just be damned sure that you don't run short of cash."

As if to punctuate that sentence, a gunshot reached Glatman's ears, echoing from the Badger's Tail barroom.

B LISS MOSSMAN SHOULDERED through the bar's front swinging doors, with Mike Limbaugh and Job Hooper immediately on his heels. The Bar X boss was carrying his Winchester '73, his two companions bearing a Springfield Model 1871 and a Bridesburg Model 1861 respectively, besides the pistols on their hips.

Across the room, four men wearing gun belts were bellied up against the bar. None of them looked familiar from behind, or in the backbar mirror, but an instant failure to identify them did nothing to put Mossman at ease. He had not seen the men who'd run off with his steers last night, except as shapes on horseback, racing through the dark and firing randomly to cover their escape.

The hinges on the batwing door to Mossman's left-hand side squealed out a plea for oil, announcing new arrivals in the barroom. One of the four drinkers glanced up at the backbar mirror, froze with his beer mug poised halfway to his lips, then glanced over his shoulder to confirm what he'd already seen.

"Jesus!" he blurted out. "It's them!"

The speaker dropped his beer, spilling its amber dregs across the bar top as his three companions turned to face the street exit. Suddenly, as one, they reached for holstered six-shooters before Mossman could caution them against it.

Maybe facing murder charges for the man and boy
Mossman had lost made them a trifle hasty, but it didn't
matter now. Dropping to one knee with his rifle shouldered, Mossman sighted on the first man who had seen
them enter, squeezing off a .44-40 Winchester round
from thirty feet or so. His bullet closed the gap in an
eighth of a second, struck his target near the midline of
his chest, and slammed him back against the bar before
the enemy's pistol cleared leather.

Nonetheless, his adversary, falling, still managed to
fire a shot into the barroom's floor, missing his own
right foot by an inch as he collapsed.

While Mossman pumped the lever action on his Winchester, Hooper and Limbaugh nailed two more of the
gunmen, their bodies dropping through a crimson mist
of blood to join their comrade on the barroom's floor.
That left one standing, pistol in his hand and firing
back, but in his haste he only blasted out one of the
windows facing onto Main Street, missing all three of
the riflemen before him.

It turned out to be a fatal error as a second round
from Mossman's Winchester ripped through the gunman's throat and left him slumped against the bar, left
arm outflung to hold him upright while his pistol wavered aimlessly. He lasted for about another second
and a half, then folded, dropping to his knees before
he toppled over on his face.

Rising, Mossman told his men, "Fan out. We're looking for the boss, maybe an office. Wherever he is, don't
let him get away."

The Sutter Ranch

Sterling Tippit found the deputy from Longwood
where he'd fallen by the barn. Inside that structure,
pocked with bullet holes over the past few minutes,

Danny Underwood and Zebulon Steinmeier had another gunman cornered in the hayloft, trading shots with him by lantern light.

Peering inside the barn, Tippit discovered that its stalls were empty, no livestock of any kind in evidence besides the stolen longhorns lowing from the paddock out in back. Steinmeier caught sight of him and called out, "This one's dug in like a tick, I'm not sure we can root him out, but if we do, it's gonna take a while."

"So, treat him like you would a tick," Tippit advised, nodding in the direction of an oil lamp standing on a shelf against the barn's west wall.

"Good thinking," Zeb replied, and scurried to retrieve the lamp while Underwood pinned down their adversary with his Sharps rifle, each shot a thunderclap inside vacant barn.

Returning with the lantern, Steinmeier ran as close as he could manage, trusting Underwood to cover him, then lobbed it overhand, an arcing toss into the hayloft. Tippit heard glass shatter on impact, and seconds later, flames were leaping as the oil set fire to musty bales of hay up there.

The hayloft sniper stuck it out another thirty seconds, give or take, before he tossed his rifle down and called out to the cowboys he'd been dueling with, "Don't shoot, all right? I give up! Just don't let me cook up here!"

Raising his voice, Tippit advised the shooter, "Throw down any other guns you've got and show us empty hands!"

"That Henry's all I had," their enemy replied. "I'm coming out now!"

And he did, hands raised to shoulder height, bareheaded, coughing from the smoke that swirled around him. Tippit looked the gunman over with his own Sharps carbine centered on the fellow's barrel chest.

"All right," he said. "You can start down the ladder. Make it slow and careful."

"Coming down, yessir!"

But as he reached the hayloft's overlook above them, one hand darted to his back and came out clutching a revolver, smallish, probably a .32 or .36. Three rifles cracked and boomed as one and blew his ragdoll figure backward, sacrificed to the voracious flames.

"Clear outta here," Tippit ordered his men, and led the way outside.

They reached the farmyard just as their companions— Guenther, Reyes, and McCormick—were returning from the ranch house, prodding an unarmed old man in front of them.

"We left the other two around in back, *jefe*," Reyes explained. "They won't be going nowhere now."

"And who's this?" Tippit asked.

Their captive answered for himself. "Joe Sutter, mister. I'm no part of this fight."

"But you let 'em stash our cattle here," Tippit reminded him.

"You don't know what they're like," Sutton replied. "Run roughshod over everyone in town and here-abouts. This place is all I have."

He glanced back toward the barn, smoke pouring from its loft, flames visible, a roaring sound emerging that reminded Tippit of a dragon's snore. "I take that back. It's all I *had*."

"Remember who's to blame for that if anybody comes around here later, asking," Tippit cautioned him. "The county sheriff may not charge you if you sell him on the notion you were forced to go along."

"And that's God's truth," Sutter averred.

"Best leave God out of it and make it known how weak you are, no backbone, all of that."

"So, you ain't gonna kill me, then?" asked Sutter.

"Did you want us to?" Sterling replied.

"No, sir! Can't rightly say what I'll be living for from here on in, but if it's my choice, I'll play out my string."

"Suits me," Tippit agreed. Then, to his drovers, "Best be clearing out those steers while we can handle 'em, before the fire gets them all riled and ready for another run."

Longwood

"You came without your boss this time?" Bert Whitesell asked.

"He's busy elsewhere," Catlin said.

"Trying to wrap it up another way, I guess."

"You're not as stupid as you look," Art told the marshal.

Whitesell shrugged, his right hand still concealed beneath his desk's top. "Well, I won't deny feeling a little foolish now," he said.

"Just so you know," Catlin informed him, "we've got people taking back the steers you people stole."

"I didn't take 'em," said the lawman. "Hell, it wasn't even my idea."

"You played along, though. Looking for your cut."

"Who wouldn't have?"

"The fact you have to ask tells me that you're unfit to wear that star."

"It looks good on me, though, don't it?" The marshal teasing him a little.

"Not for much longer."

"You here to kill me, then? Don't wanna call the boy you left outside to help you?"

"That's your call," Catlin replied. "My preference would be to lock you up, along with all the rest involved with this, and send a rider for the county sheriff once we're on the road."

"That's one way it could go, I guess," Whitesell agreed.

"Play nice in court, give up the others, and you might even reduce your prison time."

"Makes sense, I guess," said Whitesell. "But I gotta tell you, I ain't big on the idea of living in a cage."

"At least it's living," Catlin said. "You can direct us to the others and we'll bring 'em here to you. You-all can sit around commiserating till the circuit judge shows up."

Whitesell made no response to that, prompting Catlin to say, "We'll get them, one way or another. Say your mayor to start, that lawyer—if he even is one—and your so-called justice of the peace."

"Nobody else?" the marshal asked him now.

"Maybe a couple more. I'd like to see the one who called himself Jay Fielding when he joined the drive."

"His real name's Findlay, if that helps you. Jed, not Jay, unless he lied to us about that, too."

"Where might I find him?" Catlin asked. "I'd call you 'Marshal,' but I'm worried I might choke on it."

"I feel that way from time to time myself. Last time I seen him, he was headed for the Badger's Tail, wanting Glatman to pay him off."

"Who's Glatman?" Art inquired, although he had a hunch, remembering Bliss Mossman's words from their last time in camp.

Whitesell's laughter surprised him. "Murray Glatman? Why, he's nothing but the man behind this whole damned thing. He thought it up and talked us into it, though I admit it didn't take a too much persuasion."

"Runs the bar and whorehouse, does he?" Catlin asked.

"And more besides. Good luck with him. He'll likely chew you up and spit you out again."

"I'll take my chances," Catlin answered.

"That's about how I feel," Whitesell said, and whipped his right hand out from under cover, fingers clasped around the butt of a Schofield revolver.

Catlin's Colt Navy revolver beat him to it, belching a .44 slug that ripped into Whitesell's chest, pitching him over backward and his chair along with him. The only part of him still visible after he fell was from the knees down—or knees *up*, as he landed. From where Catlin was standing, he could see a hole in Whitesell's left boot sole.

Pathetic.

Luis Chávez poked his head inside the marshal's office, scanning left and right, while Catlin walked around the desk to verify that Whitesell wasn't getting up again without a man or two to hoist him, turning back to Chávez as they heard gunfire across the street, coming from the direction of the Badger's Tail.

Catlin and his companion reached the Main Street sidewalk as that firing ceased. Off to their right, a sound of rattling and clopping hooves alerted them to other people on the move. As they stood watching, lawyer Tilman Crull broke from the livery, astride a palomino, racing toward the northern end of town without a backward glance. Close on his heels, the hunched form of Judge Butler occupied a buckboard drawn by what appeared to be a sable roan.

Luis Chávez had his Colt Navy pistol raised, was lining up a shot, when Catlin pushed the weapon's muzzle down. "Forget about them," he instructed. "It's high time we paid a call on the saloon and him that owns it."

The Badger's Tail

"Sounds like our company's arrived," Glatman advised Jed Findlay, rising from the padded swivel chair behind his desk, drawing a Colt Pocket Police revolver from its chamois leather harness under his left arm. "Shall we go down and meet them?"

"Nope. I reckon not," Findlay replied.

"Say what?"

"I changed my mind," said Findlay. "You can deal with 'em yourself. I'm clearing out."

"You'll go without your ten percent, then," Glatman cautioned him.

"It's looking more like ten percent of dead," said Findlay. "I can do without that, thank you all the same."

"You're running out on me, you bastard?"

"Fast as I can travel," Jed affirmed. "And for the record, my parents were married."

Glatman raised his six-gun, tried to keep the motion smooth and fast, but Fielding drew his right-hand Peacemaker with deadly speed and fanned a shot almost before the gun cleared leather, echoing like thunder inside Glatman's office.

Glatman had no opportunity to fire his Colt. A .44-caliber bullet drilled him through the breadbasket and punched him back against the built-in bookshelves ranged along the wall behind his desk. Eyes glazing over in a rush, darkness descending like the curtain at a theater, he toppled forward and felt nothing as his face collided with the nearest corner of his desk.

Glatman was stone-cold dead before he hit the floor, staining the office carpet with his blood.

A RT CATLIN RAN around the back side of the Badger's Tail while Luis Chávez watched the front.

Before they split up, Catlin saw Bliss Mossman in the barroom with Job Hooper and Mike Limbaugh, standing over dead men, with their rifles primed to deal with any more who might appear. He left them to it, dashing down a narrow alleyway beside the Badger's Tail and winding up out back just as a figure shoved through the saloon's back door.

"Findlay!" he called. "That's far enough."

"I'd have to disagree with you on that, Art," Findlay answered back. He stopped, though, hands dangling loosely over his twin Colt Peacemakers. "Who tipped you off about my name?"

"The fake lawman they used to have."

"No longer with us, is he?"

"Gone to his reward."

"Can't say I'm sorry, but I sense there's something else you want to ask, before we tie this up."

"There is," Catlin agreed. "I understand you helping steal the longhorns. Money talks, and all that. Even burning up Tim Berryman the way you did, I guess some might call that a kind of accident."

"And they'd be right. I didn't plan on anything like that. The fire was just a signal to them other boys, you know?"

"I'll leave that for a judge and jury, but I'd like to know why you stuck Wolford with that boot knife."

"Turns out that he saw me do something way back, and it was eating at him. Hell, I couldn't have him tattling to Mossman right before the raid, could I?"

"That one will get you hanged, regardless of the rest," said Catlin.

"Only if they catch me," Findlay answered.

"You're already caught."

The gunman smirked at that. "You've got a high opinion of yourself."

"Feel free to prove me wrong."

"Well, now, I might just—"

Moving while he spoke, leaving his comment incomplete, Findlay went for both of his Colts at once, his right hand slightly quicker than the left. It hardly mattered, though, as Catlin cleared his holster, cocked his Colt Navy revolver on the rise, and drilled his opposition's Adam's apple from a range of fifteen feet or so.

Blood spouted from the wound as Findlay fired both Peacemakers at once, shots wasted on the open ground between himself and Catlin. Art saw Findlay's eyes roll back, only the whites showing before he toppled over backward, hit the ground with force enough to raise a small dust cloud, and lay still as the dust settled over him.

When he reached the Badger's Tail barroom, he found Mossman, Chávez, Hooper, and Limbaugh huddled there around Mayor Cyrus Harding. Harding had his hands raised, fingers interlaced atop his head, eyeing his captors as if one of them might gun him down at any second.

"Who was that out back?" Mossman asked Art.

"You'd know him as Jay Fielding," Catlin said.

"I take it that he won't be joining us?"

"Not in this life, boss. What about the man behind all this? The marshal claimed they call him Murray Glatman."

"Dead upstairs," the Bar X boss replied. "Looks like he had a falling-out with Fielding, or whatever that trash called himself."

"We missed the judge and lawyer," Chávez said. "Sorry, boss."

"No need to apologize," said Mossman. "They were just the small fry, anyhow. I'll put the word around when we hit Independence. And speaking of that . . ."

"We've got a cattle drive to finish," Catlin said.

"We do indeed," Mossman replied. And for the first time Catlin could remember, the boss smiled.

EPILOGUE

June 13

Independence, Missouri

"TWO MONTHS AND less four days, plus thirteen," Bliss Mossman said, while counting out greenbacks. "I make that ninety-two dollars I owe you, and I'm adding five for all the trouble we ran into on the way."

"Obliged, sir," Art Catlin replied. He took the cash, not counting it, and wedged it down into the left-hand pocket of his blue jeans.

"No, Art," Mossman answered. "*I'm* obliged to you and all the rest for getting here at all. We could have lost it all, three times I'm sure of, and I won't forget it."

"Well . . ."

They sat across from one another at a window table in the Blue Bird restaurant, removed sufficiently from the stockyards that diners wouldn't be reminded con-

stantly of where their steaks and chops came from,
before they wound up butchered, aged, and grilled.

"I don't suppose you've given any thought to what
comes next?" Mossman inquired.

"Just thought I'd take a few days off and have a look
around," Art said.

"Sure, sure. I understand," the Bar X boss replied.
"I'd feel that way myself, but I've been missing little
Danny back at home. We're late already, what with one
thing and another. Gayle might think I'm up to some-
thing that I shouldn't be, the longer that I'm gone from
Santa Fe."

"I guess it was a rough one," Catlin said. "Not that
I have a lot to judge by."

"Worst I've seen for trouble," Mossman granted. "If
I'm lucky, there won't be another like it."

"Then I wish you luck, sir."

"From your lips to God's ears, son. And if you're
ever back in Santa Fe, looking for work . . ."

"Yes, sir. And thanks. I'll think on it."

They rose, shook hands, and parted, Mossman exit-
ing the restaurant while Art moved toward the counter
and a menu mounted on the wall. He realized that he
was hungry, but the last thing that he wanted was a slab
of beef.

He'd told Mossman that he'd consider going back to
the Bar X, but even as Art spoke those words, he knew
they didn't have the ring of truth. In fact, after the grueling trip he'd had, with all the blood spilled between
Santa Fe and Longwood, he was reconsidering a trade
he'd given up as lost.

Or maybe he could make it new again, try it a slightly
different way.

From a hip pocket, Catlin drew a folded sheet of
paper, opened it, and scanned the "Wanted" poster on
a highwayman and murderer named Milton Keynes,

alias "Martin Cain," alias "Mickey Crowe." Missouri offered seven hundred dollars for his capture, breathing optional. His list of crimes included two bank robberies, four coaches stopped and looted, plus a former sidekick killed in Henry County when they squabbled over cutting up the proceeds from one or their holdups.

Henry County, Catlin knew, lay eighty miles southeast of Independence, something like a three-day ride if he relaxed and took his time about it. If he could get a line on Keynes and run him down, it wouldn't be a bad use of his time.

Why not? Art asked himself, and got no answer that dissuaded him.

This time around, he thought, he'd be more careful about where and when he braced a fugitive, more mindful of civilians getting in the way.

The more he thought about it, the more Catlin's doubts evaporated, taking flight.

And what else was he any good at, after all?

Ready to find
your next great read?

Let us help.

Visit prh.com/nextread